Crazy For Love

Tahnee Fritz

Crazy For Love is a work of fiction. Names, characters, places, and incidents are the products of the author's imagination or are used fictitiously. Any resemblance to actual events, locales, or persons, living or dead, is entirely coincidental.

Copyright © 2014 Tahnee Justus

ISBN-10: 0991279115

ISBN-13: 978-0-9912791-1-1

For Megan
The craziest redhead I know.

One

"It's over." Those two, small words burned through Colton Wischmeier's mind like a spark igniting a flame.

He thought they would always be together. The last three years were the best of his life. She was the main part of it which only made it better. He poured his heart and soul into their relationship, even when she never did the same. When rock bottom came soaring into the picture, he knew things would be okay as long as they were together. He never thought she would actually want to end it and his heart shattered into a million pieces when those words fell from her lips.

"Please, just give this thing one more chance. I'll do whatever it takes to keep you from leaving." He pleaded as he followed her through the apartment.

"There's nothing you can do. This is something that *has* to be done and I'm doing it." She refused to look at him as she gathered some of her belongings. "I'm tired of feeling stuck in whatever kind of relationship this is and I feel like I have to force myself to *want* to be with you. That's not what I call a being in love, Colton."

"Is this because I lost my job and haven't had the best of luck finding a new one? Is that why you want to leave?" he asked.

"No, that's not why. I just can't do this anymore." Was her response.

"Come on, Amy, I can't let you give up on us so easily," he said. "I mean, we're still in love and we have to stick by each other even when things look horrible."

Colton followed her to the door, the only thing stopping her from leaving any faster. Before she opened it, she turned to him, a calm expression written on her face. He looked at her beautiful auburn hair gently caressing her bronze shoulders. Her big, blue eyes showing no sign of remorse for the heart she was in the process of breaking. That was when he started to wonder if she was still in love with him at all.

He could feel his eyes swelling up with tears as he stared at her perfect face, "*Are* we still in love?"

He waited for an answer. Anything to prove to him there was a chance he would be with her. The longer they stood there staring at each other, he knew he had no chance at getting the answer he longed for. Her only response was a simple shrug of her shoulders and a slight shaking of her head. Not a single tear in her eyes or a look of sadness on her face.

"I can't give you what you want anymore, Colton." She stated then put her hand on the doorknob.

"Yes you can." Colton felt like he was begging as he tried to stop her from going. "You just need to stay. You need to see that I'll change. I'll do whatever you want me to do so we can still be together. You don't need to give up on what we have."

Amy shook her head, then said, "I'm not giving up. I just want to move on."

She twisted the doorknob and pulled the door open. She didn't bother looking back as she started walking away from him. Colton stood in the doorway, letting the breeze from outside flow into the apartment. She disappeared from his view and was gone.

He pushed the door closed and listened to the latch echo through the empty apartment. He couldn't bring himself to chase after her. As much as he wanted to, he knew how pointless it would be. She already had her mind made up and it would take a miracle to get her to change it. Amy was the kind of girl who could be hard to convince when something was worth saving. To her, their relationship wasn't. She wanted what they had together to be over and done with. Forget they ever had a love life together and move on. She was the best that ever happened to Colton. He didn't *want* to move on.

He spun around and stared at the empty living room. He didn't have much when he first moved there. A twin sized mattress, a small couch and TV, and a folding chair and table for the dining room. Then she came along and spiced the place up a bit. She hung pictures all over the walls to add color and put bright orange pillows in the corner of his dull brown sofa. They were so happy at the beginning and the apartment showed that happiness. She stole it all away and left only a dull reminder of how awful his life was without her.

Colton thought moving to the big city would be worth it. Taking the great job he got after college would never end up being a bust. Meeting the girl of his dreams was the one thing that put the icing on the cake. Something *had* to go wrong. He *had* to lose his high paying job forcing her to pay for everything. He could barely afford to buy bread and he knew she was beginning to hate being the only one with a salary. That still wasn't a good enough reason for her to leave. Colton thought the people who loved you, those that cared about you more than anything else in the world, were supposed to be there for you when times were tough. He felt like an idiot thinking she was the kind of person he hoped her to be.

He pulled himself away from the door and walked through the apartment to the bedroom. The closet door in the room was wide open and empty. His clothes were kept in a dresser because Amy took up too much space in the closet. The bare hangers are the only reminder of what he used to have.

He walked to the tall dresser next to a window that overlooked a small garden two stories down. Loose change and other odds and ends cluttered the top of the dresser. She took the picture of the two of them at Times Square along with the stuffed bear she got him when they first met. More of his heart that she ripped away from him. The only picture to remain on the dresser was that of him and his parents when he graduated high school. He had his arms draped over their shoulders with smiles on all of their faces.

He lifted the picture from the dresser and stared at it for a moment. It's been a while since he's seen them. Living half the country away from them made it hard to get home whenever he wanted. He hated growing up in that small town, but there were people who cared about him there and they'd be more than happy to see him again. He'd hate himself for leaving, but with the thought of Amy being out of the picture forever, he might not have much of a choice.

Two

"So, what are you going to do now? I mean you can't possibly afford that apartment even with a decent job." Stated Jacob, Colton's best friend since high school. "The rent on that place is more than my house payment."

Colton sat at a booth in the bar down the street from his apartment building. The two of them have met there every Friday night since they graduated high school and moved to New York. A tradition they thought would never die, until Colton lost his job. He had the *wonderful* economy to blame for that.

He shrugged as he took a drink of his beer, "I don't know. Without Amy, I feel like I could die. She was the one thing I thought I would always have and she left."

"Hey, you'll always have me and I ain't going anywhere." Jacob joked. "You know you can move into the basement at my place. There's plenty of room."

Colton shook his head, "I know, but you have a kid on the way and there's no way I could impose on your family like that. I moved here to be on my own, not mooch off my friends."

"It wouldn't be imposing. You'll be in the basement, it's like a whole house down there." His friend was trying to be as helpful as he possibly could.

"No, I can't do that. Amy broke my heart and I can't rely on you to fix it." Colton said as he stared at the table.

Jacob finished his drink then set the bottle on the table, "Well, if you don't get a job and pay your rent here soon, you'll be out on the streets. This is New York City, no way in hell I'd wanna be caught homeless on *these* streets."

Colton forced a smile, "Yeah, me neither. We both know I wouldn't last a night on my own like that."

"That's for sure."

A young waitress approached their booth and set a two more brown bottles on the table for both of them. She was a petite woman with blonde hair and a gorgeous body. Something that would make any man drool over. She tossed a smile to Colton who couldn't return the favor. His heart only belonged to Amy.

The waitress strolled away from them and Jacob leaned forward in the booth, "Dude, that chick was totally checking you out. Why don't you go for that?"

"Amy *just* broke up with me. I'm not that big of a dick to go for the next girl I see just for pointless rebound sex." Colton replied.

"I'm just saying, a one night stand would take your mind off things."

"Not gonna happen, so drop it."

"Okay, sorry." Jacob replied.

Colton ran his fingers through his shaggy, brown hair. He stared at the table in front of him, thinking to himself how he was probably the only person in the whole bar who was depressed. While everyone else was having a good time with their friends, he felt sad and alone with no idea what to do next.

He left everything to come to the city for school and a

6

good career. Left his home in a small town to live out his dream which shortly became shattered. His parents would definitely welcome him back with open arms, but they don't even know what happened. Colton didn't have the courage to call up his folks and explain to them how he lost his job and his girlfriend all in a few months. They wouldn't judge him for being down on his luck or make him suck it up and move on. His parents care and sometimes too much.

"What are you thinking about over there?" Jacob asked.

Colton shook his head, "I don't know. I think I might have to move back home with my parents."

"Hell no, I can't let that happen. I don't care what you say, you can live in my basement till you die, but you cannot move back to that shithole of a town in Iowa." Jacob protested.

"I have no other options. I can't stay in the city anymore. Amy will never take me back and being here is just a constant reminder of what I'll never have again. Going home is the best possible solution for me." Colton replied.

Jacob stared at his friend. They've gone through just about everything together. Their houses were right next door to each other as they were growing up and they even shared a dorm together at the University. Losing his best friend would be hard, but Jacob knew it would be for the best.

Finally, he nodded in agreement, "If there's nothing I can do to change your mind, then I guess it has to be done. I'm really gonna miss you though, bro. No matter how gay this might make me sound, I love you, man."

Colton let out a slight chuckle, "Yeah, I'll miss you, too."

"Then, here's to some of the last few drinks we'll have together. At least in this city." Jacob said as he raised his bottle for a toast.

Colton did the same with his and said, "Let's make them last."

The clink from the glass bottles could only be heard at their table and each of them smiled as they took a drink.

7

Three

The air was a lot fresher when Colton climbed out of his two-door Honda. He was back home, standing in the street of his old neighborhood, wishing he was still sitting in the air conditioning of his car. Iowa was always hot and humid in the summer and having to move what little belongings he had, made the heat seem worse. Sweat was already beading on his forehead as he stood outside the car.

He took a deep breath as he shut the drivers' door and looked around the neighborhood. Nothing has changed. The old man in the brick house across the street was sitting in the porch swing, glaring at the kids skateboarding in the middle of the road. The black lab next door seemed a little greyer and didn't bark much anymore. It used to bark and growl at anything moving within a foot of his lawn.

Then Colton turned around and stared at his own house. The swing on the tree in the front yard was still there. His father put that up when he was five years old. Hours were spent on that swing with his father right behind him the whole time. His mother's grey minivan was parked in the open garage with his dad's squad car parked right behind it. Colton was sure the neighbors were intimidated knowing a sheriff lived right next door.

He walked around to the trunk of his car and popped it open. He didn't have any furniture to bring back with him, so moving home was almost a breeze. Only needed to fill a few trash bags and one duffle bag of his clothes and the important things he couldn't live without. Everything else, he let Jacob keep in the basement of his house in case of the off chance he'd make it back to New York. Colton grabbed a couple bags of his things then headed for the front door.

His feet carried him along the path cutting through the bright, green grass leading to the house. His parents still weren't expecting him. During the long road trip home, he contemplated calling them to explain his situation, but he could never put the right words together. Everything seemed too horrible to explain over the phone. Surprising them was the only thing he could think of. It was a good thing his parents loved surprises.

The trash bags fell from his hands and he approached the red, front door. He nervously pressed the doorbell and listened to the annoying chime his mother picked out. It's been the same ever since he was a little kid.

A few seconds passed before the door burst open and his father, Carl Wischmeier, stood before him. He never got as tall as his father, who was over six feet. Colton was a few inches shorter and in worse shape. It wasn't his fault. His job didn't call for him to be muscular at all. He sat behind a desk all day designing web pages for different types of businesses. He wasn't overweight, he just lacked the muscle definition an extremely toned man would have. His father on the other hand, needed to be in great shape to chase down whatever bad guy he came across. Another intimidating aspect.

"Hi, dad," Colton said, smoothly.

A puzzled look shot across his father's slowly aging face, followed by a smile, "Get in here and give your old man a hug, boy."

Colton smiled as his dad wrapped his big arms around him and gave him a tight squeeze, "I've missed you, too, dad."

"Is that my baby boy out there?" came his mother's soft voice from inside the house.

Denise Wischmeier walked up behind her husband and a huge grin crossed her face the second she saw her son. Colton was released from his father's grip and he glanced over to his mother. It looked like she hadn't aged a day since he saw her two years ago. Her hair was dyed brown to hide the grey and her face was wrinkle free. Colton could only hope he would get that lucky when he ages.

He wrapped his arms around his mother and kissed her cheek as she embraced him. He could smell the sweet scent of lavender coming from her hair. She pulled away from him, then glanced down at the bags on the floor next to him.

"What's that, sweetie?" she asked.

Colton looked down at his feet and shrugged his shoulders, "I had some bad luck, I guess."

"Bad luck, huh?" his father asked.

Denise shook her head as she elbowed her husband, "Help him bring his things down to his bedroom, then the two of you can come into the kitchen for some tea."

"Thanks mom." Colton added as she walked away.

His dad reached down and grabbed one of the bags as Colton grabbed the other. He followed his old man into the house and closed the door behind him. Carl built his son a bedroom in the basement when he turned thirteen. The only thing his father could think of to stop the loud music from being upstairs in the main part of the house. Unfortunately, the laundry room was right next to his new bedroom so he would constantly hear the washing machine going.

They stepped into his old room and Colton flung his things on the floor next to his old twin-sized bed. Memories flooded his mind as he stared at all of his things. Trophies from playing baseball in high school covered the shelves across from his bed. Posters of female models, half naked and gorgeous, covered the walls all around him. Everything was just as he left it when he went away to college.

"Can I ask you what you're doing here, boy?" his father finally asked.

Colton took a deep breath as he faced his father, "I lost my job a few months ago and haven't had the best luck finding a new one. Amy left me last week and I didn't have much choice but to come back home."

Carl nodded, "Why didn't you call? We would have sent you some money to get by."

Colton shook his head, "I can't ask you guys for money. I was too ashamed to even tell you what happened."

"You have nothing to be ashamed about, Colton. It's a bad time for everybody in this country." His dad sounded caring as he spoke. "You can stay here as long as you need to. Let's get upstairs before your mother yells at us, then we'll get the rest of your stuff."

The two of them shared a quiet laugh then headed back upstairs. Colton was finally able to get a look at the few changes made to his childhood home.

Everything in the living room was different. A black couch replaced the old green one they've had for as long as he could remember. A flat screen TV hung on the wall which replaced the bulky monstrosity that used to sit in the corner of the room. A glass coffee table sat on top of a black and white area rug. Even the small, brown Pomeranian lying on the couch was a new addition.

His father noticed him staring at the new setup in the house, "We changed this up last winter. Your mother thought it would be a good idea to finally upgrade to the new styles. Even made me buy her that damn dog over there and all he does is shit and whine."

Colton smiled, "Well, it looks nice in here."

"Wait till you see the kitchen. Had that remodeled over the spring." His father lead him into the kitchen.

Just as he said, everything was different. The cabinets

and countertops were all brand new. The white appliances were some of the latest models that could be bought. Just about everything in his home had changed. Lucky for him, his parents were still the same, quirky couple they've always been.

"Have I really been away this long? I mean so much has changed around here and I feel like I missed it all." Colton stated.

The last time he'd been home, was two years earlier for his mother's birthday. He stayed for three days then hopped on a plane heading back to New York. As much as they begged him to come back home, he always had some excuse as to why he couldn't. Work got in the way most of the time along with Amy only wanting to hang out with her friends and her family during the holidays. He forgot how important his own family was and instantly regrets never coming home all those times.

Denise met them at the small kitchen island and set a couple glasses of tea on the marble countertop, "Well, it has been awhile, sweetheart. We couldn't go on living with the same old stuff forever. That doesn't mean this isn't the same home you grew up in. There are still chores to be done while you're living here and I expect you to do your part."

"I know mom. I'll help out with whatever you want until I can find a job and a place of my own out here." Colton replied as he took a sip of the cool drink.

"What are your plans for the night, son? I don't expect you to stay in when there are plenty of your old friends dying to see you again." Carl asked.

Colton shrugged, "I guess I could call up the old gang and get together."

"You don't need to call them. Just head down to Lonny's Pub." Denise chimed in. "Most of your friends are down there almost every night."

"Where's that?" he asked, ignoring the fact that his mother knew where his friends from high school hang out.

"Downtown. That boy Lonny Henderson opened it about

a year ago and it's quite the popular spot nowadays." His mother said with a smile.

He didn't want to ask how she knew so much about the bar. He was almost embarrassed to think of his parents going to a bar for a drink and running into his friends from school. He was beginning to notice that so much has changed while he was gone living a great life in New York City. He could only hope his old friends would still be there for him.

Four

Colton finished setting up his old room that afternoon, then joined his parents for an early dinner. His father grilled steaks while his mother made sweet corn and mashed potatoes. A good, hearty meal only his family could provide for him. Living in the city was tough on his diet. He mostly ate pizza or hot dogs whenever he passed a stand. Amy was never the best cook and it was much easier to order take out than get something to cook on the stove.

When he was finished eating and helping his mother with the dishes, he hopped in his little car and headed downtown to Lonny's Pub. Along the way, he drove by some of his old hangout spots in the town. There was the park by the middle school where he made out with his first girlfriend, Betsy McMann, when they were just twelve years old. He was sure her heart was broken when he ended things after a month.

He went passed the old high school and was flooded with memories. Skipping class with his friends to go to a matinee to see whatever their favorite movies were at the time. Then sitting in detention with them after school and being grounded for a week for goofing off instead of being where he was supposed to be. A smile crossed his face as he continued driving.

Finally, Colton made it downtown and discovered the bar on the corner where he was headed. There was no way he could have missed it. A giant neon sign hung on the building with the name of the bar in glowing red letters. The windows on the front were tinted dark and had neon beer and alcohol signs hanging in them. Quite a few cars were parked out front and around the corner. He was lucky to find a spot across the street and walked to the bar.

He couldn't help but feel nervous about seeing some of his old friends. Most of them have lost touch with him or he eventually quit talking to them for no apparent reason. There were still a few that he's managed to speak to through online messaging or texts back and forth. He was really hoping he would run into them at the bar.

A bell above the door rang as he pulled it open. The smell of grilled chicken filled his nose and loud chatter filled his ears. The place was slightly crowded and he could tell someone was celebrating their birthday. A bunch of people were wearing party hats and dancing to whatever song was on the jukebox. A rap song with a good beat to it. He smiled at the few people crowding around the door and said "hello" to a few of them as he passed. Most of them were younger girls, probably just turned twenty-one, and they were out celebrating with their girlfriends and boyfriends. Not a bad way to spend a birthday.

"Oh my god! Is that Colton Wischmeier?" shouted a male voice from a few feet away.

Colton turned his head and immediately recognized the man walking toward him. Seth Donohue. Other than Jacob, he was another of Colton's closest friends from school.

It didn't take long before everyone in the bar was staring at him. Some of them shouted his name and cheered for him while others were trying to figure out who he was. He couldn't have asked for a more heartwarming welcome.

"When the hell did you get back in town, man?" Seth asked as he reached out for a manly hug from his friend.

"Early this afternoon," was Colton's reply.

"Sweet. So, how long you in town for?" Seth said.

He sighed, "I don't know. I moved back in with my parents. Things didn't go the way I hoped in New York."

"Awe, shit man, that really sucks. C'mon to the bar, I'll buy you a drink and we'll catch up a bit." Seth said and the two of them strolled through the place to the bar.

A few people Colton knew from school stopped him along the way to say their hellos and ask how he was doing. He was surprised that so many people still thought of him as a friend and cared enough to ask about him. He half expected most of them to ignore him or smile instead of stopping to catch a few words.

He sat on a stool with Seth sitting beside him. The bartender walked up to them and put her hands on the counter. Colton shook his head and smiled as he caught her eye.

"Well if it isn't the infamous Colton." She said with a sly smile.

"How're you doing, Sarah?" he asked.

She brushed her wavy, black hair away from her face as she spoke, "Great. Married the best man in the world and opened this bar with him. I guess I should thank you for that one. If you wouldn't have ditched me for school, I could still be stuck with you."

"It's nice to see you too, Sarah." Colton replied.

She smiled, "I'll get you some beers. The first one's on the house."

"Thanks." He and Seth said at the same time.

"I still can't believe you dumped the hottest girl in this town for college." Seth stated.

Colton shrugged, "I had to move on, man. A lot of good that did me."

He thought about Amy. No matter how hard he tried, he couldn't get her off his mind. He was still in love with her and it would take a lot more than a few beers with his old friends to change that.

"What all happened in New York? I know you had a good job and a girl back there, so what went wrong?" Seth asked.

Sarah brought them each a beer and Colton immediately took a drink, then replied, "I lost everything. First my job, the economy destroyed that. Then my girlfriend left me a week ago without much of a reason. I had no other choice other than coming back here."

Seth shook his head, "Man, I'm sorry about all that. You know if you ever need anything at all, you can always call me. I know it's been awhile, but I'm still here for ya."

Colton smiled, "Thank you, that means a lot."

He spun around on the stool to get a good look at everyone else in the bar. There were a few people he recognized from high school. They were surrounding a table, laughing and having a real good time. Some of them smiled when they noticed Colton staring at them. Relief fell through him at how nice and caring everyone was being. It was a good thing those people still thought of him as a good guy and not someone who abandoned them when he drove off for a chance at a better life.

There were other people in the bar which he didn't recognize. Some older gentlemen sitting in the corner wearing suits and ties. They must have gone straight to the bar after a tough day at work. Colton's eyes passed over them and he caught a glimpse of a young woman sitting at the other end of the bar. She was concentrating hard on a computer screen sitting on the counter in front of her. The only person in the place who didn't appear to be having a good time with friends or drinking the night away. She seemed like she was there to get some work done.

Her hair, a brilliant shade of red that shimmered in the dim bar lighting was the first thing Colton noticed about her. Red had always been his favorite color and attracted him the most. He could see the green of her eyes when she glanced up from the monitor. Her skin, slightly pale and he spotted the freckles on her arms and her cheeks. She was beautiful. Everything Colton would ever look for in a girl. He just wasn't looking at the moment.

The woman noticed his stare as she took a drink of her apple martini. She stared back at him for a moment then tossed him a smile. He couldn't bring himself to do the same. Instead, he shook his head and spun around on the stool, facing Seth.

"Who's that red head at the other end of the bar?" he asked.

Seth looked past him, then smiled, "Oh, you have a good eye, man. That's Sidney Jenison, most people call her Sid. She moved here about a year ago. Does something in journalism, I think. She is probably the hottest chick that comes here. Always turns me down."

"Why doesn't that surprise me?" Colton joked.

Seth gave him a friendly punch on the arm, then took a drink of his beer. Colton let out a chuckle then glanced back toward the woman. Her eyes were still fixated on him. There was something in those eyes that seemed to be telling him something. He couldn't quite pinpoint what they were telling him and had to turn away from her before he gave her the wrong impression. Romance with a woman was the last thing he wanted.

Five

It was an early night for Colton. He didn't stay out much past ten before heading home and going to bed. Seth begged him to stay out for a few more drinks and catching up. He wound up accepting a rain check and the two plan to meet up again in a couple days. There was still a lot on Colton's mind and he was hoping sleep would help take some of it away.

The next morning, Colton woke up to the smell of bacon filling the whole house. The same smell that used to wake him up early for school when he was younger. He smiled as he pulled himself out of bed and rushed to the stairs. The issues on his mind were put to rest for the time being and he was looking forward to a nice breakfast with his mother. As he made his way to the kitchen, he could hear the bacon sizzling in the pan on the stove and heard the toaster pop up.

"Good morning, mom," he said as he sat in a stool at the kitchen island.

"Morning, did you sleep well last night?" she asked.

He shrugged, "I actually slept really good. I think the

lack of the big city noise outside the window seemed to help a bit. Where's dad?"

"Oh, he goes in early some days." Denise said as she pulled the toast from the toaster and put it on a plate next to three strips of bacon.

Colton watched her scoop scrambled eggs onto the plate as well. She strolled across the kitchen and set it on the counter in front of him. Then she went back to the stove and made a plate for herself.

"Eat up. I'm sure you have a big day today." She said as she sat next to him. "Got any plans?"

He shrugged after taking the first bite of eggs, "Yeah, I'm gonna drive around, see if there's any place I can apply for a job. Maybe catch up with some old friends or something. What about you?"

"Oh, I'll be headed downtown in about an hour. I'm teaching a pottery class over the summer for kids and young adults. There are surprisingly quite a few of them that want to take the class." She replied.

"That's good." Colton said.

Once he was finished with breakfast, he helped clean up the kitchen and washed the dishes while his mother got ready to go. He almost missed being home to help out around the house. He hated it when he was a teenager, but for some reason it felt relaxing now that he was older. He felt needed in the house and knew any amount of help he offered his folks, the better he'd feel about his current situation. Doing chores and other random things for his family made him feel less of a mooch and more of a person who was able to contribute to something.

When his mother left and after he was in and out of the shower, he sat on the couch searching the want ads in the local newspaper. The small Pomeranian curled up on his lap as he read through the listings. There wasn't much in there that pertained to his line of expertise. He was really good at web design and had good job in New York before the company went belly-up. Unfortunately, in a town of only three thousand people, that line of work was hard to come by. There were mainly ads for paperboys or cashiers at the grocery store. Nothing in an office and nothing with computers. He was a little disappointed with the lack of opportunity he found.

He tossed the paper on the couch next to him and stared through the bay window. The dog was soft against his skin and he ran his fingers through its fur. The dog enjoyed being rubbed and scratched and started licking Colton's hand. There wasn't a whole lot going on outside as he stared. It was before noon and the neighbor kids weren't out roaming the streets on their bikes yet. The old man across the street was sitting on his front porch, like always.

Colton set the dog on the floor and stood from his seat. He walked through the house, going back downstairs to his bedroom. The keys to his car were sitting on the dresser against the wall. He forgot to put them in his jeans' pocket after he got dressed. Sitting next to his keys was an old picture of him and his friends from high school graduation. All of them were standing with their arms folded across their chests and a serious look on their faces. He remembered the day his mom took that picture. She told them to look grown up and that's why all of them chose that pose. One of his favorite memories he had with his friends.

He shook his head as he grabbed the keys and headed back upstairs. He locked the door on his way out and jogged along the path to his car. He wasn't sure where he was going yet, but he knew he had to go somewhere to find a job. Sitting on the couch would get him nowhere and it was getting a little boring being alone with a lap dog.

He hopped in the car, stepped on the clutch, and started the engine. The first thing he noticed was the gas light flashing at him. He was never good at remembering to fill the tank. Even after a long drive home, he still forgot to fill up. Now, he's forced with doing the annoying task. He rolled his eyes as he pulled away from the house and headed for the gas station a few blocks away. He glanced at a few houses as he drove, trying to remember the fun times he had while growing up.

There were so many times he got caught sneaking out to a few of these houses. Mainly to hang out with his friends while their parents were out of town and they decided to throw a *little* party. It never helped that his father was a cop and always on the lookout for rambunctious behavior. More memories that brought a smile to his face as he drove to the station.

After putting close to forty dollars of gas in the tank, he walked to the glass doors of the convenience store. There were two other people in the building. The cashier and a man unloading soda and beer into the coolers. That man was far too busy to pay any attention to Colton as he walked inside. He strolled through the place to get a candy bar and a soda. Then he walked to the counter and set his items down for the cashier to ring up.

"I also got gas out there." He said as he dug his wallet out of his back pocket.

"Colton Wischmeier?" the woman behind the counter asked.

He raised an eyebrow, "Yeah, that's me."

"I thought you looked familiar. It's me, Betsy McMann, from middle school." She replied.

He cocked his head to one side as he stared at her face. It took him a few seconds to recall the short time he spent with Betsy. They only dated a month, but he always felt that she got more out of it than he did. Finally, he was able to recognize the woman standing across from him. She still wore her glasses and kept her hair cut short in the bob style. Her clothes didn't change much either, now that he recognized her. Still the same type of plain colored t-shirt and Capri-pants. He can't figure out why he didn't realize it was her until she spoke her name.

"Oh, Betsy, it's been a long time." He finally said.

She smiled, "It has. You still look really good, like always."

"Yeah, so do you." Colton replied, hoping she would give him his total soon.

"So, what have you been up to?" she asked as she pushed a few buttons on the register.

He shrugged, "Just moved back to town. Trying to find a job and catch up with old friends. How about you?"

"I'm the store manager here now. Not my dream job, but it pays the bills and has great benefits." Betsy looked up from the machine. "It's gonna be $43.76."

He pulled the cash from his wallet and handed it over to her, "Well, it was nice to see you. Maybe I'll see you out sometime or something. Then we can catch up on old times."

She handed him his change, "That would be great. I'm looking forward to it." she sounded very eager with that last bit.

"Alright. Thanks." Colton grabbed his soda and candy then walked out of the station.

He let out a much needed sigh of relief as he headed for his car. He was always a little tense around her. After their break up, she would not leave him alone. She would leave little love notes in his locker using cut-out letters from magazines in an ill-attempt form of being cute. Every day he would find her waiting for him before school started so she could talk to him. It took all three years of middle school to get her to realize that he didn't want anything to do with her anymore. He could tell she was upset and was hoping she accepted the end of their relationship. There was still something weird about her whenever he saw her in high school. She gave him a longing look whenever his eyes passed over her. He felt lucky that he didn't get that same look inside the gas station.

He climbed in his car and started the engine. He knew he was just being nice in there, telling her they should meet up sometime. There wasn't a single part of him that wanted *that* to happen. The further he stayed away from her, the less awkward things would be between them. As far as exes go, she wasn't one he'd enjoy staying in contact with.

Six

Colton applied at a few different places downtown. Nothing he really wanted to do, but they were the only places with a "Help Wanted" sign in the window. There was a manager's position open at a hardware store and a teller position at a bank. He also applied for a janitor's position at the small theater on Main Street. That one was definitely not something he ever imagined he'd be doing, but he had to get a job. He couldn't live with his parents forever.

By the time he was finished searching the town for work, it was dinner time. He knew his mother would be making a nice home cooked meal, but he didn't want to go home. Instead, he found himself back at Lonny's Pub, sitting in a booth, drinking a beer alone. He noticed the bar was pretty empty for a Wednesday evening. He thought if Tuesday was so busy with people, the rest of the week should be as well.

Sarah brought him one of her famous giant tacos over-stuffed with everything he loved. Lettuce, tomatoes, onions, the works. She walked away from him, letting him sit and eat in peace. He took a few bites of his meal then realized it was much spicier than he anticipated and nearly drank all of his beer to calm his tongue.

He blew out a deep breath as he looked up from the table. His eyes passed over the few people sitting in a booth across the bar. A few girls out for dinner showing off pictures on their phones. Sitting at the stools were two older men arguing with each other about politics or something, Colton couldn't really hear them. Then he saw the red head.

She was sitting alone at the bar with a laptop in front of her, doing the same thing he found her doing the night before. Her red hair cascading gently on her shoulders, glistening in the dim light. He couldn't help but stare. She was more than gorgeous, with a body to die for. Any man would be lucky to have her on his arm.

It didn't take more than few seconds for the woman to notice Colton's stare. He quickly looked down at the table when she saw him, too embarrassed to look anywhere else. He took another bite from the taco, his tongue instantly felt on fire. Then, he flooded his mouth with beer and heard footsteps heading his way.

He glanced up to see who was coming toward him and saw the red headed woman. She was wearing skin tight blue jeans with leather, knee high boots. Her grey and black shirt was tight and showed off the perfect amount of cleavage. Her long shoulder bag brushed against her perfectly curved hips. He tried not to gawk at her as she strolled up to his booth and sat across from him.

She put her laptop inside her shoulder bag then smiled at Colton, "You stare a lot."

He shook his head, "I'm sorry."

"It wasn't a complaint," she stated with a smile. "I'm Sidney by the way, but my friends call me 'Sid'."

"Colton," he replied.

"Nice to meet you." She said with another smile. "Can I ask why you're sitting here alone on a Wednesday evening?"

He shrugged, "I don't know, just trying to clear my head

I guess."

"Oh yeah. What are you trying to clear?" she asked.

"The past five years, since I took a stupid job in New York." Colton replied.

"Things didn't work out up there, I take it." The smile faded from her face.

"Not at all. I thought I had everything figured out, but apparently I was wrong." He couldn't understand why it was so easy to talk to this strange woman. "Then I met this girl. I thought she was the one, I was wrong about that too."

"That's not good." Sid stated.

"I'm sorry, I'm probably dragging your night down talking about my problems." Colton looked away from her.

She shook her head, "Not at all. You've had a rough patch in life and now you're trying to fix it. I get it. I've been there."

"You have?"

"Yeah, that's why I moved here. To get away from someone who I couldn't be around anymore. I got lucky that I can do my job online and through video chat if I need to do." She stated. "How about I buy us each a drink and we can clear our minds together?"

Colton leered across the table at her. He stared at her green eyes and still couldn't figure out what they were trying to tell him. There was almost a look of determination hiding behind them. She definitely appeared to be the type of girl who always got what she wanted. He got this strange feeling she was hoping to take this night somewhere outside the bar and get a little frisky. Not that he hadn't thought about that, he just wasn't ready for that kind of relationship.

"That sounds nice and all, but I have to tell ya, I'm not really looking for a relationship or anything. I just got out of something really serious and that is the last thing on my mind." Colton explained.

There was a slight hesitation before she spoke, "Who said I was looking for a relationship? I was just offering to buy you a drink and give you a friend to talk to, but if you don't want that, I can leave."

Sidney grabbed her bag and started scooting out of the booth. Colton stopped her before she could stand up. A big part of him didn't want to see her leave. If she was willing to be a friend when he needed one, then he wanted to get to know her a little better. To be a friend in return.

"You don't have to go. I'm sorry for thinking that's what you wanted. I mean, a pretty girl like you, I guess I expected that." Colton apologized. "It would be nice to have someone to talk to though. You can stay if you want and I'll buy the drinks."

She tossed him another smile as she slid back to her spot, "That would be nice."

"Sarah!" Colton called.

The waitress quickly walked up to the table and said, "Yeah, what's up?"

"First of all, this taco was insanely spicy, thank you for that." Colton joked, "Secondly, bring us some nachos and a couple drinks. Beer for me and a martini for Sid."

Sarah grabbed the plate of food from the table, "Be back in a few."

Colton smiled as she walked away from the table. He glanced to Sidney who seemed surprised by what he had just done. She had a sly smile on her face as she stared back at him.

"How do you know what I drink?" she asked.

He shrugged, "That's what you had last night."

"You have a pretty good memory."

"I try sometimes." Colton said.

She let out a slight chuckle, "For someone who's not looking for anything beyond friendship, you sure know how to turn on the charm."

He took a deep breath, then said, "What can I say? I've been with the same woman for the last three years and I got good at turning the charm on in the relationship. It's a tough habit to break, I guess."

"And one you probably shouldn't lose. That's a hard

quality to find in a man." Sid stated.

Sarah was back with their drinks and a plate filled with cheesy nachos. She set everything on the table, then walked away. Colton reached for a nacho and carefully took a bite. He didn't want to look like a slob in front of, what he hoped was his new friend. Sidney took a sip of her drink, then reached for a nacho herself. The evening was beginning to look up for him.

Seven

It was almost midnight by the time Sidney strolled to the front door of her small house. The front porch light was left on, illuminating the small stoop. The gold of the mailbox shimmered in the yellow light. The stars were shining and the full moon brightened up the night's sky. She's never felt happier, never felt so alive before. Ever since she left the bar, the smile hasn't left her face.

The keys dangled in her hand as she unlocked the door. She stepped inside the house and closed the door quietly behind her. She always left the living room light on so she never had to come home in the dark. Something her mother always told her to do. Her house was a small, two bedroom rental found by her father when she moved to town. The neighbors were always friendly enough to wave whenever they saw her and that's what her father wanted for her. Someplace nice where the people looked after one another.

She took a few steps into the living room and tossed her keys and bag on the chocolate brown couch. Next, she leaned against the wall beside it and smiled. Her heart had been racing ever since she met Colton in the bar downtown. She pressed her hand against her chest just to feel it beating.

Her eyes closed for a moment and he was all she could see behind them. His perfect brown hair, his amazing hazel eyes, and his perfect body. She couldn't wait to see him again. Couldn't wait to hear his sweet voice or stare into his amazing eyes. Colton was the man of her dreams. The one man she could envision herself falling in love with and growing old with. He was funny, charming, and she could talk about anything with him. He was everything she had ever wanted. There was only one flaw about him.

He didn't want the same thing.

She opened her eyes then pulled herself away from the wall. No matter how perfect the night may have gone, the one thing that ruined it was when he said he just wanted to be friends. It was the only time she'd ever been rejected without asking for a date first. The only time any guy had ever been straight forward with her about what he wanted. No part of her cared for that at all because all she wanted was him. She wanted to take him home and spend the night with him. She wanted him to still be there in the morning and never want to leave. She couldn't understand why he didn't want any of that.

Sure, he might have given Sidney his phone number and would love to hang out again sometime, but that wasn't enough for her. He showed her his true colors and showed her what kind of man he was capable of being. The perfect man for her. The kind of man that would always be there when she needed him. To be the shoulder to cry on or the ear she needed to talk to. Being friends was the last thing she wanted from him.

She needed to have more.

She paced across the living room floor, trying to come up with some logical explanation as to why he wouldn't want to be more than friends. Her figure reflected off the flat screen TV hanging on the wall as she walked. She knew he was still in a fragile place after being dumped by his longtime girlfriend. Part of her understood that. Something else was telling her that he there were other reasons for his need for only friendship.

"Is there something wrong with me? Is that why he doesn't want me?" she said to herself. "I saw the way he looked at me last night and he gave me that same look today. Why would he do that if he didn't want me?"

She ran her fingers through her hair, unable to wrap her mind around whatever was going through Colton's head. She knew the way he looked at her was that of a man who wanted more than friendship. It was the same look she got from any other guy in town. The look of lust and she knew she deserved that look. She was gorgeous, a ten on the guy scale of hotness. She had the perfect body, the perfect hair, and she always made herself look amazing before setting foot outside of the house. But, for some reason, Colton still did not want her in the serious way she wanted him.

"Sure he just got out of a long, probably horrible relationship. That girl never deserved him in the first place. That's still not a good reason to just stay friends. I could understand if he was dying or something. Then he wouldn't want to get attached to anyone." Sidney ran her fingers through her hair again. "But no, he just doesn't want to be with me. Why can't he see I'd be perfect for him? I could take care of him and give him whatever he wants. We would be absolutely amazing together. Yet, he doesn't want to give that a chance."

Finally, she stopped pacing and walked through the short hallway and turned left into the bathroom. She flipped the light on and stepped foot on the marbled floor. The walls were painted a light brown color, matching the darker shade of the tiles and the mahogany cabinet. She stood in front of the mirror above the sink and stared at her reflection.

There were no visible flaws she could identify on herself. No pimples, moles, or scars of any kind. She made sure to show off the freckles on her nose and cheeks because she knew guys loved that look on a woman. She never wore too much makeup so she didn't look like a woman of the night. Not a single strand of hair was ever out of place. There wasn't anything wrong with her reflection that would get him to not be physically attracted to her.

Her personality definitely couldn't be the reason either. Never would she tell an embarrassing story about her life or admit to some terrible thing she did in the past. Guys didn't like that in a woman. She made sure to keep a smile on both of their faces and make him laugh at whatever silly joke she had to tell. Colton's smile crossed into her mind and she took a deep breath trying not to overwhelm herself. Seeing that smile was more than enough to get her to crave him all the more. The one thing she hated more than anything else in the world, was not getting the things she desired most. That feeling was enough to drive her mad.

As she stared at herself in the mirror, she knew there was only one thing she could do in order to get Colton to realize she was the one he needed to be with. He needed to see that he couldn't go another day without her in his life. She needed to get herself stuck in his heart so deeply, that he couldn't get her out even if he tried his hardest. There should be no one on his mind besides her.

A serious expression crossed her face as she stared at her reflection, "I have to make him fall in love with and I'm going to do whatever it takes to get that."

Sidney took a washcloth from the shelf above the toilet. After turning the warm water on, she got the cloth wet then brought it to her face. She gently rubbed the makeup away letting her mascara and eyeliner run down her cheeks. There was a devious plan pacing through her mind. One she absolutely couldn't let herself fail. It was the perfect way to get the man of her dreams to fall head over heels in love with her.

Eight

Colton woke up the next morning feeling refreshed. He spent most of the last night talking about everything with Sidney. He told her things he found hard to tell Amy sometimes. Even some things Amy never cared to hear about. He told her about his life, his past, and what it was like for him to grow up with a cop for a dad. Sid hung onto his every word and seemed overly interested in whatever story he had to tell. She would make a great friend and he was hoping he made it clear to her that was all he wanted.

He walked upstairs and joined his mother in the kitchen. This time, she had donuts sitting on the counter for breakfast. He poured himself a glass of orange juice, took two donuts from the box, then sat down next to his mother. He took a bite from a chocolate donut and smiled as he chewed. He hasn't felt so happy to be home since he was a little kid.

"You seem to be in a good mood today." Denise asked, looking up from the newspaper.

He shrugged, "I made a new friend last night. She's

pretty cool."

"Ah, a new girlfriend already? Seems kind of fast to be moving on from Amy." She stated.

"No, we're just friends. I told her I wasn't ready for anything like that and she understood."

"Does this girl have a name?"

"Sidney Jenison. I guess she moved here about a year ago." Colton replied, then shoved half of the donut in his mouth.

"Well, I'm glad you're making new friends. I would hate for you to come back home and not have anyone to talk to." Denise said, taking a sip of her hot coffee. "I need to get going though. My class starts in an hour and I have to get things set up."

She set the newspaper on the table then stood from her chair. Colton's eyes followed her out of the room, then he went back to eating his breakfast. He glanced across the room to the clock on the stove. Ten-thirty in the morning. Seth would be at work, along with many of his other friends still in town. It would be another day of driving around looking for a job, ultimately ending up at the bar downtown.

"Love you, sweetheart," his mother called from the living room on her way out.

"Love you, too, mom," he shouted back.

The front door shut and he took a drink of orange juice. He set the glass down, then dug into his shorts' pocket for his cell phone. There weren't any new messages or missed calls, not that he ever expected to hear from Amy after the break up. She seemed very clear that she wanted nothing to do with him after she left the apartment that day.

He tried calling her a few times since then. Left her a message every time and hoped she would call him back. He wanted to hear her voice again, wanted her to say that she still loved him and wanted him to come back to New York. He would leave his home in a heartbeat for her. But, after the week and a half that's gone by, doubts were starting to emerge in his mind that she would call him back. He still felt that he needed to hold out for her. He knew there was something between them and he wanted that back. Love was always the greatest feeling in the world to him.

As he stared at the phone in his hands, it started to vibrate with a new text message flashing across the screen. He quickly unlocked the touchscreen, hoping that his prayers would be answered and Amy was finally coming to her senses. Instead, it was a message from Sidney. He cocked his head to the side out of confusion and read the message.

"Sorry to bug you so early, but I wanted to know if you had any plans for lunch?" read the message.

A smile crossed his face as he thought of a reply. Of course he didn't have plans for lunch. He was unemployed, living in a town where all of his friends had jobs, and he was stuck being alone. Anything would be better than sitting at home doing nothing.

"No plans. Did you want to hang out today?" he texted back.

He set the phone on the table next to his glass of juice. He finished his second donut as he waited for her response.

He still couldn't believe how cool she was being about just staying friends. Normally girls who looked as good as she did would storm away at the thought of not getting anything. He liked that she was laid back about it and wanted to be his friend as well. The first good thing to come out of moving back home.

Finally, his phone buzzed and he quickly read the new message, *"I know the mall isn't that great in this town, but you wanna meet there around noon?"*

Colton glanced at the clock one more time. Three minutes went by since the last time he checked. He needed to take a shower and get dressed, but he would most definitely be ready by noon in order to meet her at the mall. It's not like he took an hour and a half to get ready and get cleaned up.

"Sounds like a plan. I'll see you there." He replied, then took the last drink of juice.

He stood of from the chair, grabbing his dirty glass, and

walked across the tiled floor to the kitchen sink. He rinsed the glass out, then headed back the table to get his phone. There was already another message from Sidney waiting for him.

"*I can't wait.*" was all it said.

He walked through the house until he got to the bathroom down the hall from the kitchen. His parents' bedroom was across the hall and his old bedroom was right next to theirs. His mom turned it into a computer room, a sewing room, and whatever other project she was working on room. She changed it the same day he moved down to the basement. There was another bedroom at the end of the hallway. His father used that as his personal storage room and no one was allowed to go in there. The one time Colton got caught behind that door, he was grounded for a month and he *more* than learned his lesson. Even now, as an adult, he stayed far from that door. His father might not punish him like when he was a teenager, but just the mere thought of getting yelled at by his dad, made him shiver. He hated getting his parents upset.

He walked into the bathroom and shut the door behind him. He reached into the bathtub to turn the hot water on. He set it to shower mode and closed the curtain. He made sure to get a towel ready for him and set it on the counter. Next, he slid out of his shorts and boxers, then climbed into the steamy shower.

Nine

As Sidney stated, the mall was nothing impressive. There was the main store at the west end of the building and a movie theater on the east. In between, were only six stores spread around the place and three restaurants in the food court. The town thought it would attract more people to live there if they built the place. They spent a lot of money, made room for plenty of shops and kiosks. It turned out to be a big waste of money. The only thing keeping the mall alive was the cinema and the town was lucky for that.

Sidney stood outside the main entrance waiting for Colton to pull up. She made sure she looked absolutely amazing just for him. Again she wore skin tight blue jeans with brown leather boots going up to her knees. A tight, buttoned down, pink and white plaid shirt over a red tank top covered her top half revealing the perfect amount of cleavage. Her hair had the perfect amount of wave to complete the look. There was no way he could resist that.

It was a few minutes past noon by the time he showed

up. He parked in a stall up close to the entrance then climbed out. As he strolled up to her, she couldn't help but stare at him. He was a guy worth taking the time to check out and she would continue to do that until the end of time.

He had on a pair of faded jeans and a red t-shirt with some sort of symbol on it. His hair was a mess, like he had just rolled out of bed and Sidney absolutely adored that look on him. He gracefully approached her with a smile on his face and his hands in his pockets.

"Sorry I'm a little late. I had to let my mom's dog out before I left." Colton said.

She shrugged, "No problem. I haven't been here long."

She stared into his hazel eyes waiting for him to compliment how she looked. Longing for him to tell her she looked amazing. Her heart began to race and she was sure he could tell. It was something she couldn't control around him. She was only a few feet away from him and she was already swooning. Staring at his lips, wanting his arms to be wrapped around her. She wanted to feel those lips on her own, to taste the warmth coming from them. She knew she needed to give him some time, wait it out a few days at least. It was going to be a hard few days of waiting.

"You look really nice today. I'm not saying you didn't look nice last night or anything. Just making an observation." Her wait was over.

She tossed him a big smile, calming her breathing a bit, "Thank you."

"Should we go inside?" he asked.

She nodded her head, then allowed him to walk past her to open the glass door for her. She walked inside, with butterflies in her stomach and ran her fingers through her hair in a failed attempt to calm her nerves. Having him act like the perfect gentleman, only made her feelings grow.

The food court was to their left and Colton motioned for her to follow him to a restaurant. She willingly went along, thinking to herself how things were going good so far. She hoped things would get even better and the little date of theirs

38

would end up at either of their houses.

"Pizza sound good?" he suggested.

"Whatever you want," was her reply.

"Okay. I'll get us a couple slices and a pop. You should find us a table and I'll meet you there."

Sidney headed away from him toward one of the few tables in the middle of the food court. There weren't many visitors at the mall so there were plenty of tables to choose from. She picked one with two chairs instead of four. It wasn't far from the pizza place and she sat in a chair facing Colton so she could stare at him while he waited for their meal.

Words couldn't describe the feelings she had inside for that man. There was something about him that was driving her crazy. Something that told her she needed more. She tossed and turned throughout the whole night, thinking about him and picturing his face every time she closed her eyes. She was sure that sleep would be scarce until she had him all to herself. She couldn't stand seeing him behind her eyes and waking up to an empty bed. Every time she rolled over, she wanted him to be there with a smile on his face. She wanted him to be there to hold her in his arms. She knew she could fall fast asleep in those arms.

Colton finally made his way to the table with two slices of pizza and a couple sodas. He set everything on the table then sat down across from her. He handed her one of the drinks and she smiled as she took it.

"Thank you for lunch." Sid said as she took a small sip of her pop.

"No problem. Thanks for inviting me out today. I was positive I'd be stuck at home with my mom's dog all day." Colton replied.

"We can't have that." She joked.

He shook his head as he took a bite of the pepperoni pizza. Sidney waited a few seconds before biting into hers. She enjoyed watching him do things. It made wanting him even more unbearable.

A few teenagers walked into the food court. Each of them being loud and obnoxious. Her eyes watched as they went to the Chinese restaurant and ordered their meal. Colton noticed them as well and shook his head as one of them slid a table across the marble floor making a screeching sound. The echo filled the food court and probably drifted throughout the mall for everyone to hear. It was a few feet from where they were sitting and he was positive they weren't going to behave like normal people in the middle of the mall.

"I can't believe I was like that when I was their age." Colton remarked.

"Really?" Sid smirked. "I can't picture it."

He shrugged, "Hard to believe, I know, but when I was in high school, my friends and I ruled this town. We could go anywhere and it wouldn't be long before we were kicked out or our parents were called. You were a teenager once, weren't you like that?"

She shook her head slightly, "Not really. I mean there were a few times I got caught under the bleachers at the football field with one of my old boyfriends, but nothing too terrible."

"Yeah, I've been there." Colton said.

"So, you're saying that you've been caught making out with one of your *boyfriends*? Glad to know that." Sid joked, then took a drink.

"Hey now, you know what I meant." Colton tried defending himself.

"Are you sure about that?" she asked with a playful smile.

He shook his head and smiled. Sidney loved that smile. She could stare at it for days and never grow weary of seeing it.

The teens sat at the table and began their loud chatter about whatever drama was going on in their lives. There were four boys and two girls sitting together. One of the boys was talking about the girl he wanted to ask out while another was talking about which girl he wanted to sleep with first. The girls were busy making fun of some other girl they went to school with. The normal life of a teenager in high school. Filled with drama and sex.

Sidney ignored the kids next to them and kept her focus on Colton. He was finishing up with his pizza and she was doing the same. She took the last sip of her pop then stared across the table at Colton.

"So, what now? You wanna walk around or something?" Colton suggested.

"Sure. I could go for some shopping." She replied.

He grabbed their trash from the table and said, "I said walking, not shopping. I know how you girls get the second you enter a mall. You have to look at everything."

She stood from her chair, grabbing her purse, "I'm not like that. If I don't see something that interests me, I leave it alone and go on to something more important."

Colton tossed their plates and cups into the garbage, "I'll believe it when I see it."

The two of them walked through the food court and out into the open mall. A few older couples were doing laps through the hallway to get their exercise. Some mothers were taking their kids clothes shopping to get ready for the new school year. Sid was more than happy to be so close to Colton. She could feel the warmth coming from his body. It was comforting knowing he was next to her. Their arms brushed together and she had to bite her lip to keep herself from tackling him to the floor, forcing their lips together.

Sidney glanced at the few stores they passed trying to take her mind away from the one thing she couldn't do. None of them were catching her interest as a place she wanted to shop at. There was a sale going on in a shoe store that would normally have her running inside to buy whatever boots or sneakers she could find. She didn't want to appear like every other girl in the world, jumping at the sight of the latest trends. She needed to play things just right for him.

Her eyes passed over a sign hanging above a small shop down the hall. A smile came to her face as she saw the garments hanging on the racks and covering the walls. It would be the perfect place to be irresistible and charming. A place Colton might actually do something in her favor.

"You know, there is something I need this summer." Sidney stated.

"What's that?" Colton asked.

"A swim suit. I just realized I don't have one and the weather in this town is just beautiful in the summer time. You wanna help me pick one out?" she asked.

Colton was a few inches taller than her so he looked down to see the smile on her face, "I don't think that would be a good idea."

"Why not? It would be fun." She said.

He sighed, "Look, Sid, you're really hot and, to be completely honest, I would love to see you in a bikini. I just don't think it's a good idea to make you think something will come out of it. You know what I mean?"

"I see," she said, the smile fading on her face.

Rejection was something she was never good at handling. She's had to deal with it before and hated every minute of it. Being turned down by someone she cared about or not getting something she wanted was the worst feeling in the world. Things like that, drove her over the top sometimes and she really had to force that horrible feeling down. She more than wanted to drag him into the nearest bathroom and throw herself at him. Make it impossible for him to say "no" to her anymore. That's what she truly wanted at the bottom of her heart, ignore the rejection and take what she wanted regardless what he said. She just couldn't do that to him, not yet anyway.

"I get what you're saying, Colton. Believe me I understand and I don't want to make you uncomfortable." She said, smoothly. "I'll just look at them, I don't need to try anything on today."

"Thank you for understanding. You're seriously like the coolest girl I've ever met." Colton said.

"I do try sometimes." she said as they headed through the

mall.

Pretending to be happy about the situation would have to do for the time being.

Ten

Colton followed Sid through the mall until they came to the bathing suit store. It was only open during the summer months and changed to a snow gear shop in the winter. This little store was another thing that helped the mall keep its doors open.

As they strolled down the hallway, Colton thought about what he just said to her. He knew that any normal man would jump at the thought of seeing Sidney half naked wearing nothing other than a bathing suit. She had a great body and, in the back of his mind, he would love to see more. He wasn't ready for that. There was no telling when he'd be ready for a new relationship with another girl. His heart was still holding out for Amy even though she wasn't calling him or getting in touch with him like he had hoped for. Although, he couldn't help himself when it came to staring at his new lady friend, regardless what his heart was telling him.

There were three other women in the store when they walked inside. A young woman behind the counter reading the latest fashion magazine. Two others were looking at life jackets and laughing about something. No one was paying them any mind at all.

Colton followed Sid to the wall filled with bikinis and tiny swimsuits. He stared at her as she searched through them. His eyes moved up and down her body, suddenly finding it hard not to stare. She was doing something to him that was forcing him to want more. The way she was standing, with her hand on her hips as she sorted through a few of the suits on the wall. That cute smile she threw at him every chance she got. It was more than Amy ever did and he was starting to enjoy it.

She pulled one down and held it against her body to show it to him, "What do you think of this one?"

He took a good look at the swimsuit. There were tiny black stars on the white bikini top and the bottoms were just plain black with a silver star on the right side. Something he would love to see any girl wearing.

"I like it," he replied.

"Me too. I have a thing for stars." She said. "I even have a tattoo on my back of three shooting stars. It was my eighteenth birthday present from my friends. Pissed my dad off all to hell, though."

He felt his lips quivering as he tried smiling. There was something about a girl with a tattoo that made him weak in the knees. Amy never liked the idea of, in her words, ruining her body with permanent ink. She always looked down on the people who covered their body in ink or even just the tiniest little tattoo in a hidden place. To her, it was the ugliest form of art. Colton still thought it was sexy for a girl to have a tattoo. Seeing ink on a woman, especially an attractive woman like Sidney, was always a turn-on for him.

"Where at on your back?" he asked.

"My left shoulder. You'll have to see it sometime."

He nodded and kept his eyes glued to her. The words he spoke out in the hall, completely vanished from his mind. Everything he said to her about just wanting to be friends was gone as well. All he could think about was seeing that tattoo on her back.

"I would love to see it sometime." He finally said.

Sidney bit her bottom lip as she took a step closer to him. He could hear her breathing nervously and could see her chest moving up and down with every breath she took. That wasn't the only thing he was noticing about her chest and he had to force himself not to stare. He could see the sly smile on her face as she lifted her hand and rubbed her fingers along the length of his arm.

"Do you want to see it now?" she asked.

He took a deep breath and swallowed hard. Unconsciously, his head bobbed up and down wanting nothing more than to see whatever she was hiding under her plaid shirt.

She turned away from him and led him to the back of the store where the fitting rooms were. They went into the furthest one away from the main part of the store. He followed her inside the small room and let her lock the door behind him. She dropped her purse on the small stool and hung the bathing suit on the wall hook. She faced him and began unbuttoning her shirt.

Their eyes were fixated on each other as she slid her arms out of the sleeves and tossed the shirt on top of her purse. His eyes drifted down to the red tank top she was wearing, it hugged her body so tightly. Then, she slipped the strap over her left shoulder and turned slightly so he could see the shooting stars on her back.

"They're beautiful." he whispered.

Without being able to control himself, he took a few steps closer and brushed a few strands of hair out of her face. He stared into her eyes for a moment, letting the feeling of wanting her flow through his mind. He couldn't stop himself from pressing his lips against hers. He wanted to taste those lips and nothing was going to keep him from doing that. No thoughts of *just* friendship. No thoughts of any past relationship. Sidney was the only thing on his mind and, for the moment, he was okay with that. The two of them closed their eyes and kissed in the dressing room. Not anything Colton would have ever done with Amy. Another thing he was starting to enjoy about Sid, doing things he could never do with Amy.

He felt Sid wrap her arms around his neck and he gently shoved her against the wall, feeling the flimsy material shake a little. He ran his hands up and down her body, feeling her every curve and her smooth skin. He was totally lost in that perfect moment, never wanting it to end. Never wanting to go out and face whatever the world had to offer him, because he was caught up kissing a beautiful stranger. The stranger he was very attracted to.

Just as things were beginning to get really steamy between them, a thought popped into Colton's mind. Nothing blocked it from showing up and nothing would make it disappear. Amy's face was all he could see and she was crying over what he was doing. She was upset because he didn't wait for her. He didn't wait because he was too busy being charming to a random girl he just met.

The kissing ceased, even though he could tell Sid wanted more. He pulled himself away from her and looked into her eyes. Panic started to fill his mind, driving out the very thought of wanting to kiss her any longer.

He shook his head quickly, then said, "I'm sorry, I shouldn't have done that."

"It's okay." She said as he started to back away from her.

"No, this was a mistake. I...I have to go." He unlocked the door and walked out of the room.

His feet quickly moved through the store, leaving Sidney behind in the dressing room. He couldn't believe the mistake he just made. How would Amy ever forgive him for doing something like that? For making out with a complete stranger? He never should have agreed to meet at the mall with her in the first place. He should have known she wanted much more than friendship out of him.

Colton walked into the hallway and picked up the pace. The more space he put between himself and Sidney, the better it would be for him. His quick steps weren't enough to keep her from catching up. She was buttoning the last few buttons on her shirt as she walked beside him.

"Where are you going?" she asked as she flung her purse over her shoulder.

"I have to go. I never should have done this." He stated, making his way to the nearest exit.

He sped up, getting a further away from her. There was an exit to his right and he took it. He pushed the glass doors open, not realizing Sidney was right behind him and she quickly caught the door before it slammed against her. The fresh air was just what he needed to clear his head and get the bad feelings out of his body.

"Colton!" Sidney called after him. "You don't have to leave."

He quickly walked toward his car, "Yes I do. You don't understand what I'm going through."

Sidney met him halfway to his car and grabbed a hold of his arm, stopping him from going any further. Finally, he turned to face her and could see the pained look in her eyes. He knew it matched the same look in his own.

"I do understand what you're going through." She stated.

"How?" he asked.

"I just do. The reason why I left my home town, the reason I *had* to get away from somebody," she began, "I was in a terrible relationship that ended with the guy not wanting anything to do with me. We were together for two years and I thought we would be together forever. He just didn't love me the way I loved him. So I moved on and came here to start over."

He lowered his head, "I'm sorry, Sid. I'm sorry you had to go through that. I'm just not ready to start over." He turned around and took the last few steps to his car.

Eleven

Colton could still see her face in the rear view mirror as he drove away from the mall. He hated leaving her like that, but he had no other choice. He couldn't risk being around such an attractive woman while he was still so vulnerable from his breakup with Amy. He didn't want to feel like he was taking advantage of the situation or that she was taking advantage of him. He wasn't ready for anything physical or emotional. He did what he thought was the logical thing to do, he drove home and tried not to look back.

All evening, he stayed home with his parents and decided to spend time with them. He enjoyed a nice dinner his mother prepared and even watched an old western with his father after they ate. It was just like old times, when he was a kid still trying to grow up. Only now, he was using this time with his parents to help him forget about the mistake he made with Sidney. A task that wasn't easy to accomplish.

It seemed everything reminded him of that girl. The spaghetti they ate for dinner, the red of the sauce had him thinking of her long, gorgeous hair. He loved how natural and soft it looked. The woman in the movie reminded him of Sidney's sweet side. He never had that problem with Amy. There weren't a lot of things that made him think of her, no matter how much he missed and loved her.

The sun went down and his mother went to bed for the night. She had to get up early for a doctor's appointment in the morning, leaving Colton alone with his father.

"How come you didn't go out with your friends tonight?" Carl asked as he turned the volume down on the TV.

Colton shrugged, "I just felt like staying home."

His dad snorted a chuckle, "Never in all my years of knowing you have you ever said such bullshit as that. What's really going on, boy?"

Colton let out a sigh, "I did something I really regret today."

"Care to talk about it?"

"I had a moment with a girl at the mall. This girl I just met last night and I told her right from the beginning I didn't want a relationship. I just wanted to be friends." Colton said.

"She didn't want that, did she?" Carl asked.

"I don't know. It's hard to tell what she's thinking." Colton ran his fingers through his messy hair. "At the bar last night, she was more than willing to be friends. Then, today at the mall, there was this moment when we were alone and I kissed her. It didn't last long and I left right after that, but I'm sure she'll never want to see me again."

"Well, that's just how women are. When they see something they want, they do whatever it takes to get it. That girl obviously saw something she liked in you and really wants it." Carl stated.

Colton shook his head. He knew he played the charming guy more than he should have. It was a mistake he would most likely make again and there wasn't too much he could do to stop himself. He learned from his father how to treat a woman and he knew he had to treat her right. Even with a complete stranger like Sidney, he couldn't bring himself to be rude. Apparently his charming side was the one thing she couldn't resist.

"Well, if you're done complaining about a girl, I'm hitting the sack. Another early shift in the morning." Carl said as he stood from the couch.

"Goodnight, dad." Colton said.

"You too, son."

His father strolled across the living room then disappeared down the hallway to his bedroom. Colton heard the door shut and he was left alone on the couch. Even the little dog was curled up in bed with his mother. He hated being alone when his mind was wrapped around things he shouldn't be thinking about.

He reached into his pocket and took out his cell phone. No missed calls or new text messages. There was no way Sidney would ever talk to him after what happened at the mall. He really thought she was a nice person and was actually looking forward to having her as a friend. She was so easy to talk to and get along with, she almost seemed like one of the guys.

He clicked the contacts button on the phone and scrolled through the list of people. He went all the way to the bottom of the list and found her name in big bold letters. All he had to do was click on it, then he could call and apologize to Sidney. Not that it would do any good, but at least he would feel slightly better about himself. Instead, he scrolled back to the top of the list and selected a different person to call. It was highly doubtful she would answer, but he tried anyway.

"Hello?" came an annoyed voice from the other end of the phone.

Surprised, Colton leaned forward on the couch and said, "Amy, I'm so glad you answered. I've been trying to get ahold of you for the last week."

"I know, Colton. I can see all of your missed calls and texts. The only reason I answered the phone was to hopefully get you to stop calling me." She replied.

"Why? Don't you think we should talk about things?

You know I'm still in love with you. You know you're all I think about." Colton said.

A sigh came through the phone, "Listen, Colton, you need to get me out of your head. You need to think of other things and give up on *whatever* you think will happen between us. It's over and no matter what you think, it will always be over. I don't want to pick up where you think we left off. I wasn't happy and I have the chance to be happy right now. So, just stop calling me and move on with your life."

The phone went silent. He couldn't hear her breathing coming through the speakers. He pulled the phone away from his ear and glanced at the screen. The call had ended. She got angry with him and hung up. It felt like she was breaking up with him all over again. His heart ached and the lump in his throat expanded. The tears in his eyes were forming already.

He couldn't give up on Amy. Sooner or later she would realize she made a mistake and she'll want him back. She'll see that things were better when they were together. He had to keep waiting for the day she comes to her senses and calls him begging to take her back. Of course, he would take her back in a heartbeat because he was that in love with her.

He shoved the phone in his pocket and stood from the couch. He grabbed the remote from the arm of the sofa and turned the TV off. Then he walked through the house, going down into the basement and finally ended up in his bedroom.

The light was dim as he switched it on, almost time to change the bulb. He sauntered over to the bed and plopped down on top of it. The box spring squeaked as the bed bounced underneath him. It was the same old mattress he's had since he was a teenager. He took a moment to look around at his things. There weren't too many reasons why he had some of his childhood stuff cluttering his room. Like the old notebooks he had when he was in school. Some were filled with notes from the class while others were filled with doodles from being so bored sitting through English. They were stacked in a neat pile on the bottom of the bookshelf across from his bed. One day he'll get up and throw things away.

He closed his eyes, then laid back on the bed. Maybe sleep would come quickly for him so he could get the terrible day over and done with. He couldn't go another second with that mistake playing through his mind. He didn't want to relive the conversation he had with Amy, but he knew it would continue to play over and over again. It would be a night filled with tossing and turning and forcing his eyes to stay shut even though they demanded to be open.

Colton rolled onto his side and grabbed his pillow shoving it under his head. It was soft and smelled like the laundry soap from when his mother washed it. He kept his eyes closed, thinking only good thoughts, and tried to fall asleep.

Twelve

Sid rolled the window down, letting some fresh air inside the car. It was another muggy night in Iowa, but she didn't let that bother her. She was used to the weather in the Midwest and enjoyed it most of the time. Getting to wear tight t-shirts and short shorts in the summer and the cutest boots and sweaters in the winter. Dressing as nice as she possibly could was one of her favorite things to do. She loved looking good for the world.

She found the house she's parked in front of completely by accident. While on her way home, she decided to take a longer way than normal. She wanted to explore some of the back roads she hadn't taken yet. She turned onto one of the streets not far from her house and recognized Colton's car in one of the driveways. She even saw him outside helping an older man with yard work. She memorized the address and made a mental note for herself to come back a little later, when the sun went down.

Exactly what she did.

Sidney kept her gaze focused on the house. The lights were on and she saw people moving around inside. Three of them were sitting in what she assumed was the living room. The blue glow from the TV illuminated the window. The blinds were open and she could see the family perfectly. His parents on one end of the sofa and he was on the other. She was lucky it was dark out so they couldn't see her sitting in the car watching them.

The older woman got up, disappeared, and never came back. The other two were still sitting on the couch and Sid could tell they were talking. From where she was parked, she could see their lips moving, but she couldn't make out what they were saying. She had a sneaky suspicion they were talking about her and the incident at the mall. It gave her goose bumps at the very thought of him telling his parents about her.

Just thinking about that kiss at the mall made her heart race. It was more than she was hoping for, his lips pressed against hers. He practically threw himself at her and she was more than willing to let him do so. That's what she was planning all along, to get him to realize that he had to have her. He ruined everything by storming out of the place. He left her there, and she had to force herself to watch him drive away. She knew he wanted her. She saw it in his eyes every time he looked at her.

There was something holding him back.

She knew he got out of a long relationship with some girl back in New York. A girl that Sidney knew didn't deserve him. How could someone throw away a good man like Colton? He was the most charming, handsome man Sid's ever seen. She didn't want to be *just friends* with him. She wanted the whole package. She wanted to be with him morning, noon, and night. To wake up next to him and smile the second she saw his face. He was definitely worth the wait, but she wasn't sure how long she could control herself until he finally comes to his senses. All she could hope for, was that he didn't take too much time doing so.

The older man in the house got up from the couch and left the room. Colton was the only one left sitting there. She could see his face and see how upset and alone he looked. She saw him take his phone out of his pocket. Hoping she was the one he was thinking about, she dug her own cell phone out of her purse and held it tight in her hands. When he pressed his phone to his ear, she stared at hers, begging it to ring. The black screen taunted her as the seconds ticked by. The phone never played the tune she picked out specifically for him.

She turned her eyes back to the window of the house. He was definitely talking to someone and she could barely make out that it wasn't going well. He seemed more upset than a few seconds ago. Almost like he was getting bad news from someone he wanted to hear great news from. She could give him the great news he needed to hear. She could give him more than that if only he would let her.

Sidney thought about calling him as she clutched the small phone in her hand. She wanted to talk to him and make things better. But, if he knew that she knew he was upset, he could find out she was right outside, watching him from a distance. She couldn't give herself away.

It wasn't long until he was leaving the room. The glow of the television went to black, then all she could see was the dark outline of his perfect form. Her eyes followed his shadow as he disappeared from view. She waited for him to return, waited longer than she should have. She stayed parked outside for a little while longer hoping he would come back into her sight.

He never did.

The engine under the hood of her small sedan was a quiet hum after she turned the key in the ignition and started it. A feature which every vehicle she's driven in her life has had. It made sneaking out easier and sneaking back home a breeze. Her eyes glanced back toward the house as she put the car into drive and slowly pulled away from the curb. She was still hoping he would go back into that room. Hoping she would get to see him one last time before she had to go home.

Soon, she was driving away from the house and on her way to her own. Another sleepless night with Colton on her mind was on the horizon. Only a day has gone by since they met, but he already haunted her dreams. What little sleep she got the night before, he was there, behind her eyes with that gorgeous smile of his. No other man on the planet had that effect on her. He was the only one who made her fall in love with him so quickly. He was the only one who had her wanting more and hating every second she had to go without him. Seeing him, even just for a moment, made things better. She felt like the day mattered and she could finally breathe again. That feeling faded the second he was out of her view.

She turned onto the crossing street and it was just a few blocks to her house. Her eyes passed over the houses as she drove. Most of them had their lights off and the owners were probably in bed already. There were a few that had a couple lights on and one with a teenaged girl outside with her little dog. She didn't look too happy to be outside walking the dog instead of doing whatever she wants on the computer like most kids her age.

Sidney pulled up to her house and shut off the engine. The only lights coming from the place were on the front porch and in the living room. She put the car in park and killed the engine. Her eyes stared at the front door to the house and she took a deep breath before opening the car door. Loneliness was the only thing waiting for her on the other side of that door. Until she had Colton all to herself, she would hate going inside that house.

Thirteen

Colton didn't get out of bed until noon the next day and he still found himself tired. After a long night of tossing and turning on the mattress, he found it extremely hard to peel himself away from the bed. He couldn't figure out why sleep eluded him. Amy didn't pass through his mind more than once and she was normally the cause of his insomnia since the breakup. Sidney, however, trudged through his mind like wildfire.

The kiss he shared with her in the dressing room at the mall, played over and over in his mind. He practically felt her lips on his every time he closed his eyes. The passion, the raw emotion of being with a complete stranger kept his heart racing and he could never fall asleep. As much as he hated thinking of that mistake, he enjoyed it just the same.

He lay in bed, staring up at the ceiling, trying to push Sid from his mind. His phone rang on the nightstand next to the bed. He leaned over and glanced at the screen. A number he didn't recognize flashed across the screen and he knew he had to answer. Quickly he pushed the green answer button and held the phone to his ear.

"Hello?" he answered, groggily.

"Is this Colton Wischmeier?" an older man's voice spoke into his ear.

"Yeah, that's me."

"This is Greg Olson from the All Star Theater downtown. I looked over your application for the maintenance position and I was wondering if you were available for an interview."

"Yeah, that would be great." A lie, but he had to get a job somewhere.

"Would this afternoon work? Around two?" Greg asked.

"I'll be there." Colton replied.

"Just ask for me when you get here. I look forward to seeing you."

"Thank you."

The call ended and Colton lowered the phone from his ear. He wasn't expecting to get called for an interview so soon, but was grateful. It definitely wasn't something he would look forward to doing. After living the last few years making over fifty grand a year, working as a janitor would be a drastic pay cut. He was only hoping he would be able to make a living on that.

Colton stood from his bed and walked through the room. He pulled himself up the stairs and into the living room. His mother's dog was asleep on the couch with its tongue hanging out of its mouth. Colton smiled at the little animal as he made his way to the kitchen for a quick lunch.

On the counter, his mother left him a few blueberry muffins she made for breakfast. It was the perfect lunch for a guy who slept in so late. He grabbed the plate of food and sat down at the table to eat. Then, he checked his phone for any other missed calls or texts as he munched away.

There was one call from Jacob, followed by a text from him saying how much he missed his best friend. Colton smiled as he read the text and replied saying something similar. After going his whole life with Jacob always being around, it was a little weird not having his best friend within walking distance. After that text, Colton noticed three messages from Sidney. All within ten minutes.

"Sorry about yesterday. Hope we can still be friends." Was the first.

"I really hope you're not avoiding me. I was hoping you would text back by now." Was the second, three min-utes after the first.

"Well, since you won't text me, I'll just let you know I'll be at the bar tonight. Hopefully you'll be there too and we can hang out again. I really like spending time with you." Was the third.

Colton's jaw dropped as he read her messages again. He liked how she apologized for what happened at the mall. He was glad she still wanted to be friends, but she could have left it at that. She didn't need to text him back right away thinking he was avoiding her. That's nothing any other girl has ever done to him before. If he didn't text back right away, that should tell her he was busy or he didn't hear the phone. The text messages didn't seem like the Sidney he hung out with at the mall. They seemed like someone who wanted more.

He took another bite of his meal and thought about saying something back. She was being a bit persistent about wanting to spend time with him again. He felt that if he didn't text her back, she would do something else and sound even worse. He figured he'd at least tell her he'd be at the bar later on, but he wasn't going to suggest they'd hang out. If they run into each other, they run into each other, as Colton liked to think.

He set his phone on the table, after sending the message, and finished eating. Then he took the dirty plate to the sink and rinsed it off. He went to the refrigerator next and grabbed a bottle of water from inside. He drank nearly half the bottle before putting it back on the shelf. He walked through the kitchen, picking his phone up on the way out, and turned down the hall getting to the bathroom. He took a towel from the linen closet and set it on the counter next to the sink. He turned the shower water on to hot, then closed the brown curtain. Then the pulled his t-shirt over his head and tossed it on the floor.

He caught a glimpse of himself in the mirror and stared at his reflection for a moment. He always considered himself lucky that he didn't get his father's hairy chest. He would rather have a nice smooth one instead of hair sticking out the neck of his shirt. He looked good for not working out since college. That was five, long years of eating takeout and doing the occasional set of crunches on the floor of his apartment. He still wasn't in the kind of shape he should be in at that age. He used to work out at the gym and go running all the time. He was lucky if he could run halfway down the street without getting winded now.

As he stared at himself, he found it really hard to come up with a conclusion as to why Amy left him. They looked good together and made one hell of an awesome couple. Whatever fight they got into, they always worked it out, until the ones during the last few months. That was after he lost his job. Things took a turn for the worst and he knew he should have seen the relationship falling apart. He just didn't want to. He loved Amy and thought she loved him in return, but maybe that's why she broke up with him. He must have thought wrong about her loving him as well.

He took a deep breath as the ran his fingers through his messy hair. He had about an hour before he needed to be downtown for his interview. Not that he was looking forward to sweeping floors all day and mopping up whatever mess the bathrooms held in store for him. He just had to keep thinking that anything was better than nothing and soon enough he would get another good job like the one he had in New York.

He turned around and opened the shower curtain. He stuck his hand under the running water, making sure it was at the right temperature. After adjusting it slightly, he stepped out of his shorts and climbed into the bathtub, letting the warm water caress his body.

Fourteen

The interview went well. Too well, according to Colton. Greg offered him the job after they were done speaking and he agreed to start on Monday giving him the weekend to prepare himself. He was given a decent starting wage of eleven dollars an hour. More than what he was expecting, but much less than what he wanted. He would work eight hours a day and some nights on the weekends when there were shows going on. Something he was not looking forward to.

"Well, congratulations, Colt." Seth sat next to him at the bar. "I know it's not as glamorous as web design or anything, but at least Greg is an awesome guy to work for. My dad went to school with him and has only nice things to say about him."

Colton took a drink of the beer in his hand and said, "Yeah, he was really nice in the interview and I was really surprised he offered me the job so quickly. I was still kinda hoping for something better though."

Seth shrugged, "Sometimes you gotta take what you can

get. Not everyone is lucky enough to get a job after only one interview and three days of searching."

"You got that right." Colton agreed.

He kept moving his eyes around the bar. Searching for that one familiar face with the long red hair. It was late enough and he thought for sure she would have been there. Of the few people sitting at the booths and the two old men sitting at the other end of the bar, she was nowhere to be seen.

He couldn't help feeling relieved knowing he didn't have to face her after that awkward moment at the mall. The thought of trying to say something without making a big deal about their kiss was giving him a headache. He rubbed at his temples trying to soothe the pain. He still felt that he needed to clear things over between them.

"Who are you looking for?" Seth finally asked after watching Colton look around the bar for the last few minutes.

"That girl, Sidney. She told me she was going to be here tonight and I guess I need to talk to her." Colton replied.

Seth smiled and raised both eyebrows in amazement, "Oh man! I can't believe you got her. I've tried a dozen times and she would never give me the time of day, but you come in and get her in one shot. *God*, I'm jealous."

Colton shook his head, "Don't be. Nothing's going on between us. I told her I just wanted to be friends and she was fine with that."

"Really? A hot girl like that was okay with just being friends?"

"I thought so, until yesterday. She wanted me to meet her at the mall to hang out and get to know each other better. Then we went into this store, she showed me her tattoo in the fitting room and we sort of kissed." Colton stated, then took another drink.

"That sounds like she wants to be *best* friends to me." Seth joked.

"No, it was a mistake." Colton retorted. "At first I wanted to kiss her, she kind of pulled me in, but then I thought of Amy and I had to stop."

"You're still stuck on that girl?" Seth asked. "You really need to get over her."

Colton shook his head, "I don't know what it is, but I swear to you, she was the one. She'll come back eventually and I have to be waiting. I can't waste my time with a girl like Sidney."

"Okay. I'm not going to be the one to change your mind." Seth said.

Colton spun around on the stool and stared at the few people in the bar. For a Friday night, it wasn't very busy. He thought for sure there would be more people. One table was crowded with a few couples who were laughing and having a good time. There were the two old men sitting at the bar drinking their lives away. A few college students were crowded in the corner of the bar. Each with a fruity drink in their hand. Other than that handful of people, it was relatively dead.

The door to the bar opened and Colton turned his attention to it. Her red hair glistened in the bar light as did her smile. He couldn't help himself as he stared at her. She always dressed nice and her hair and makeup were perfectly done. He watched as she strolled up to the bar and sat in the stool next to him, setting her leather purse on the bar counter. Colton spun around to face her.

"Glad to see you came out tonight." Sid said with a smile.

"I kind of have a reason to celebrate." Colton replied.

"Oh yeah?"

He shrugged, "I got a job today. I'll be a janitor at the All Star Theater."

"You don't sound too excited about that." She said. "I'll just have an apple martini." She ordered when Sarah app-roached her.

"I'm going from an awesome job where I mattered, to a job where I'll be cleaning up after people. Not something to get excited about." Colton replied.

"At least it's something." She stated.

"I guess." Colton said. "I have to talk to you about something, Sid."

She turned a little so she could see him better, "Okay. What's up?"

"It's about what happened yesterday."

She stared into his eyes and waited for his next words. He could tell by the look in her eyes that she was hoping he would say he wanted to be with her. It's like she was telling him to say that by staring at him with a look of determination on her face. A part of him started to feel bad because that's not what he wanted to say.

"I know things got a little heated in that dressing room, but you have to know, it didn't mean anything. It was just a kiss." Colton said.

The smile completely faded from Sid's face and she said, "Just a kiss?"

He nodded, "I'm sorry, but to me it was."

She rolled her eyes and shook her head, "Okay."

"I do still want to be friends, Sid. You are a really cool person and you're super awesome. I just don't want things to be weird, ya know."

She nodded, slightly, "I know and I'm not going to lie to you. I kinda wish you would change your mind about all that. I know you just got dumped and all, but you'll have to move on sooner or later. Why not make it now, with me?"

He shook his head, "I can't. Not right now. I'm still in love with my ex and I can't move on until I know for sure things are completely done between us."

Sarah brought Sidney her drink. She stared at the light green liquid as she lifted the glass from the counter. She brought it to her lips and drank all of it in one, quick swig. Colton watched as she did this and had the sneaking suspicion she wasn't happy with how their conversation was going.

"You do understand what I'm getting at right, Sid?" he asked.

She nodded, "Oh, I understand completely. I just wish you would change your mind."

"I can't. Another mistake like that would only make things worse." Colton replied.

"It wasn't *that* big of a mistake. It's not like you're still seeing that girl." Sid protested.

"I still shouldn't have done it."

"Whatever." Sid forced herself to look away from him.

She set the glass on the bar top, harder than she should have. She could feel his eyes gazing at her and wanted to look back at him. She wanted to stare into his wonderful eyes and get lost in whatever he had hiding behind them. Every part of her wanted to be with him, to hold him in her arms, never letting him go. He just wanted to be friends. He didn't want anything more than someone to talk to whenever he needed it.

Sid took a deep breath, grabbed her purse, then said, "I think I'm gonna go."

She reached inside her purse and took out her wallet to pay for her drink. She handed the money over to Sarah then stood from the stool.

"You just got here." Colton questioned.

"Doesn't mean I want to stay, especially with someone who doesn't want to make another mistake." She snapped.

"Sid." Colton called as she began walking away from the bar.

His eyes followed her to the door where, only moments ago, he watched her walk inside. Now, she was leaving and he was certain he just ruined whatever chance of friendship he had with that woman.

Fifteen

Sidney sat in her car outside the bar for the rest of the evening. A few tears shed from her eyes and she let them. She was never ashamed to cry over not being able to have something she so badly desired. She knew Colton was the man of her dreams. Knew he was going to be the one she would spend the rest of her life with. He was doing his absolute best to make it complicated for her to get what she wanted.

He called their kiss a mistake. To her, it was much more than that. The feelings that rushed through her body when their lips met, she knew he felt the same. It was far from a mistake. It was the beginning of something that could be wonderful between them. A love like no other love the world has ever seen.

"How could he call it a mistake?" she said to herself in the rearview mirror. "The only mistake that was made yesterday, was him not wanting more than a kiss."

She turned her eyes to the bar. She was waiting for him to walk outside with his friend. It was getting late and she knew he would be heading home soon. She had to be the one who made sure he got there safely. After a few drinks at the bar, it wouldn't be wise for anyone to drive themselves home. Who knows if they would make it anywhere without getting hurt or hurting someone else. She was only going to do the right thing and there was no law stating that she couldn't.

A small crowd came outside. She quickly sat up, scoping out each and every one of them. A brunette with extremely long hair and short shorts came out holding hands with her girlfriend. An older man came out to have a smoke and leaned against the wall of the bar to do so. Then she saw his friend stumble through the doorway. There was a woman with him, holding him up so he wouldn't fall on his face. Colton was right behind them.

He laughed at his drunken friend and helped get him in the passenger seat of the woman's SUV. Sid kept her eyes on him as she started her car's engine, preparing herself to follow him. She waited to turn the headlights on until she was sure he wouldn't notice her. She didn't want him to know she'd be right behind him his whole drive home. Colton walked away from his friend and headed toward his own car. Just as he walked past the entrance to the bar, he was stopped.

There was another woman who grabbed his arm. She had short, blonde hair and wore black framed glasses. Even from across the street, Sid could see the flirty smile on the girl's face. She was being playful with him, trying to coax him to play back. She rubbed Colton's arm and moved closer to him while he was taking a few steps back. This woman kept trying to push herself against him, their bodies were already too close for Sid to be comfortable with it.

As Sid watched this new girl come around trying to steal her man, she could feel the jealous anger rise in her stomach. Part of her wanted to jump out of the car and run across the street to knock that girl to the ground. She wanted to rip her hair out and shove it down her throat for even talking to Colton. But, she held herself back and forced herself to stay in the car. She had to bite her lip in order to keep the jealousy from really boiling up when the girl put her hands on Colton's face, moving her fingers through his hair.

Colton was trying to keep some distance between the blonde and himself. He was backing further away from her, making his way to his car. Sid could tell he wanted no part of whatever that girl was offering. She finally smiled when Colton was safely in the car and that girl stood on the sidewalk with her arms folded across her chest. There was no way Sid would let any other woman on the face of the planet steal him away from her. She would make sure of that.

Colton was backing out of the parking spot and slowly headed down the street. That was Sid's cue to pull out of her spot and follow him. With the headlights flipped on, she drove by the blonde, getting a better look at her face. There was a determined look written all over it. A look which Sidney knew all too well. That girl would try again and Sid was going to make sure she would be there to stop it.

She followed Colton down Main Street then turned the corner leading them uptown. At first she kept her distance, making sure he couldn't tell that she was the one behind him. It became hard to do that when they got to a red light.

She pulled up behind him and waited patiently for the light to turn green, ever so thankful there weren't any street lights at this corner in town. That way he couldn't see her face as she stared at the back of his head in his car. All she could see was a black blob in the shape of his head, looking from side to side wondering why the light was taking so long.

He inched forward in hopes of triggering the light to change. She stayed still, listening to the quiet newscaster on the radio. She didn't want the volume turned up too loud or else it would break her concentration. She had a bad habit of singing along with whatever song that came on the radio. Doing that would cause her to take her eyes off Colton's car and she could lose him. He might be going home right now, or he could be going somewhere else. She had to know where he was going, regardless where that was.

When the light turned green, both of them took off down

the street. They left the downtown area and headed to the residential part of town. Sid kept some distance between them as she followed him. She made sure there were at least two car lengths between her car and his. There weren't many other cars on the streets this time of night. Most of the town was asleep, except for the lucky third shifters working at the local fertilizer plant.

As she followed him, she couldn't help but wish he was in the car with her. To hear his voice, smell whatever cologne he was wearing, things would be much better for her. She imagined herself growing old with that man. Getting married, having a beautiful ceremony in the park next to the fountain. Having a couple of kids together and raising them to be absolutely perfect. Then, when they were old enough, they could retire and travel the world together. They would have the perfect life and die in each other's arms. A smile crossed her face at that thought.

She would love nothing more than to be with Colton for all of eternity. Other people would think it's crazy of her to fall in love only a few days after meeting a guy, but she was sure she found her one and only someone. She wasn't going to rest until he saw that in her as well.

Sidney followed him onto his street. His house was coming up quickly and she knew it was almost time to say goodnight. She saw the turn signal on his car flicker on and off then he slowed down. He pulled into the driveway at his house, right next to his father's squad car and she watched his every movement.

She slowed her car down to a crawl and peered through the tinted window. She needed to see him get out of his car before she drove away. Just one glimpse of him and she might be able to sleep. He opened the car door and stepped out into the night's cool air. He walked to the front door of the house, stumbling a bit as he walked. She could see the keys dangling in his hands as he stood by the front door. Before he unlocked it and went inside, he turned around.

Sidney knew he was staring right at her car, watching as

she slowly rolled down the street. The windows on her car were so dark, there was no way he could see inside. She wasn't even sure if he knew what kind of car she drove at all. Not like it mattered. If he knew she followed him, he would simply call and ask why. She would come up with some lie saying how she was worried about him driving home drunk. Colton was too sweet and charming not to believe anything she told him. He believed she actually wanted to be friends, instead of something much more.

Colton stared at her car a second longer before shrugging his shoulders and facing the door again. She watched him open the door and disappear into the darkness of the house. Then, she stepped on the gas and headed home.

Sixteen

Colton met with Seth for lunch on Saturday. They got together at a small, Mexican restaurant and sat in the corner away from everyone else. The restaurant was busy regardless what day of the week it was. It was one of the few in town and the most popular one to go to. They were lucky they found a table to sit at without having to wait. They just had to wait a few extra minutes to get their food which the waitress promised she'd bring out soon.

Colton had his phone in his hand, fidgeting with it. Every few seconds, he'd unlock the screen to make sure he didn't miss anything. He was hoping Sidney would text or call him or do something to let him know she wasn't upset. He couldn't stop thinking about what he said to her at the bar and how she didn't take it very well. He hated when people were upset with him. It was all he could think about and he knew he had to make things right. They might have just met, but she was starting to get to him. He was afraid he ruined whatever friendship they could have had by what he said at the bar.

Their kiss wasn't a mistake. He couldn't admit it at the time, but the more he thought about it, the more he realized he might be wrong. They had an intimate moment together and thought it was terrible to have feelings for someone else so soon after his breakup. He ruined things at the bar by telling her it was a mistake. After she stormed out, all he could think about was wanting to go after her and tell her to stay. He loved being in her company, it just took him a while to realize it. When he was about to call her and apologize, Betsy showed up and stopped him.

Betsy hung onto him like they were an item. She kept flirting and joking around with him the entire evening. Even when he tried to leave the bar, she followed him outside, begging him to stay a while longer. She even asked him to go back to her house so they could be alone. She was the last person he wanted to be alone with and she got really upset when he told her "no". He saw the look in her eyes and knew she wanted more than just a simple talk at the bar. She wanted him, after all the years of not talking to each other, she still seemed crazy about him.

Colton drove straight home after that, wanting nothing more than to close his eyes and sleep. The entire way home, he thought someone was following him. He didn't recognize the black car with tinted windows behind him. He knew it wasn't Betsy. She was still standing outside the bar as he pulled away. Whoever it was, stayed in the rearview mirror all the way to his house. They made him nervous about going inside. He knew the person in the car was staring at him, he just couldn't see who it was. Good thing his dad was a cop and happened to be home at night. That thought took some of the edge off and he was able to get inside the house a little easier.

"What are you thinking about? You keep staring at your phone and the lady brought your food like five minutes ago." Seth stated. "Something you wanna talk about?"

Colton hadn't realized his enchilada was on the table, his

eyes were glued to his phone, "I don't know. I just thought someone was going to call me or something."

Seth rolled his eyes and tore into his taco, "What'd you do after the bar last night?" he asked with a mouth full of food.

Colton shrugged, "Went home and crashed. I think I was followed though."

"You think it was Betsy?" Seth asked.

"No, not her. I don't know who, but they were behind me until I pulled in the driveway and went inside." Colton replied.

"Oh, I see. That's not good. Did you tell your dad about it?"

Colton shook his head, "I didn't get the chance. He was gone by the time I woke up and I don't want to worry my mom about it. You know her, she'll take things *way* out of proportion and lock me in my room for a month."

"Yeah, like when we were in ninth grade and there was that rumor two guys from the prison fifty miles away escaped and she said you weren't allowed to leave or else they would kill you."

The two of them laughed as they thought of that memory. Colton was only allowed to go from home to school until his mother was sure nothing bad would happen to him. Even when it was proven to be a rumor, she still kept a tight grasp on him. He didn't want to go through that again.

"Good times." Seth added.

"Yeah, they were. But what should I do if someone *is* following me? I'm not exactly prepared for something like that." Colton asked.

"I don't know. I wouldn't worry about it too much unless it happens again. Who knows, maybe you have a hot stalker after you." Seth joked.

"Or I could have a deranged psychopath after me who wants to wear my face as a hat." Colton said, quietly.

Seth grimaced as he pictured someone actually doing that, "Gross dude, I'm trying to eat."

"Sorry, I just wish I knew who it was. It would make me less worried." Colton stated.

"Maybe it is Betsy. Maybe she had someone else follow you home so she could stare at you from afar. She was all over you at the bar and tried even harder every time you backed away from her. You do remember, she was absolutely obsessed with you in middle school." Seth said.

Colton took another bite of his meal as he thought about middle school. After he broke up with her, there were times he caught her following him home. She tried to hide in the bushes whenever he turned around, but he always saw the branches shaking and her feet sticking out. Betsy *was* all over him at the bar, maybe turning her down so many times, made her mad and she wanted to do something about it.

"I guess I could ask if it was her. I could swing by the gas station she works at and ask, right?" Colton said.

"Dude, would you be honest if the person you were following asked you the same question? Of course not. You would lie through your teeth and keep doing it. That's what crazy people do." Seth retorted.

Colton nodded, "You're right. I guess if we go to the bar tonight and it happens again and she's not there, I can assume it's her. If not, I don't know what to do."

Seth shrugged, "Me neither, man. All I can say, is I'm glad it's you and not me."

"Thanks." Colton replied, sarcastically.

He took a drink of soda, then set the plastic cup on the table. His eyes wandered around to the other people in the small restaurant. Most of them were families, sitting together and enjoying a nice meal. There was a table of three teenaged girls who were clearly gossiping about something that was really funny. Each of them were laughing and carrying on with the conversation. He didn't recognize them and didn't think they would be responsible for following him home. They were too young to be driving anyway.

He turned his attention back to his meal and took another bite. They were sitting next to a window and he happened to glance outside at the passing cars. A red pickup truck drove by with a car trailer attached to it. A small, grey minivan was right behind the truck and he could see a rowdy group of kids in the back. On the other side of the street was a red sports car cruising by with too much bass because Colton could hear it all the way inside. Then behind that, was a black car with tinted windows. Something that looked strangely familiar to him.

Colton did a double take, thinking his eyes were playing tricks on him. He was already paranoid about the whole idea of someone following him. His mind could be imagining the car to make him think he was crazier than he seemed. But it *was* the same car driving slowly by the restaurant. The same dark tinted windows and black paint. The windows were too dark for him to see the driver and his heart started pounding. There *had* to be someone following him, he just knew it. He wished there was some way of finding out who it was. That was a long shot though. His best bet was to pray they mess up and he'd be able to catch a glimpse of them. Until then, he'd have to be careful about things.

Seventeen

Colton was a little devastated when Sidney didn't show up to the bar that night. He was hoping he could see her to apologize and make things better. He tried texting her, to see if she was coming out, but she never responded. He wound up spending another evening with Seth and a few friends from high school. They had a good time and reminisced about the good ol' days when they ran the town.

He stayed at the bar until midnight, drinking a few beers. He felt good enough to drive home and was certain he would make it there unscathed. He wasn't wrong about that and made it home just fine, except for the whole being followed part. The same black car with dark windows was in his rearview mirror all the way home, just like before. There was no trying to lose the car, they already knew where he lived and it seemed pointless to try. He still couldn't tell if Betsy was the one responsible or if it was somebody else.

He pulled into the driveway at his house and the black car crept by. He got out of the car and walked to the front door, keeping his eyes on the black sedan the whole way. They weren't really trying to hide the fact that they were following him. A normal person would have sped up and kept going after being spotted. The driver of this car, waited until he went inside the house before they drove off. He thought it was a little odd, but he'd rather not question the mind of a stalker.

Once he was safely on the other side of the front door, he locked the knob and the dead bolt. He didn't want to take the chance of having someone break into the house and come after him while he slept. He turned around and took a deep breath. Slowly, he walked down the basement stairs to his bedroom and didn't bother to turn on the light. All he wanted to do was get to sleep and not think about someone coming after him.

Colton could see enough in the darkness to plug his cell phone into the charger and set it on the nightstand. Then he collapsed on the bed with his face on the pillow. He didn't bother changing out of his day clothes into something more comfortable. This was how he spent his nights during high school, along with most of his adult life, when he got home later than he should have.

He tucked his arms under the pillow and closed his eyes, praying sleep would come swiftly. He didn't want to stay up anymore to worry about someone breaking in the house and stealing only him. Of course, trying not to think about it only made him think about it even more.

He could picture it perfectly. A madman, picking the locks on the front door. Rushing down into the basement to see him shuddering in the corner of his room because he was too afraid to fight anyone. Then the madman would tie him up and carry him off into whatever sick fantasy the guy was thinking about. No one would ever see him again and would always wonder what happened.

Colton rolled over to face the rest of his bedroom and tried to push that image from his mind. He thought of something better to fill the blackness behind his eyes. An image that made him smile, a person to take the edge off things. That person used to be Amy and he almost wished it was her. Instead, he found himself falling asleep to the gorgeous red hair flowing around Sidney's perfect shoulders. Thinking of her calmed his heart and his mind and he was finally able to drift off to dreamland.

By three o'clock in the morning, his sleep came to an abrupt halt. There was a loud noise going off somewhere nearby. It was driving him crazy. He was too tired to figure out where the noise was coming from and was more than relieved when it stopped. He held onto his pillow and tried to fall asleep again.

The noise screamed through his bedroom once more and he forced his eyes to open. He could see the screen of his phone lit up on the nightstand, illuminating the area around it. He let out an annoyed groan as the phone continued to ring. There was no reason someone should be calling him so early in the morning.

He reached for the phone and squinted as he looked at the number on the screen. There was no number or a name. All it said was "Blocked Call". He pressed the answer button and held the phone to his ear anyway.

"Hello?" he said, groggily.

There was no answer on the other end of the line. Colton pulled the phone from his ear for a second to make sure the call was still connected. Sometimes calls had the tendency to drop when he was in the basement. Not this time. The call was still going and he put the phone back to his ear.

"Hello?" he said again, this time more clearly.

Still, there was no answer. Nothing but the chilling sound of silence coming through the phone. He gave it a few seconds, thinking maybe Seth was playing a prank on him. His friend was known for scaring people when he knew they were already freaked out to begin with. Colton was certain Seth was the one behind this phone call and he would get to tell him all about it the next time he saw him.

"Okay, whoever this is can take their phone and shove it.

This isn't funny, waking me up at three in the damn morning. And Seth, if this is you, you better prepare yourself for my retaliation tomorrow." Colton lowered the phone and ended the call.

He set the phone back on the nightstand and attempted to get comfortable again. Just as he laid his head on his pillow, the annoying ringer of his phone went off again.

"What the hell?" He yelled into his pillow, then reached for the phone.

It was that same blocked number again. He didn't want to answer it. He wanted to hit the ignore button and let it go to voicemail. A bigger part of him wanted to yell at the person on the other end of the call. It was too early in the morning for this type of nonsense.

He reached for the phone and answered, "Seriously, whoever the fuck this is, please stop calling me. I'm fucking tired and would like to go to sleep." He shouted into the phone.

This time he got a response. Not a voice or words or anything. There was only breathing. Light, creepy, heart racing breathing. Colton felt a chill climb up his spine as he listened to the sound. The tiny hairs on the back of his neck rose and he sat up in the bed.

"Whoever this is, please talk to me. Please tell me who you are. Are you the one who's been following me the last two nights?" he asked, unsure to still assume it was Seth on the other end of the phone.

The only answer he was able to get, was the breathing. He couldn't tell if it was from a man or a woman through the phone, but it was enough to creep him out. He pulled the phone away from his ear and ended the call again. This time, he held the power button until the phone shut off. It was the only way he'd be able to get some sleep without hearing the constant sound of the tone.

The very second he let go of the phone, he found himself feeling unsafe in the darkness. He could feel his heart racing as he looked around the room. Everything seemed darker.

The tiniest sounds were louder with an eerie hint to them. He didn't want to be in that room anymore.

Instead of forcing himself to stay in the basement, he grabbed his pillow and a blanket from the bed and headed for the stairs. He kept his feet quiet as he walked through the house. The only light came from a plugin night light on the wall at the top of the stairs. He walked into the living room and tossed the pillow on the couch, then laid down on top of it. He covered himself with the blanket and had to force his eyes to stay closed. All he could think about was the weird breathing on the phone. He thought he could still hear it in the house. That slow, raspy breath coming into his ears sent shivers up his spine all over again.

Colton opened his eyes quickly when he heard something approach the couch. Whatever it was, wasn't big enough to hurt him and definitely nothing that should scare him. He did jump however when he felt something hop onto the couch with him. The little feet walked across his back and he leaned up a bit to see what it was. His mother's small dog was staring back at him and he gave it a little smile.

He let out a sigh of relief, then allowed the dog to crawl under the blanket with him. He cuddled with the soft animal, not feeling any safer, but felt more relaxed with something else in the room with him. At least he wasn't alone any longer.

Eighteen

"Colton, time to wake up." His father's deep voice startled him awake.

He was still lying on the couch in the living room. His father was sitting on the coffee table, a worried look crossed his face. There was a small glass of water along with a pill bottle on the table next to him. Colton rolled onto his side then slowly sat up, rubbing the sleep from his eyes. His head was pounding as he looked into his father's eyes.

"You want to tell me why you slept on the couch last night? You were obviously downstairs at some point because you brought up your blanket and pillow." Carl couldn't sound more concerned even if he tried.

Colton took a deep breath and asked, "Can I have some aspirin?"

His father shook his head, "Not until you tell me what happened last night."

"Where's mom?"

"At church with your grandparents. I'm on call this

morning so I couldn't go." Carl replied. "Now, tell me what's going on."

Colton ran his fingers through his hair as the early morning phone call played over in his mind. He could still hear the raspy breathing in his ears and he didn't want to think about it happening again.

"I don't know. It's probably nothing or Seth playing a joke on me." Colton began, "Just the last two nights, I got followed home by some black car with tinted windows. Then, at three this morning, I woke up to my phone going off and no one said anything the first time so I hung up. They called back and all I could hear was breathing. It freaked me out and I didn't want to sleep downstairs."

"You think it's Seth?" his father asked.

Colton shrugged, "I don't know. Seth is an asshole sometimes, but he's not normally one for doing the same prank twice in one night to the same person."

"You need to find out for sure if it is him."

"And if it's not?" Colton asked.

His father reached over and picked up the water and aspirin from the table, "Then, we'll deal with it."

Colton took the water and pills from his father. He took two aspirin from the small, white bottle, followed by a drink of water. His father stood up from the table and walked toward the kitchen. Colton set the stuff on the table and grabbed his pillow and blanket from the couch. Slowly, he stood up and sauntered toward the stairs.

Once he was in his bedroom, he flicked the light on and tossed his things on the bed. His feet carried him to the nightstand where he left his phone. The screen was black as he lifted it and held the power button until the screen flashed on. As he waited for it to power up, he went to his dresser and started picking out clothes to wear for the day. Jeans and a green t-shirt.

He looked back at the phone in his hand and his eyes grew wide. There were fourteen missed calls and he had a pretty good idea who they were from before he even checked it out. He unlocked the touch screen and clicked on the call menu. Every one of the missed calls was from that same blocked caller. Each one was placed exactly two minutes after the last. This was something his father needed to see.

Colton grabbed his clothes and headed upstairs, practically running into the kitchen. His father was leaning against the counter, waiting for his morning coffee to brew. His eyes grew wide when he saw the frantic look on his son's face. Colton set his clothes on the counter and walked over to his dad with the phone in his hand.

"They called me *fourteen* times after I shut my phone off, dad." Colton said in a panic. "I know for a fact Seth wouldn't do that. He's not that persistent with his pranks."

Carl took a look at the missed calls on his son's phone, "Did they leave a voicemail?"

Colton went through the apps on the phone, searching for a new voice message from the mysterious caller. The voicemail menu was empty, other than a few he left on there from Amy and Jacob. He thought it was probably a good thing the stranger didn't leave a message. He didn't really want to hear their raspy breathing again.

He did notice a new text message flashing in the upper right corner of the screen. A part of him was afraid to open it, thinking it was a demented message from his stalker.

"Anything?" his father asked.

Colton shrugged, "No voicemail, but there is a new text."

He hesitantly clicked on the new message and let out a sigh of relief. Just a message from Sidney and he was more than grateful to see her name instead of something from the blocked caller. He didn't want to think of the type of message they would leave.

"It's just a message from a friend." Colton stepped away from his father as he opened the message to read it.

"*Sorry I wasn't at the bar last night. I wanted to come out, but had to work. Why don't we meet up for lunch today? My treat!*" he read quietly.

He looked away from his phone and glanced at the clock

on the stove. It was almost eleven in the morning. He couldn't believe his father let him sleep in that late.

"Everything okay, boy?" his father asked.

Colton nodded his head, "Yeah, Sid just wants to meet up for lunch today. Thank god it wasn't whoever was calling me all night."

"Yeah, but we need to find out who's bothering you. If this is something serious and you let this continue, it could graduate into something worse than an early morning phone call or following you around town." Carl sounded demanding.

"We'll figure it out, dad." Colton said, paying more attention to his phone than to his father.

Sidney's message was still open on the screen. He couldn't believe how happy he was to hear from her. After going a full day thinking she hated him, he was relieved to know she still wanting to hang out. He read her message again before hitting the reply button.

"Sounds great. I'll meet you at the Deli on Washington Street downtown." Was his response.

He grabbed his clothes from the counter and walked out of the kitchen, going to the bathroom. He locked the door behind him and set his things on the counter surrounding the sink. He got the shower water prepared and realized that little message from Sidney was enough to calm his nerves a bit. Amazing how a simple text message was enough to do that to him.

Nineteen

Colton had a table picked out for the two of them when he got to the Deli on Washington. A small booth next to a window so he could keep an eye out on the street. He's been a bit paranoid since the random phone calls that morning and getting followed home. He wanted to make sure he could see whatever vehicle pulled into the parking lot. He didn't see the black car, but he had a feeling it would be around.

Sidney arrived not long after he did and he didn't see her drive up to the building. He smiled at her as she approached the table and she gave him one of her irresistible smiles in return. She sat in the seat across from him and brushed her bangs out of her eyes.

"I've never been here before." She said.

"Really?" Colton asked.

She shrugged, "I honestly don't eat out too much. I have a lot of ramen noodles in my cupboards and hot pockets in the freezer."

"That's no way to live." Colton said with a smile.

"Well, when it's just me, there's no point in cooking." She lifted the menu from the table and asked, "What's good here?"

"I like the chicken teriyaki sub, but everything's good. A friend of my dad's owns this place. He opened it like twenty years ago." Colton replied.

"What an interesting fact for the day." Sid joked. "I think I'll have this turkey sandwich with provolone cheese. It looks pretty good."

A young waitress approached the table with a notepad in her hand, "What can I get you two today?"

Each of them placed their order and the waitress walked away from the table with the menus in her hand. Colton was trying his best not to look out the window every few seconds. He wanted to spend this time with his new friend, but he was too nervous about seeing that car again. He never imagined having a stalker and hated that he had to worry about that now.

Sidney noticed his strange behavior, "Are you okay over there?"

He nodded quickly, "Yeah, I'm fine. Just nervous I guess."

"Nervous? Why would you be nervous?" Sid questioned.

He let out a brief sigh then leaned over the table to get closer to her, "I think I'm being followed. The past two nights, the same black car followed me home from the bar. I think they even called me this morning at three o'clock."

"Really? That's strange." Sid acted surprised at the information she was hearing.

"I know. My dad told me I needed to find out who it was otherwise it will get worse. I'd like to think he knows what he's talking about since he's a cop and all."

Sidney glanced at the others in the restaurant. She had to try to look the part of a concerned friend. Acting like she was looking for someone suspicious or something that might not belong. Everyone was doing things they would normally be doing in a deli, ordering their lunch and eating a nice sandwich. She was the only one guilty of doing anything wrong. She just wasn't about to tell Colton any of that. It was best for her to keep it all a secret and laugh about it later on.

"You should calm down, Colton. I'm sure it's no one to be worried about. Probably just a prank or something." Sid tried to sound reassuring.

"I really hope you're right, Sid." Colton replied.

After a few minutes, the waitress came back with a tray of food and two drinks for each of them. She set the tray on the table, smiled, then walked back to the front to greet customers. Colton took his sandwich from the tray, along with his drink, as Sidney did the same. He nervously took a bite, then looked through window again.

There was still no sign of the black car. He didn't see it drive by and the only cars he could see in the parking lot were two trucks and a green minivan other than his car. He was hoping that was a good thing, thinking maybe that person only waited for him at the bar.

He glanced across the table at Sid, trying to push the thoughts of being watched out of his mind. She was taking a bite from her sandwich and tossed him a playful smile. He couldn't believe after all he said the other night and how weird he's been around her, that she still wanted to be friends and hang out. She really was the type of girl he's never had in his life before.

"So, I have to ask, why did you leave the bar the other night? I know what I said and I know you obviously didn't like it, but I just wanna know why." Colton asked.

Sid took a drink of her soda, then said, "I don't know. I guess I was kind of hoping you would change your mind about the whole friend thing. I really like you and I like hanging out with you. I'd rather be your friend than nothing at all. We might not know that much about each other and I'd really like to get to know you a little better."

A smile crossed his lips, "Me too. You're pretty awesome."

She shrugged, "I do try."

They went back to eating their lunch and, eventually, Colton took his mind off the black car. He stopped thinking about the possibility of being followed home again. He wanted to focus on enjoying his lunch date with Sidney and not constantly worry about what could be waiting for him outside.

He watched her take small bites from her sandwich. Not a crumb fell as she ate. He stared at the freckles flowing across her nose and cheeks. The green of her eyes stood out beautifully in the dim corner of the deli. They smiled every time her lips did and he was beginning to adore that about her. He couldn't admit it yet, but deep down, she was the perfect candidate for a future relationship.

Sid finished her sandwich, then wiped her mouth and hands on a napkin. She took the last sip of her soda and waited for Colton to do the same. The waitress came back and handed them the bill, which Sid left the money on the table along with a tip. Then the two of them stood up and headed for the exit.

Colton followed Sidney outside into the fresh summer air, "Thanks for lunch, Sid, but what now?"

"I have no idea. You start your new job tomorrow so this is your last day of freedom." Sid replied as she walked across the parking lot.

Colton walked right beside her, his eyes glancing to the minivan that was backing out of its parking spot. He froze in his tracks as he stared at the car parked on the other side. The van was blocking it so he thought he was safe, but there sat the black sedan with tinted windows that had been following him and driving him crazy. He noticed the car was empty and his eyes darted back to the deli. He thought he'd see the culprit waltzing out after him, but no one was there.

Sidney didn't hear his footsteps beside her anymore, so she stopped walking. She turned around and saw him frantically searching the parking lot. There was a panicked look on his face and, as soon as she saw what he was staring at, she knew the reason why. She had to play this just right in order for him not to suspect anything.

"What's wrong?" she asked.

Still staring at the car, he replied, "I need to get out of here. They followed me here and I don't even know how."

"What are you talking about, Colton?" Sid asked, looking around the parking lot like she had no idea what was going on.

"That black car over there. It's the same one from the last two nights, the one that's been following me." He pointed to the car across the lot.

Sid looked to the car and acted nervous about seeing it parked there, "What do want to do about it?"

He walked up to her and said, "Can we take your car? I'd feel better if we were in something they didn't recognize."

"Umm," she had to come up with a lie quick, "I didn't drive today. Running low on gas so I walked. That's why it took me a little longer to get here."

"Shit." Colton said under his breath. "We'll have to take mine then. I'll take you home, but I just gotta get outta here."

She nodded her head, "Okay. Whatever you want to do is fine with me."

She watched as he glanced back to the restaurant. He was still looking for the person that wouldn't be there. The person he thought was following him. She never meant to scare him like that or have him thinking his life was in danger. She would never hurt him or bring any kind of danger his way. The look on his face as they walked to his car on the other end of the parking lot, had her thinking. Maybe she was doing the wrong thing. Maybe she should stop with the following and leave him alone.

She climbed into the passenger seat of the car and buckled her seatbelt. Colton quickly got behind the steering wheel and started the engine. He sped away from the deli and kept checking the rearview mirror. There was nervous tension written all over his face, a look she didn't like seeing on him. Then, something happened. Whatever fear was boiling in Colton's mind took over his body, getting him to latch onto her hand and clutch it tight.

Sidney looked down to see his hand on top of hers. She wasn't sure if he meant to grab it or if he just needed something to help take the edge away. This reaction to the fear she had brought him, was something she enjoyed and she suddenly didn't feel so bad for following him. She wanted more of his touches and was willing to do anything to get it.

Twenty

Sidney directed Colton to her house. Since he already knew the town like the back of his hand, she didn't have to give him too many directions. They pulled over on the street outside her house and he shut off the engine. He let go of her hand, but she could still feel his grip on her fingers.

She unbuckled her seatbelt then grabbed her purse from the floor, "You wanna come inside and relax for a little bit. I just got cable hooked up a month ago. I don't really watch it, but I'm sure there's something good on."

Colton took a deep breath and said, "Sure. That would probably help take my mind off things. Just as friends though, so we're clear."

She nodded as she reached for the door handle, "Just as friends."

She pushed the car door opened and stepped outside. As long as Colton didn't ask her where her car was, things would go great and she could force herself to make this a friendly hangout instead of begging him to make it something more.

She walked up the small set of wooden stairs to her front porch, then fumbled with her keys before unlocking the door.

"This is a nice place." Colton stated as he checked out the outside of the house.

"Thanks," she finally found the house key, "my dad picked it out when I moved here. I found an apartment downtown above some antique shop, but he insisted I move into a house. He paid for the first month's rent so I couldn't really complain."

She unlocked the door, then headed inside with Colton behind her. She shoved her keys inside her purse then tossed it on the recliner in the living room. Thankfully she cleaned the place up a bit over the last few days, otherwise she would have to explain her messiness to the man of her dreams.

"I say your dad made the right move. This is much nicer than any of those places downtown. For one, you don't have to worry about being woke up early in the morning when the shops open." Colton commented.

"That's exactly what my dad said." Sid replied as she walked further into the living room.

"So, you're a journalist, right?" Colton asked.

Sid nodded and said, "I write a few articles for my dad's sporting magazine. I'm the only woman who works for him, other than his assistant. He just needed a woman's voice to add in the mix and he says it helps."

"Wish I still had my awesome job like that." Colton said.

"Everything happens for a reason you know." Sid tossed him a smile.

She took the remote from the coffee table and pressed the power button to turn on the TV. Some old cartoon movie popped up on the screen and Sid quickly changed the channel to something more adult like. The cartoon channel was the only thing she ever kept the cable set to. She never cared for getting cable in the first place, but having to get up and change movies every two hours was getting to be a pain and she needed some sort of noise while she wrote on her laptop.

Colton was busy looking around at all of her things on

the bookshelf next to the couch. It served as a side table as well as her miniature library. All of the books she had on the shelves were about monsters or things that would never in a million years happen. She hated reading about normal, everyday things. Getting lost in a good monster book was her favorite past time.

"You read the same kind of books I do." Colton stated as he glanced over some of the titles.

"Yeah, I could never get into those romance novels or whatever girly-girls read. I have to have something to keep me on edge, something that keeps my heart racing throughout the entire thing." She replied.

"I never quite understood why girls enjoy reading about love and romance and happy endings. Amy was always into that kind of stuff and it drove me crazy. Forcing me to go to every chick flick made and telling me these soppy stories about her friends." Colton said. "Glad to know there's at least one normal girl out there who enjoys the good stuff."

Sidney found an action movie that had just started and left it on that channel, "What can I say? I am one of a kind." She set the remote on the coffee table, then asked, "You want anything to drink? I think I have pop in the fridge."

"Sure." Colton replied.

He followed her into the small kitchen. There wasn't a dining room so the kitchen was right off the living room. All of her appliances were stainless steel and spotless. The countertops were cleared off as well. It was the cleanest kitchen Colton had ever seen. Sid opened the refrigerator and bent over to get a better look inside and he found himself staring at another flawless thing in the room. He didn't mean to gawk at her, he was just enjoying the view.

"I do have a couple Cokes in here. Apparently I have gone shopping lately." She took two sodas out of the fridge then stood back up.

She turned around and handed one to Colton. He smiled as he took the drink then went into the living room with a dumb look on his face.

"So, did your mom help you decorate this place? 'Cause you did a great job." Colton asked as he headed for the couch.

Sidney stopped walking and stood in the doorway. She never really spoke about her mother to anyone. It was always a sore subject with her. It had been such a long time since anybody's asked about her, that it felt a little strange. They didn't have the best relationship and she always regretted not getting to spend as much time with her as she should have.

Colton turned to face Sid and noticed a sad look on her face as her eyes stared blankly at the floor. He could tell right away that he asked about the wrong person.

"Sid, are you alright?" he asked, taking a few steps closer.

She nodded, "I'm fine. It's just been a long time since anyone's brought up my mom. Kinda hard to think about her sometimes."

"Oh, I'm so sorry." Colton apologized.

"No, it's okay. I never told you about her so you had no way of knowing." She replied. "It's just," she paused and thought of the right thing to say, "my mom passed away a couple years ago. She got sick with the flu and refused to see a doctor for it."

"That's terrible." Colton set his soda on top of the bookshelf-side table, then moved closer to Sid. "I'm really sorry that happened to you."

She shrugged, "Things like that happen to the best of us."

"You're right about that." Colton said. "You need a hug, I can tell."

She stayed put and let him approach her with a warm embrace. She wrapped her arms around him as well and smiled as she rested her chin on his broad shoulder.

Twenty One

Colton stayed at Sidney's house until dinner time. His mother called to say she was making his favorite meal and that was his cue to leave. He kept glancing into the rearview mirror on the drive home, making sure no one was following him. He hadn't seen the black car since he left the Deli. Not that he was complaining or anything. He'd rather not get caught up in that mess again.

He pulled his Honda into the driveway and parked next to his father's squad car. As he made his way to the front door of the house and could smell one of his favorite meals. His mother's spaghetti. She knew how to put just the right amount of zest and spice in with the sauce. Just thinking about it had his mouth watering.

He burst through the front door and practically ran into the kitchen. Both of his parents were already at the dinner table with plates of spaghetti in front of them. Denise already had a plate ready for her son along with two pieces of garlic bread on the side. He went to the fridge for a can of soda then headed for his spot at the table.

Carl glanced at his son, then asked, "Where were you all afternoon?"

Colton finished chewing the bite of pasta before answering, "At a friend's. We went out for lunch, then back to her place for a movie."

"A girl, huh?" his mother chimed in. "You're finally over Amy?"

Colton shook his head, "No, not yet. Sidney is just a friend and she knows that."

"Does she know someone's following you?" Denise asked.

Colton set his fork on the glass plate then glared at his father. He was really hoping his mom would never find out about that. All she would do is worry herself to the point of getting migraines and he would never hear the end of it.

"I thought you weren't going to tell her, dad." Colton said.

Carl shrugged, "I'm sorry, son. When it involves your safety, both of us need to know what's going on."

Colton let out a sigh of exhaustion as he rolled his eyes. He picked up his fork and twirled more spaghetti on it. He shoved the bite into his mouth, avoiding his mother's question. He shouldn't have told anybody about the black car following him home the last two nights. It would only lead to worried phone calls whenever he's out and a million questions about his day when he gets home. He'd never forgive himself for that mistake.

"Your mother asked you a question, boy, you better answer." Carl demanded.

His father was never a mean man. Never really raised his voice to any member of his family unless it deemed necessary. However, he had a great deal of respect for women, it was how he was raised. So, whenever his son ignored Denise or was rude to any woman at all, Carl made sure to say something about it and things always got resolved.

"Fine." Colton finally said after his mouth was empty.

"Yes, Sid knows somebody followed me home. That was why she invited me to her house to relax."

"Were you followed today?" Denise asked, getting more concerned about her son.

Colton remembered seeing the black car at the deli with Sidney. It made him nervous all over again just thinking about it. He glanced to his mother and saw the concern on her aging face. He hated worrying them over something that's most likely nothing. It was pointless to go on and on about some random car following him everywhere.

"Nope." Colton figured lying was the obvious choice to avoid further questions about the matter.

He shoveled another bite into his mouth, hoping the conversation was over. He couldn't take any more questions about something he was slightly embarrassed to talk about. He was a grown man and shouldn't be afraid of someone following him around at night. He could take care of himself if the time ever came, which he was hoping he wouldn't have that problem. It might just be someone following him and calling him in the middle of the night at the moment, but he knew there was a possibility of it escalating into something more. He couldn't stand thinking about his issues, especially with his parents around.

Colton took a sip of his soda, then tried changing the subject, "So, I start my new job tomorrow."

His father nodded his head while his mother spoke, "That's good, honey. I know it's not what you're used to, but at least it's something. Maybe it will lead to a better position down there."

"I doubt it, but it's a start. Hopefully I can save enough to get an apartment here in town soon." Colton replied.

"Oh, you don't need to do that, yet." Denise was practically telling her son he wasn't allowed to leave.

"Yeah, especially when someone is following you home every night. You wouldn't want to be caught alone and have them around." Carl stated.

Again, Colton dropped the fork on the plate and let out

an annoyed groan, "I knew I shouldn't have told you that. You guys are just gonna blow this all out of proportion. It's probably nothing, just someone I went to school with playing a prank on me. I don't know, but I'm just tired of hearing about it already. I mean it's only happened twice. It's not like they're parked outside the house right now."

"We're just a little worried, that's all." Denise said, softly.

"I know, but you worry too much." Colton argued.

"You don't raise your voice to your mother. I don't care how old you are, as long as you are in this house you will listen to us." Carl retorted. "If there is the possibility of someone following you in an attempt to hurt you, you will not say a damn thing about us getting worried. We are your parents and that is our job. Do you understand me, boy?"

Colton nodded his head and stared down at his plate, "Yeah, dad, I understand and I'm sorry."

"Good." Carl said, then went back to eating dinner.

There were only two things that his father did to scare Colton more than anything. The first one was the day he got elected to be one of the sheriffs in town. *What kid would want that as a parent?* The second being anytime his father got angry. The tone in his voice changed and his face got tense. Colton always got nervous when his father got angry. He tried to stay on his good side and dreaded the days when that didn't happen.

Twenty Two

After the uncomfortable dinner was over, Colton went straight down to his bedroom. He dug out his old TV and hooked it up to the cable. The first show to pop up on the screen was some reality show about dancing. Something he didn't care for so he flipped through the channels for something better to watch. An old action packed comedy came across the screen, so he decided to watch it.

While staring at the small screen, he dug his cell phone out of his pocket and unlocked it. He went to his contact list and scrolled through the names. He thought about calling Amy again. To tell her how much he still missed her and how badly he wanted to be with her. The only thing stopping him was knowing she didn't feel the same. She made it very clear to him the last time they spoke that she did not want to be with him anymore. If only there was some way to change her mind.

He closed out of that screen then set his phone on the nightstand. He had to set his alarm clock for eight the next morning so he could get ready for work. Something he wasn't looking forward to, but was hoping it would go well and he would like it. He laid back on the bed to get comfortable while he watched the movie.

A few hours went by and he eventually fell asleep with the TV and the bedroom light still on. He woke up during the middle of the night to what he thought was his alarm clock going off. He smacked it a couple times trying to get the sound to go away and that's when he realized it was his cell phone ringing.

He opened his eyes and sat up. He grabbed the phone and stared at the screen. Another call from the blocked number. Instantly, his heart began to race.

Hesitantly, he answered the call and held the phone to his ear, "Hello?" he said, nervously.

There was no answer, just like before. He could hear someone breathing, but it wasn't as loud as the last time. The breathing was calmer and he was wondering if it was even the same person. Maybe there were two people harassing him in the middle of the night with strange phone calls. That would be his luck.

Colton ran his fingers through his hair, "If someone's there, will you please answer me and tell me who the fuck this is?"

The breathing stopped and Colton listened more intently to the other end of the phone call. He waited for an answer. With the eerie silence coming through the line, he expected the caller to say something. Even if it was something simple or something that would scare the living daylights out of him, he felt he deserved an answer.

He stood from the bed and walked toward the stairs, thinking if he got his father on the phone, things could get straightened out. It was a slim chance, but a chance none-theless.

He made it to the living room and, just before he turned down the hall, he happened to see a light flicker off outside the house. He turned toward the living room window and figured he would see someone standing outside. No one was out there, but that didn't stop him from going to the window to see what the light had come from.

With the phone still pressed to his ear, he went to the window and peered outside. His car was parked in the driveway next to his father's. All of the neighbors were sound asleep and their lights were off. The streetlamp was still lit on the curb outside and he stared at the car parked in the spotlight. The black windows were rolled up, making it impossible for him to see inside it. That didn't matter because it was the *same* black car with the dark tinted windows. The one he's seen in his rear view mirror the last few nights and the same one parked outside the deli when he was with Sid.

The breathing began again in his ear as he stared at the car outside, "Please will you just tell me who this is?" he begged quietly.

There was another pause on the phone, followed by a whisper, "I just had to see you again."

The voice was so quiet, he couldn't make out who it came from. The one thing he knew for certain, was that it came from a woman. The whisper was not deep enough to come from one of his friends or any man he knows. It definitely had to be a woman. Not that the notion was enough to calm his nerves one bit. Women can be even *crazier* than men sometimes.

Colton lowered the phone, still keeping his eyes glued to the car outside, "Dad!" he called through the house, "Dad, I need you!"

The driver must have heard him yelling for his father. The headlights flickered on, shining a light blue haze down the street. He heard his father's footsteps rushing down the hallway toward the living room. The light came on and the car outside sped off down the street just as his father joined him at the window.

Colton glanced to the screen on his phone. The call had ended.

"What's the matter, son?" his father asked, staring

through the window, puzzled.

"That was them." Colton said, calmly.

"Who?" Carl asked.

"The black car that followed me. They were outside and they called me again." Colton replied.

His father turned to look at him, "Did they say something this time?"

Colton nodded, "It was just a whisper, but I could tell it was a woman. When I got to the window, she said she just had to see me again."

Carl put his hand on his son's shoulder in hopes of comforting him. He was never really good at being the sentimental fatherly type. He was better at being the overly protective, do what I say kind of dad.

"What do I do, dad? It might be a girl, but she sure has a way of making me nervous." Colton stated.

"We'll figure it out and we'll find out who this woman is. For now, just try to get some sleep and worry about work tomorrow. Just turn your phone off at night from now on." Carl stated.

Colton nodded then walked away from his father and headed back downstairs to his bedroom. Along the way, he made sure to power down his cell phone. He never had to worry about doing that before.

His mind went back to the phone call. That quiet voice still played in his head like a broken record. He'd be lucky if he got any sleep at all for the rest of the night.

Twenty Three

Colton was pretty tired at his first day of his new job. He found himself having to force his eyes to stay open during the hour long maintenance training video. Luckily, he wasn't tested on anything otherwise he might have failed. Losing a job before it's even started wasn't exactly on his list of things to do.

The job was relatively easy. Change a few light bulbs, sweep the theater area, mop up the bathrooms. Any type of maintenance job, he had to do it. There was an older man who was showing him the ropes and how to do everything. He was retiring in a week which was why Colton got the job so quickly. They had to make sure he learned all he needed to know before he was left on his own.

After the video, he spent the rest of the morning follo-wing the old man around with a broom. There wasn't much going on at the theater for the next few days, so all he had to do was busy work. They swept the lobby and dusted the glass doors and windows. When the old man went home after lunch, Colton spent the rest of the day cleaning chairs and the small party room. By the time the day was over, he felt like time had gone by so slowly that a month had passed. He almost wished it had.

It was five o'clock when he was able to leave for the day and he was both relieved and tense at the same time. His gut was telling him there would be company on his drive home. He walked to his car, keeping his eyes peeled for the black sedan. All he wanted to do, was get home without them following him.

Once he was in his car, he locked the doors and started the engine. He put it in gear then backed out of the parking spot. The only other vehicle around, was the grey truck his boss drove and that man always stayed late.

Colton pulled away from the building then turned down the next street that would take him home. He made it all the way to the first set of stoplights before he saw the car pull up behind him. He shook his head as he stared at the car in the rear view mirror. Even though it was light out, he still could not see the driver's face. All he could see were the white hands gripping the steering wheel.

It was like that for the rest of the week. He could count on seeing that car pull up behind him every day after work. They never did anything to threaten him on his short drive home. Never tried to run him off the street or slam into the back of his car. All they wanted to do was follow him and they followed him *everywhere*. To spruce things up a bit, Colton would take a different route home. Turning down a street taking him even further away and that car would stay right behind him the whole time. He even tried to lose them more than once, but apparently the little car was faster than he expected it to be and stayed caught up, even when Colton got on the highway.

The phone calls were still coming. He kept his phone shut off at night, obeying his father's orders. When he turned it on and checked it the next morning, there were at least three missed calls from the blocked number. They never left a voice message and they never gave up. Once Friday hit, he was more than ready for a drink at the bar with Seth. Part of him was nervous about being out, especially when some woman was stalking him every night. Another part of him needed interaction with other people. He needed to take his mind off things and he knew a night at the bar would help with that.

He sat next to Seth who was busy checking out the group of girls sitting at a booth in the corner of the bar. They were probably on summer break from college and enjoying a night out as friends. Each of them had a fruity drink in their hand and huge smiles plastered on their faces. A couple of the girls even tossed a flirtatious smile his way, but he shrugged it off.

Colton let Seth flirt back with the girls while he kept his focus on the beer bottle in his shaking hands. He emptied it a few minutes after Sarah brought it to him, but it wasn't enough to clear his mind.

"You seem really tense tonight, Colton. Can I ask what's up?" Sarah brought him another beer.

He met her eyes and kindly replied, "I just had a really bad week. Haven't been getting much sleep and I'd rather not talk about it."

"I understand. We've all been there before." Sarah stated, then walked to another customer.

Colton took a small drink of beer, then glanced to Seth. His eyes were glued to the pretty girls at the booth. Apparently he was much too busy to help his friend relax, especially when he needed it the most. So, he was forced to sit there, basically alone, to think about whether or not he would ever figure out who's been following him home.

He knew none of his female friends would be that crazy to tail him like that. Amy would never drive that far for the sole purpose of stalking him, although he was secretly hoping it *was* her. He would absolutely love it if she were his stalker. It would mean there was still a chance for their relationship and he could get her back without trying too much. But, the more he thought about it, the more farfetched it seemed that

Amy would ever do something so crazy as that. Getting caught for speeding was probably the most reckless thing she's ever done, so stalking was definitely out of the picture.

He was so caught up on trying to figure out which woman was the one following him that he didn't notice Betsy sitting on the stool next to him. When she ordered a drink, he finally lifted his head and turned his eyes to hers. He wasn't exactly convinced that she wasn't the one following him and wanted to be careful with their conversation.

"Hey, Colton. How're you doing?" she asked in an ever pleasant tone.

He shrugged, "Had a rough week."

"Awe, that's too bad. Hopefully after this weekend, things will start to pick up for ya." Betsy replied.

"I doubt it." He said, taking another sip of beer.

"You care to talk about it?" she asked with a smile.

He shook his head and answered politely, "Not really. This isn't a problem I care to share with the entire world."

"I understand that." Betsy stated. "I still wish there was something I can do to put you in a better mood."

He shrugged as he stared at the playful smile on her face. He could tell exactly where she wanted to take things. The way she licked her lips as she stared at him, how she couldn't help but move her eyes all over his body. That idea was the furthest from Colton's mind, especially with Betsy.

"You know," she put her hand on his thigh, "there is one thing that will put you in a better mood."

He gently grabbed her hand and set it on her own leg, "No thanks. That is the absolute last thing on my mind right now."

"But you know it will make things better. Maybe you should give me a chance." She suggested with a sly smile.

Colton let out a sigh as he shook his head, "No thanks."

"Please." Her brown eyes were pleading with him.

He turned to Seth once more but his friend had disappeared. He went over to chat up the girls in the booth. He knew a few other people in the bar, just not well enough to spark up a random conversation. The only other option he had was to leave and he was positive she would stop him from doing so.

"All I'm asking is for one night. We can go back to my place, have some fun, and when you wake up in the morning, you can decide whether or not to go further." Her persistency was driving him crazy and he was desperate for a way out. "Although I know you'll want it to go further."

He shook his head and tried focusing on the counter. There were droplets of beer in a few places and some scratches in the wood. It was the only thing for him to focus on while Betsy was invading him with her eyes.

"Colton! I'm so glad to see you out tonight." Sidney's voice came from behind him.

He turned his head and tossed her a relieved smile as she sat in the stool on the other side of him. He could see her look past him and snarl at Betsy. A hint of jealousy was written on her face, but he would take that over the relentlessness of Betsy trying to get him to leave with her.

"Yeah, I haven't been in the mood to come out lately. I'm sure you can guess why." He stated.

She nodded, "Things will get better. You're a trooper."

Betsy felt ignored, so she put her arm around Colton's shoulder and glared right back at Sid, "We were having a conversation and you interrupted us. It was kinda rude so you can just go back to the mall and buy yourself some more shoes. I'm sure that's you really want to do."

Sid let out a little chuckle as she took a drink from Colton's beer. She wasn't much for the back and forth banter most women do in those situations. Not that drama and gossip weren't her strong points, she was just slowly getting away from all that high school melodrama some girls carried with them throughout the entirety of their lives. Sid would come up with a witty remark in hopes of winning whatever little battle they had going on and continue with her life. By the look on Betsy's face, she knew it wouldn't take much to get that win.

"Desperation does not look very good on you, sweetheart." Sid said as she set Colton's beer back on the counter, "I think Colton would much rather have a real woman than a desperate piece of garbage hanging all over him. So why don't you just save yourself the embarrassment and crawl back to whatever shithole you call a home."

Sid kept her eyes glued to her opponent. They were locked on each other for what seemed like an hour and Sid could keep her glare for as long as she needed to. Betsy, on the other hand, gave up and removed her arm from Colton and backed away. Sid could see the jealousy on her face and smiled knowing she had caused it. She wasn't the type of girl to let another woman come along and steal her man. Especially when that man was Colton. Betsy grabbed her purse and strolled to a different part of the bar, a spot where she could still keep her eyes on Colton.

"I can see you don't take shit from anyone." Colton commented.

"It was how I was raised," Sidney replied with a shrug, "and that girl is outrageously annoying."

"That she is." Colton said. "Thank you for getting her to leave, by the way."

"No problem. When I got here, I saw you were looking for some help away from her. Luckily I got here before she could do anything else."

"Never in a million years would I let that woman do anything else to me."

"That's what I like to hear." Sid said. "So, how was your first week of your new job?"

"It was pretty good, really easy and extremely slow though. Until I left the place, then things got horrible. Got followed home every day by that same person, but I've come to the conclusion that it's a woman." Colton replied.

Sidney looked away from him for a moment, "I see. How do you know that?" she said, trying to hide the nervous tension building up inside.

"She called me one night and whispered in the phone.

I'm not positive, but it was much too high of a whisper to be a man's voice." Colton replied.

He didn't get an answer after that. He could tell she was thinking about something and he didn't want to bother her about it. It was best if the subject was dropped so they could go on with their evening without more talk of bad things.

Twenty Four

Colton wasn't followed home that night. He was actually surprised when he saw the empty street in the rear view mirror. He expected to see the car right behind him at every turn, but it never showed up. He thought he saw it parked at the bar when he left, but he must have thought wrong. It was the first night in the past week and a half that he was able to get home without a problem and without being nervous.

He pulled in the driveway around midnight and quietly went inside the house and to his bedroom. He wanted to see if his follower was really gone, so he chose to break his father's rule and left his cell phone on. There'd be a chance of them calling him in a few hours, but he was willing to take that chance. He needed to see if they were going to start leaving him alone.

When he woke up Saturday morning, around eleven, he checked his phone and smiled. There were no missed calls at random hours of the night. He was quite relieved knowing no one bothered him and he was able to get a decent night's sleep for once.

After his shower, he met his father in the kitchen for lunch. His dad was sitting at the dining room table with a cup of coffee in one hand and a magazine in the other.

"No work today, dad?" Colton asked as he started to make himself a sandwich.

"Nope, not today." Carl said as he stared at the article on the page.

Colton put together a turkey and mayonnaise sandwich then closed the refrigerator. He joined his father at the table and sat down across from him. He checked his phone once again, still proving to himself there were no missed calls. He actually liked seeing a blank screen.

"You seem like you're in a good mood, son. What's going on?" Carl asked.

"Well, I had a good time last night. I hung out with my friend, Sidney, at the bar for a while, then I came home and did not get followed. No one even called me at two in the morning." Colton replied.

Carl lowered the magazine, "That's real good. Let's hope it stays like this from now on."

"Yeah, I'm hoping so. It's just weird though. They followed me home from work yesterday, but not from the bar. You would think they would follow me everywhere I went." Colton said.

"Yes, this is true. Let's just hope something made them change their mind. Maybe they saw something they didn't like about you anymore and are going on with their life." Carl stated. "You talk to anyone that might have seemed suspicious last night?"

Colton took a moment to think about it. There was that whole ordeal with Sidney versus Betsy, but that wasn't weird enough for him to think anything of it. Seth went home with one of the girls at the bar and that was completely normal to him. The whole night was great after Betsy left and he was able to talk to Sid about his issues.

He lowered his sandwich and stared at the wall in front

of him. There was something a little off with Sid after he told her about the phone call. She didn't have anything to add to the conversation and chose to change the subject. He didn't notice at first, but the more he thought about it, the more he started to see how she hated talking about the person following him. She was quick to tell him things were going to be okay, quick to change the subject, and she never looked him in the eyes whenever they spoke about it. He hated the ideas that were going through his mind about her, but he needed to get to the bottom of it.

Colton finished what was left of his sandwich then said, "I need to go."

He left his father alone at the kitchen table and strolled through the house. He dug in his pocket and pulled out his car keys. It was a short walk to the front door and he burst outside into the warm, summer air. His mother was busy digging in the garden under one of the windows and she passed him a smile when he walked by. He waved and gave her a big smile right back, then headed for his car.

He unlocked the drivers' door, sat in the seat, and turned over the engine. Once he backed out of the driveway, he put the car in gear, then headed for his destination. He buckled his seatbelt as he drove down the street.

Colton felt his heart pounding faster as he got closer to the street he was looking for. He was praying his instincts were wrong, hoping he was mistaken and had the wrong person on his mind. She just started to act so strange after their conversation and he wanted to know why.

He turned onto her street and her house was a few blocks away. He slowed the car down a bit, realizing he wasn't ready for the truth yet. If that car was parked outside of her house, he wasn't sure how he would react. He really didn't want to see it there. Sidney was starting to leave a good impression on him and he didn't want anything to ruin it.

As he drove down the street, he happened to catch a glimpse of the houses nearby. There were a few people taking advantage of the beautiful day and working outside. Some were mowing the lawn and others were working in their gardens like his mother was doing. A few kids were playing around in the hose trying to wash their parents' car, but it was turning into a water fight instead. He laughed as he stared at the kids spraying each other with the hose and squirt guns. There were days when he and his friends would have that much fun in the hot summer.

Her house was coming into view and his heart beat faster. She didn't seem like the type of girl to do something crazy and follow him wherever he went. She was a sweet girl with a troubled past similar to his. He wanted her as a friend and would hate if something ruined it.

He drove even slower as he passed her house. A red truck with a trailer attached to it was on his right. A yellow sports car was parked in front of the truck. On his left, was a white SUV that clearly belonged to a soccer mom with all the school bumper stickers on the back windshield. There was a blue coupe sitting in the driveway of her next-door neighbor's house. The owner was underneath it working on something.

He stopped his car right in front of her house and stared at the vehicle parked outside. A smile crossed his lips as he stared at the small moped parked on the sidewalk. He didn't see a car of any kind parked near her house and was hoped the moped was her only mode of transportation.

"Thank god," he said as he pulled away from her house.

Twenty Five

The rest of that day flew by and before he knew it, it was Sunday afternoon. Another Saturday night of hanging out at the bar downtown was wasted and Colton had no regrets about it at all. He didn't mind drinking a little too much and probably shouldn't have driven home, but he did anyway and somehow even managed to make it down to his bedroom. He just wasn't quite sure how it happened.

It was around one in the afternoon when he walked outside and things became very clear to him. He stared at his car, half parked on his father's perfect lawn and half parked in the driveway, mere inches from the back bumper of his father's car. Colton ran his fingers through his hair as he stared at his handy work. Shame and guilt flowed through his veins and he knew he was going to be in trouble.

His father came out of nowhere and startled him enough for him to jump back a step. He looked into his dad's eyes and would have loved to run away right then. The anger that burned in those brown eyes always had him on edge.

"Proud of yourself?" Carl asked as he folded his arms across his chest.

Colton shook his head, "Sorry, dad. I honestly don't remember this."

"You're just lucky I'm not going to write you up for this."

Colton smiled, "I know. I'm an idiot. I can promise you this won't happen again."

"Good. You're grounded though."

"Funny. I'm twenty six years old, dad, you can't really do that anymore."

"That's what *you* think. You live in *my* house and when you come home drunk at one in the morning and stomp around the house waking your parents, that's enough to ground you for the rest of your life, boy."

"Good luck with that, dad." Colton said, walking toward his car.

"Don't do it again." Carl ordered.

"I won't." Colton climbed inside his car, then started the engine.

He backed up carefully so he wouldn't damage the grass any more than he already had. There were two tire tracks and a few muddy spots as he backed into the street. He could see his father shaking his head as he drove away from the house. It would take a while, but Colton planned on fixing his little mistake on the lawn.

He didn't have any plans for the day. He needed to run to the store to get a few things, then head back home. It would have to be an early night since he had work the next morning.

A dinging sound came from the dashboard, followed by a red flashing light by the gas gauge. He forgot to get gas over the last week and was hoping he would make it to the nearest station before completely running out. Unfortunately, he knew who worked at that gas station and would really like to avoid her.

He pulled next to a pump and got out of the car. He was the only one at the gas station and did not have a credit card to pay at the pump. Cash was all he ever liked to pay with and he instantly regretted not having any other form as he waited for the tank to fill. The nozzle clicked itself off when the tank was full and Colton shook the last few drops into the tank before closing the gas cap.

He sauntered to the gas station, cash ready in his hand. All he had to do was pay the cashier and get out of there as quickly as possible. The second he saw her blonde hair glistening in the sunlight, the thought of making a fast getaway was long gone.

Betsy was the only person standing behind the counter when he pushed the glass door open. She was the only other person in the entire building. He rolled his eyes as he stepped up to the counter and was greeted with a more than friendly smile.

"How are you today, Colton?" Betsy asked.

"Good. Just got thirty on pump two." He tried handing her the cash but she was taking her sweet time to ring him up.

"Glad to see that red head's not with you today. She was really annoying the other night. Don't you think?"

Colton shook his head, "Not really. She wasn't the one who kept trying to take me home."

"Sorry about that. I think I had a little too much to drink that night and you know how things go." he could tell she was lying.

Again, he tried handing her the cash, "Well, here you go."

She still wasn't taking it, "You know, I don't really get why you hang out with her all the time. She's not really your type and she's kinda crazy. I heard the reason she moved here was because her last boyfriend got a restraining order against her. I guess she wouldn't leave him alone after they broke up."

Colton shrugged, "I wouldn't know. She never told me."

"You should ask her about it. I'd hate to see her do something awful to you. Following is one thing, but that can always lead to something else." Betsy finally took his money.

That last sentence caught his interest, "What do you mean by following?"

She put the money in the cash drawer then answered, "You know, she's been following you in that black car of hers. After you leave the bar sometimes I've seen her pull out right behind you and follow you all the way home."

"How do you know she follows me home?" Colton asked.

"Well, I'm just assuming that's where you go when you leave the bar. That's what normal people do." Betsy stated, defensively.

"Whatever. I'm sure this is just another lie in your failed attempt to get me to be with you." Colton retorted, then left the station.

His feet carried him straight to his car as his eyes were dashing in every direction in hopes of spotting the black car. It wasn't anywhere to be seen and he found it slightly odd that it had been two days since he's seen it following him. The car disappeared after he spoke with Sid about it.

He sat back in the drivers' seat of his Honda and started the car. His mind was wrapped around what Betsy was trying to explain to him. There was a slight suspicion he had of her. Thinking that maybe *she* was the one who had been following him and blamed Sid as a way to get him to hate her. Betsy was the more likely candidate to be crazy enough to start stalking him. Her jealousy at the bar when Sid came around really made him see that.

He pulled away from the gas station and headed for the department store at the other end of town. Every few seconds he would glance in the rear view mirror only to prove to himself that the black car was not behind him. He turned his eyes back to the road and attempted to shove Betsy's little rant from his mind.

118

Twenty Six

Colton spent an hour at the store. He needed some new shirts for work along with deodorant and shampoo. It didn't take him long to get those few things, but the rest of the time he spent walking around the store wasting time.

He bumped into an old teacher from high school and talked about life for a few minutes. He found an old movie he used to love watching a hundred times when he was younger and couldn't resist the temptation and decided to buy it. The line at the cash register was pretty long and this store was famous for having twenty checkout lanes and only five cashiers. But, by the time he left the store, he was more than ready to head back home.

He put the bags in the trunk of his car and the second he closed it, he happened to glance across the parking lot and see something very familiar. It was parked at the end of the lot, facing the only way in and out of the store's parking lot, and he *still* couldn't see inside. He was about to go back into the store to waste more time and hope the black car would be gone by the time he'd leave. That seemed like the cowards way out and it wasn't like this person was trying to hurt him. They were just really into following him home.

Colton looked away from the car as he climbed into his own. He backed out of his spot, then drove down the lane toward the exit. He made sure to pass by the front of the vehicle in hopes of catching the driver.

The perpetrator was definitely in the car. He could see white hands gripping the steering wheel as he got closer. Whoever was driving must have noticed him. They quickly ducked down so he couldn't see their face. The only part of him he was able to catch a glimpse of, was their hair flying through the air as they ducked down.

His mouth fell open as he looked back at the car when he passed it. He wasn't positive, but he thought for sure he saw red hair as the person hid. There was only one person in the world he knew with red hair. Maybe Betsy was right after all.

Instead of heading home, he flipped the car around and pulled up next to the black car. He couldn't see through the tinted windows, but he thought it was about time he found out who this person was. Unfortunately, they had other plans.

The second he got too close, the driver peeled out of the parking spot and drove straight for the exit. Colton quickly followed them out of the parking lot and onto the main road. Finally, he had the power and was following them for once.

The black car sped down the street, passing any other car that got in their way. Colton cautiously did the same, trying not to break too many laws on the way. Luckily, they were on a four lane street and it was much easier to pass the slower cars.

They came up to a red stoplight and Colton was prepared to stop. The driver of the black car in front of him was not ready for that and sped through the red light. Before following, Colton looked both ways to make sure there wasn't oncoming traffic. When he was positive the way was clear, he sped through the stoplight. It took him a few seconds to catch back up with the black car. They were leading him to the residential part of town and he knew they were going to try to lose him in one of the neighborhoods.

He stayed behind them as they turned on a side street with houses on both sides. There were kids playing in the yards of some of the houses and men out mowing their lawns. All of them glared as the two cars sped through their neighborhood. Colton ignored them and kept his focus on the car in front of him. He couldn't get distracted. The need to know the driver of the car in front of him was his main priority at the moment.

They turned onto another side street and the black car moved a little faster. Colton pushed the gas pedal closer to the floor, letting the car move faster as well. He caught a glimpse of the speedometer and noticed he was going well over the speed limit. A good twenty miles over it. Not a good thing to be doing in a residential part of town where children could run out in the middle of the street at any moment. Or a police car could pull up and flash their lights at you.

Colton could see the blue and red lights shining in his rear view mirror and hesitated for a moment. If he pulled over, he would lose the black car and who knows when he would see it again with this kind of opportunity. But, if he didn't pull over, he would get arrested for evading the police and he would never hear the end of it from his parents. So, gradually, he let off the gas and pulled the car over next to the curb.

He shut off the engine and watched as the black car disappeared down the street. Colton couldn't be more angry at letting them get away like that. He rolled down the window and waited for the cop to approach. It didn't take more than a few seconds before he could hear the clicking of the officer's boots on the concrete.

"License, registration, and proof of insurance." The officer said as he stood outside Colton's car.

He handed the older officer his information and waited for the same remark he got from every cop in town. Being the son of the sheriff had its perks sometimes, but when he got pulled over, things got annoying.

"Carl's boy. He told me you were back in town. Don't think that since you're his son, you're getting out of this." The officer stated.

"Believe me, I know." Colton replied.

"Do you mind telling me why you were speeding?"

Colton let out a deep breath, "I don't know. I was trying to catch up to someone, I guess."

"That's not an excuse to go forty five in this part of town."

"I know and I'm sorry. I don't normally speed like this, I just really needed to catch up with that person." Colton stated.

The officer leaned down to get a better look at Colton, seeing the distress on his face, "What was so important about getting to them?"

Colton shrugged, "If you ask my dad, I'm *sure* he'll tell you."

"Why don't you save me the trouble." The officer demanded.

He let out a sigh, "I've been getting followed home at night lately and that was the car. I was trying to get to them so I could figure out who it was before things got serious and I'd have to get my dad to do it for me."

The officer nodded, then glanced at the information in his hands, "I understand. I can see this is making you pretty upset, so I'm gonna let you off with a warning this time. I will, however, contact your father and let him deal with this. Don't let me catch you speeding again."

He handed Colton his things then walked away from the car before he could say anything else. It was already too late to think about finding the black car again. The driver turned off onto another side street and he would never be able to find it. His luck ran out on this attempt, but he was still able to go home with some hint of who his stalker might be. The red hair was a pretty big hint for him.

Twenty Seven

Sidney pulled her car into the small driveway behind her house. A gravel parking space that was impossible to see from the street out front. Her heart was still pounding after almost getting caught by Colton. She was not expecting to see him at the store and she definitely had not planned on following him after he left. She always parked at the end of any parking lot, away from the other cars. It was her way of avoiding door dings and scratches. She didn't mean for it to look like she was waiting for him.

She was only at the store to get a few groceries and ink for her printer. She didn't even make it out of the car before Colton was driving right in front of her. The only thing she could do, was duck and she thought he didn't see her. She wasn't ready for him to find out that she was the one who had been following him and calling him at odd hours of the night. How could she live with herself if he found all of that out? Running was the best option at the time and getting chased by him was such a rush.

Sid sat in the car for a few minutes, replaying the chase in her mind. The feeling of getting caught, the excitement of not knowing what would happen next. It was like an orgasm of the mind. She wanted that feeling again and more often. Almost getting found out wasn't part of her plan and neither was being chased, but she found it hard not to enjoy the rush. Part of her wanted him to catch up to her. She wanted to know what he would have done. He'd be angry with her of course. Maybe he'd grab onto her, pulling her close to him so she could feel the warmth of his breath. He could use that anger and turn it into passion.

She could practically feel his grip on her arms as she thought of him. His rough hands caressing her silky, smooth skin. His gorgeous eyes peering through hers, seeing straight into the soul that craves him. Just thinking about it was enough to make her shudder with desire. It was a feeling she wanted to feel over and over again.

Finally, she gripped the door handle and pushed the car door open. The warm summer air blew through her hair when she climbed outside. Her legs were shaking as she walked to the back door of the house. The keys were clanging together while she fumbled to find the right one. Her heart was pounding so hard, she thought she could hear it. Every beat of her heart was for Colton. It belonged to him and she couldn't wait another minute until he gave his to her.

She opened the door and walked into the kitchen. The sun was shining through the windows, illuminating the entire room. The rays bounced off the silver pans hanging from the rack above the stove. Slowly, she closed the door and leaned against it, pressing her hands to her heart, wishing they were his hands touching her.

She closed her eyes, attempting to calm her nerves. She had to get herself to stop shaking, to stop aching for him to be in the room with her. It was a task she wasn't sure she could accomplish. All she could think about was him. His face, his smile, his perfect body was all she wanted. She could shout it to the world a thousand times over and never get tired of it.

The words would never lose their meaning. She wanted him to be with her, to tell him how much he meant to her. She never wanted to open her eyes because she knew he wouldn't be there for her to stare at.

Eventually, she had to open her eyes. The grey kitchen was all she could see. The granite countertops and tiled floor were dull compared to Colton. Nothing would ever measure up to the way she saw him. The most beautiful man in the world, slightly damaged by his former paramour, giving him the perfect amount of vulnerability that she found irresistible. He truly was the man of her dreams. He has starred in them every single night since the very first time she saw him at the bar. Throughout every crazy adventure while she dreamt. She would be the damsel in distress and Colton would always be the man to come a take her away from the madness. Sometimes, she would rather live inside her head so she could have the one thing she desired more than anything else in the world. She needed to have the man of her dreams and have him need her just the same.

Unfortunately, she couldn't live in her mind.

She was stuck living in the reality forced upon her. The reality where Colton did not want her the way she wanted him. He saw her as a friend and *only* a friend. He didn't want to kiss her or hold her while they lie in bed together late at night. She didn't want to think of never getting to have him. It made her heart ache in a way she couldn't cure.

Sid moved away from the back door and walked through the house until she came to the bathroom. The reflection of herself in the mirror showed a woman starved of love and emotion. Her eyes were begging to look only into his and to see him actually looking back. To not see her as a friend, but as the woman he was going to spend the rest of his life with. The longer she went without his love, the longer she was forcing herself to starve.

There had to be a way to get him to realize that she was more than just a friend. More than someone he could go to lunch with and have it be just that. A friendly lunch with friendly conversation instead of something much more. She needed him to see that she was the girl he *had* to end up with. He needed to see that without her in his life, nothing would have a purpose. Above all, she needed his love.

With that, her life would be absolutely perfect.

Twenty Eight

Colton couldn't keep his leg from shaking under the dinner table. He couldn't bring himself to eat even a slice of the pizza his mother ordered for the three of them. His mind was far too busy being wrapped around other things than trying to eat.

All he'd been able to think about was what he saw in the black car at the store. The whole ordeal shot through his mind and, knowing that he failed at finding out who the driver was, made his head hurt. No amount of aspirin would take that kind of headache away either. All he had to do, was stay caught up with the car. He knew his car could match whatever speed they had to throw at him. He just couldn't bring himself to get arrested only to find out something he was torn between knowing.

He knew it would drive him crazy if he went the rest of his life without knowing the person that caused him this agony. It would be a long, lonely life of always trying to figure out who the culprit was. Yet, at the same time, he wasn't exactly sure if he truly wanted to know who was sitting behind the steering wheel.

He saw the hair flying through the air as the driver ducked down. He was certain what color it was, but he didn't want to be *that* certain. He enjoyed spending time with Sid, loved every minute they hung out together. She was the perfect friend, despite what happened in the fitting room at the mall. He didn't want to see her as the girl behind the steering wheel of the black car.

His father cleared his throat and said, "I guess I'll just have to eat the rest of the pizza since Colton is getting full on whatever he's got on his mind tonight."

Colton shook his head, trying to push his thoughts away, "Sorry, I just can't help but think of how close I was to finding out who's been following me."

"I know, son, but you shouldn't have started chasing them like that. It's never safe to do something *that* crazy." Carl added.

"That's what they've been doing to me. Chasing me until I ran inside and hid in my room. What difference does it make if I do the same in hopes of finding out who it is?" Colton stated.

"Life or death. That's the difference. If you found out who this crazy person is, they might not like you knowing and could do something about it. Believe me, I've seen it happen." Carl said.

Colton sighed, "I know, but if it's who I'm beginning to think it is, I really don't think she'd hurt me like that."

"And who do you think it is?"

Colton shrugged, "Sidney. I ran into someone when I got gas who said they've seen her following me home in that same car. Today at the store when I drove by, I thought I saw her red hair as she ducked down."

"Isn't that a good thing? I mean, she can't possibly be a threat, right?" his mother chimed in.

"I don't know." Colton shrugged. "I guess I don't really know too much about her. I just met her a couple weeks ago.

She doesn't appear threatening to me."

"Well, you need to find out for sure if it's her or not." Carl said.

"And what if it is?"

"Tell her to leave you alone or you'll get the cops involved. That's all you really have to do."

Colton didn't feel right about coming out and asking Sid if she was the one harassing him. He didn't think she'd even tell him the truth if it *was* her. She could be like any other girl and deny the whole thing so she could still be around him.

Finally, he grabbed a slice of pepperoni pizza from the box on the table and took a bite. The grease from the cheese flooded his taste buds as he took a second bite. It was the pizza from his favorite place in town and he loved how his mother remembered that. What kind of parent would she be if she didn't? What kind of parent would either of them be if they didn't care as much as they did? Colton couldn't picture a world without his parents being there to care so much about him.

Like his father said, he needed them to be in his life to worry about whatever choices he made. His mother bawled her eyes out the day he left for New York City while his father told him how careful he needed to be in a big city like that. He remembered getting a phone call over a dozen times a day for the first few months. All they wanted to do was make sure their baby boy was still alive and well. He loved them more than anything else in the world just because they could show him how much they care. He also hated them for that very same reason.

He took a third bite of his slice then finished it down with a big gulp of soda. Amy managed to pop into his mind for the first time that day. The first time all weekend actually. He got so used to thinking about her on a daily basis that he found it somewhat strange that this was the first time her face came to his thoughts.

She wasn't smiling in this image he was seeing behind his eyes. The only look on her face was blank. He's seen that look all too many times. The first time he saw it, was the day he told her he loved her. He should have seen it that very day and should have known they wouldn't be together forever. It took her six months to say it back and it almost seemed like she didn't mean it then.

He finished his slice of pizza, then asked to be excused. Carl and Denise nodded at the same time. He sulked through the house and headed downstairs to his bedroom. Along the way, he took his cell phone out of his pocket and went to his contact list. He scrolled down to Amy's name and hit the "Call" button. He wasn't getting his hopes up on her answering, but he needed to know one thing. The phone rang a few times and he thought for sure he would get her voicemail.

"What is it now, Colton?" Amy's voice seemed annoyed and aggravated.

Colton took a deep breath, "This won't take long. I just need to ask you one thing and I'll stop calling, but only if you will be totally honest with me. Can you do that?"

"I guess. What do you want to ask?" she replied.

He thought back to the day she finally said she loved him too. He had already told her every day for months how he felt about her and was getting restless waiting for a response. When she finally did say it, they were sitting outside the apartment, enjoying the nice summer air. It wasn't the most romantic night in the world and she said it like she was forced to do so.

"Did I pressure you into saying that you loved me?" he asked.

There was a slight pause. He could hear her breathing through the phone and, even though they were miles apart, he could still feel her breath on the back of his neck. If only it were real instead of an illusion his mind was forcing him to feel.

"Why do you want to know this? Are you trying to make me hurt you even more?" Amy asked in response.

That was all the answer he needed. She didn't come right out and say it, but she basically did. Not giving him a straight answer was the closest thing to a "yes" he could have gotten.

Colton didn't feel sad knowing he was a root cause to their relationship failing. A few weeks ago he would have. He would have laid on his bed with tears in his eyes wanting nothing more than to die. None of those feelings flowed through him at that moment. The lump didn't come to his throat nor were the tears forming in his eyes. What he did feel, was a type of relief of knowing the one thing that proved to him their relationship was completely gone forever.

"That's all I needed to know, Amy. I won't bother you anymore." He pulled the phone from his ear and ended the call.

Next, he went back through his contacts and pressed on her name for the last time. Only this time, he deleted her number from his phone forever.

Twenty Nine

Monday couldn't have gone by faster at work. A summer play was in the works, so Colton kept busy by helping get things together for the actors and stagehands. He actually felt needed, like he was going to be contributing to something worthwhile. Even though no one else would know about it, he was happy to know he would be one of the people bringing the production to life.

He left the theater with a smile on his face. There wasn't much that could bring his day down. He pulled away from the building and turned onto Main Street. After a few seconds, he saw the one thing that brought his nice day to a halt pulling up behind him. He continued to drive, knowing nothing he did would get them to stop following him. They would always be there to taunt him, to drive him crazy until he figured out who was driving.

Instead of going straight home, he headed further downtown. The bar was a few blocks away and he knew there was a good chance Seth would be down there flirting with whatever girl he could find. He was hoping the black car would follow him to the bar, park a few spots away, then wait for the right moment to go inside. That might give him the perfect opportunity of seeing the driver up close and personal.

He pulled his car into a spot right outside the bar. Quickly, he got out and watched as the black car kept on driving. There was something different about the car as he stared at it. He thought it was his stalker, but was greatly mistaken. This one was a two door and only the back windows were tinted. The person driving was a teenaged boy who appeared to still be in high school.

Colton laughed as relief flowed through him. Then he headed for the door of the bar and walked in. A few people were sitting inside and the majority of them were the same old men who were there every night. There was one person who caught his eye as he headed for the bar. She was sitting alone with her laptop on the counter in front of her. She was writing something, he could tell it was for work as he got closer.

He sat in the stool beside her and ordered a beer for himself. She tossed him a smile while she kept typing away on the keyboard. He couldn't believe how fast she could move her fingers along that thing. The words were popping up on the screen so rapidly, it seemed like she could break a world record by being the fastest typist.

Sarah brought him his drink and it was still a few minutes before Sid saved her work and closed her laptop. She shoved it in her shoulder bag, then turned to Colton.

"Sorry, I'm on a deadline for work and somehow I manage to get more done here than at my house." She laughed.

"Hmm, normally it's the other way around." Colton replied.

"How was your day?" she asked.

He shrugged, "Not too bad, actually. I talked to my ex last night about something and I think it made things better."

Sidney's expression suddenly grew serious, "Like getting

back together?"

He shook his head, "No. I just found out she never truly loved me. She was just pretending in order to make me happy."

"And *that* made things better? When I first met you, you were very determined that you were going to get her back. That was just a couple weeks ago. What changed?" Sid asked, confused.

"I don't know. She hasn't really been on my mind lately. I've been thinking of other things and last night she popped up. I got to wondering if I forced her into things and I got my answer when I called her. I didn't really like it too much, but I deleted her phone number and figured it's time to move on." He replied.

"That's good. I'm glad you're going to make room for better things to come." She said with a smile.

"Exactly. Which brings me to something I've been dying to ask you for a while now. It's been going through my mind, driving me crazy and I don't think I can go another minute until I find out."

"Okay. Ask away." Sid said, a hopeful look plastered on her face.

Colton took a few seconds to prepare himself. His heart was pounding and he could feel himself grow more and more nervous at the longing of hearing her answer. He was almost afraid of what it would be.

"The thing I need to know is...what you have to tell me honestly is," he began, his mind still reeling over asking the question or changing the subject, "are you the one who has been following me? Are you the person behind all those late night phone calls?"

Sidney stared back at him desperately trying to hide how nervous she was. That's not at all what she was hoping he would ask. She wanted him to ask her on a date, to take her for some romantic night out. She got the exact opposite of what she wanted and he wanted to hear the truth. She planned on telling him sooner or later, but now that the time has come, the truth was even harder to give than she imagined.

"What are you talking about? Why would you assume it's me?" she was hoping her questions would distract him enough from the truth.

"You know what I'm talking about. I saw the car that's been following me at the store yesterday and I just need to know, is it you?" Colton pressed.

She let out a breath, "I can't believe you would accuse me of that. I thought we were friends."

"Then why are you avoiding the question? All I want is a simple 'yes' or 'no' answer." Colton said.

She was finding it very hard to continue eluding things. If he found out she was lying, it would hurt him, but if she said the truth, that might make things worse. She looked into his eyes and thought very clearly about the next words she had to say. They would make or break whatever relationship she would ever have with him.

"Sid, I'm waiting." Colton said after a few seconds of complete silence.

She ran her fingers through her hair, "What do you want me to say? That I wanted to be *just friends* with you? That I enjoy seeing you and knowing I can't have you? Following you was the one thing that made me tolerate the friendship even though I so badly want more than that. I more than just like you, Colton, I am in love with you. From the first day I met you, I have found it terribly hard to stop thinking about you. I stay up tossing and turning every night because you're not lying in bed next to me. I can't stand going any amount of time without seeing you or hearing your voice. Following you and calling you in the middle of the night, wasn't the best choice, but it made things a little more bearable."

Colton wasn't expecting to hear *that* much of a confession. He thought she would deny the whole event and they would go on with an awkward evening. He wasn't really sure what he should say. He thought about getting up to leave, but he knew she would end up following him. That's what she was good at, apparently

"Will you please say something?" Sid begged after sitting through his silence.

Colton shrugged and shook his head, "I don't know what to say."

She looked like she could burst into tears at any second, "Just say something," she whispered.

Words weren't finding him. There was nothing he could think of to say to her. Everything in his mind was a racing blur and he couldn't make heads or tails of anything. Here before him sat a girl he thought was amazing. She was easy to talk to and seemed to be the perfect friend. By committing an act that had him afraid to fall asleep next to his phone, turned her from the perfect friend into a complete stranger.

Finally, he opened his mouth to speak, "I don't know if I should be pissed off at you or relieved to know I was right. I saw you duck down in that goddamn car yesterday and I was trying to tell myself I was wrong. I didn't *want* you to be that person. To be so obsessed with me that it completely ruins everything between us. I don't even think I can be in the same room with you anymore without having that thought creep into my head. You followed me for *two weeks*, Sid. I dreaded going home every night because I knew someone was going to be right there behind me. I just don't get why you would do something like that."

A single tear rolled down her cheek, "I'm sorry. I just needed to see you." she said in that same whisper he first heard through the phone in the middle of the night. "But I'm going to leave."

She slid off the stool, taking her bag with her and walked away. Colton followed her with his eyes as she headed for the exit. He quickly paid for his drink, then went after her. It wasn't really his first thought, but he didn't want to stay now that his night was ruined by a simple answer.

"Sid wait!" he called as soon as he stepped foot outside.

She was about to turn the corner to get to her car when she heard his voice. She slowly turned around and saw him jogging up to her.

"What? I told you everything and I'm sure you never want to see me again." She stated, wiping the tears from her eyes.

He nodded, "That's true. Part of me doesn't want to see you again. There's another part that has to know something before I let you leave."

"What's that?" again she had that hopeful look in her eye.

"You said you are in love with me. Why?" he asked.

She looked up at the sky as she wiped the tears from her face, "Because that first moment, when our eyes met at the bar, I knew there was something about you. Something that sets you aside from every other guy on the planet. You are the only one who's ever just wanted to sit and talk about whatever came to mind. I've never had that experience with anyone else and I knew I couldn't lose that." Sid explained. "I know you think it's crazy for someone to fall in love so quickly, but somehow you made that happen to me and I don't regret a second of it."

She turned and walked away from him one more time. He watched her turn the corner and head for her car. The same black car with the tinted windows he's gotten so used to seeing in his rear view mirror.

Thirty

Colton never went back inside the bar. He stood on the side-walk outside for a few minutes trying to decipher the things Sid confessed. Sure, she told him she fell in love with him the very first moment she saw him in the bar. Was that really what she meant? Or was there some secret behind her words telling him she wasn't sincere and she was just leading him on? Maybe she was *really* obsessed with him and, in her mind, that was true love.

Part of him didn't mind having a woman fall in love with him for no reason. After Amy basically told him she never truly loved him, there was something nice about having a girl fall in love with him before a relationship was even in the works. Something which made him feel warm deep inside of his heart, almost like it was healing after his recent breakup.

There was another part of him which never wanted to see Sidney again. She lied to him and got him to think that she was this sweet woman who he could easily talk to. She turned out to be someone he would never be able to trust. She was the exact opposite of what he was hoping for. He wanted her to stay that easy going girl instead of turning into the crazy stalker who followed him home every night. He was used to never getting what he wanted in life, so he should be used to this.

Eventually, Colton found himself heading for his car. Sulking to it with his eyes staring at the concrete under his feet. He knew he just met that girl, barely knew anything about her. Yet, he found himself upset at the thought of never wanting to see her again. He would miss seeing her at the bar, typing away on her laptop. Her red hair draping on her slender shoulders. He would even miss thinking about the mistake he made with her in the fitting room at the mall.

He climbed inside his car and started the engine. There was not a chance he could ever bring himself to talk to Sid again. Without knowing what she would do to keep him all to herself, he couldn't let himself be that vulnerable to a woman like that. He couldn't have a woman in his life that would scare him the way she did. The lack of sleep from worrying about seeing that car parked outside his house at night was more than enough for him to never want to see or speak to her again.

He sighed, trying to figure out why he was so conflicted over everything.

It wasn't long before he pulled into the driveway at his parents' house. The sun was just beginning its descent over the horizon and the stars were starting to show. His mother would have dinner waiting for him and his father would be waiting to play another game of twenty questions about his day. He walked inside the house and went straight into the kitchen.

He found his mother standing over the sink, rinsing off the dirty dishes then placing them into the dish washer. There was a Sloppy Joe sandwich on the stove waiting for him as he inched his way into the room. He glanced toward the dining room table, noticing his father was not sitting there.

"Where's dad?" he asked as he made his way to the plate

of food.

Denise turned her head and smiled at him, "Oh, he's working tonight. He's taking the night shift and won't be back until morning."

"I see. I must not have paid that much attention to see if his cruiser was in the driveway when I parked." Colton replied, taking a bite of the juicy sandwich.

"You sound upset, sweetie. Is something the matter?" his mother stopped with the dishes and wiped her hands on a towel.

Slowly, he nodded, "I found something out tonight that I really wish wasn't true."

She took a step closer to her son, "Do you want to talk about it?"

Of course he wanted to talk about it. He could spend hours trying to get his mother's intake on how he should react to Sidney's confession. She was always the one person he could turn to for advice on girls or love or any of that soppy romantic stuff. He just couldn't find the right words to even begin to explain everything to her.

He shrugged, "I don't know," then took another bite.

Denise saw the look on his face, he was definitely upset about something and she had an idea of what that could be, "Does it have something to do with whoever has been bothering you lately?"

He swallowed the bite as he nodded.

"Did you find out who it was?"

Another nod, "That girl I told you about. Sidney."

She leaned against the counter next to her son. He was about a foot taller than she was, but he was still her baby boy. She would do anything to make him happy and anything to make sure he was safe. She would never get used to seeing him upset and would always be right there to share in whatever pain he was feeling.

"How did you find out? Did she tell you or did you see her following you?" she asked.

"I asked and she told the truth. I guess I should admire

140

that she at least did that, but I don't really know how to react to what she told me." Colton replied.

"What did she tell you?"

He didn't want to tell her the whole story. That would take much too long and there were a few things he couldn't remember from the conversation he had with Sid. Anger sort of fell upon him as she spoke and his mind was slightly wrapped up in being mad at her than to pay attention to the words she was saying.

"She told me she was in love with me. That's why she followed me. That's why she was calling me in the middle of the night." Colton kept things right to the point.

"And how does that make you feel? Knowing a complete stranger is in love with you?" Denise asked. "I mean, she's *practically* a complete stranger. You haven't known her for too long."

"Yeah, almost three weeks now. She went into this whole thing about why she feels that way about me. Something like how I'm not like any other guy she's met and she loves that about me. I just know I'll never be able to trust her or even want to be in the same room as her. She lied to me right from the beginning, mom. Am I doing the right thing by telling her I never want to see her again? Or should I be reacting totally different?" Colton stated.

His mother took a few seconds to come up with the best answer. She's never had to deal with that kind of problem with her son before. It was normally the basics, like what he should get his girlfriend for Valentine's Day or trying to figure out why he got dumped. She's never had a problem so big and she wasn't sure she could handle giving him an answer.

"Well," she began, "I think you're right about not trusting her or wanting to see her. She betrayed you and did something that could have gotten you hurt. But, what you should be asking yourself is, are you sure you don't want to see this girl ever again? Are you sure you can handle hearing about someone being in love with you and going to this

141

extreme to show you that love and dismiss it so easily?"

Colton shook his head and shrugged, "I don't know. I think I can handle it. All I have to do is look at what she did to me over the last two weeks and go from there."

Denise went back to the sink and turned the faucet on again, "Well, as long as you keep thinking like that. That's all you can really do."

Colton finished the Sloppy Joe then took his plate to the sink. He walked out of the kitchen and went into the living room to gaze out the window. All that was left of the sun was a purplish hue covering the western hemisphere. The stars were really beginning to shine alongside the moon. It was a beautiful evening to a completely ruined day.

He glanced toward the street. A few kids were rushing home on their bikes and an older woman was out walking her small, white dog. There was a white van parked across the street at his neighbor's house. He's never seen it before and assumed the people across the street were entertaining company or something. There was a slight worry in the back of his mind about the van. The hairs on the back of his neck were standing at the thought.

Maybe, *just maybe*, Sid was so obsessed with him that she would go so far as to get a different vehicle in order to see him whenever she wanted. That was one thing he paid attention to. All she wanted was to see him more throughout the day. This white van and her car did have one thing in common for him to think it might be Sid. All of the windows were tinted, preventing him from seeing inside.

Thirty One

Sidney stayed awake in bed all night, crying for a good majority of it. There was no hope for sleep, not that she was tired at all. She was too angry with herself, pissed off that she ruined a great thing she had going with Colton. She took it too far and pushed him away before she really got to know him. Before she was able to make him fall in love with her. She knew it was part of her plan to confess everything to him, but she didn't like the feeling she got after doing so. The look on his face as she spoke to him, made her plan seem pointless and not worthwhile. She desperately wanted to go back in time to fix everything.

Her yellow pillow case was stained with mascara running from her eyes. That didn't bother her, nor did the slight chill roaming through the house. She had no intention, no motivation to wash off her makeup or cover up with a blanket. The only thing she wanted to do, was bask in the loneliness she brought upon herself.

"Why was I so stupid?" she would sometimes utter to

herself. "Why did I drive him away?"

She knew he would never want to see her again. It was the same deal with her last boyfriend. She took things too far and it got out of control. She followed him to and from work, went through his phone whenever she had the chance. Any hint of another woman drove her insane. She couldn't handle being away from him and that scared him away. Even after the relationship was over, she still couldn't get enough of him. She broke into his apartment only to watch him sleep and that lead to a restraining order against her. That's when her father forced her to pack her things and move to the small town he picked out for her. Apparently, she never learned her lesson and she lost the *true* man of her dreams.

The light in her bedroom was still on as she stared at the wall next to her. The blue paint matched the feelings she had in her heart. She just met the man a few weeks ago, but her heart still felt like it had been broken in half. The lump in her throat felt like a permanent addition to her body. She wasn't sure if she would be able to go on knowing Colton didn't want anything to do with her.

As she stared at the wall, she tried to think of a way to get him to change his mind about never wanting to see her again. Maybe if she kept her distance for a little while, he would see her in a whole new light and come running to her. Then he would finally realize she made a mistake and was willing to do whatever it took to get him back. The only thing she could do, was hope he would come around and see that he still wanted her in his life.

Slowly, Sid sat up on her bed and glanced at the alarm clock on her small nightstand. It was just past midnight and she knew there wasn't much hope of getting to sleep. She felt wide awake, but her eyes were puffy and she knew sleep would fix that problem. Her feet hit the carpeted floor and forced herself to stand.

She carried herself into the bathroom across the hall and flipped the light on. The second she saw her reflection in the mirror, she couldn't believe she let herself get that way. She was normally good about taking care of herself, but as she stared at the mirror, she saw the reflection of a homeless person.

Her red hair was a tousled mess that would take a miracle to get a comb through without catching a snag. The mascara had painted her cheeks black as it ran down her face. Her bloodshot eyes had bags under them, something she has worked hard at keeping off her face. Now they were laughing at her as she cried over a man she barely knew.

She reached for a washcloth on the towel rack on the wall next to the sink. She got it wet with warm water then brought it to her face. Gently, she wiped the black mascara away, realizing she had to scrub a little in order for all of it to come off.

It took a few minutes to wipe all of the makeup from her face. When she was finished with that, she reached for her hairbrush and got to work on fixing her hair. She hit a few tangles on the way, but soon enough her hair was almost back to normal. There were still a few strands that didn't want to cooperate with her and she ignored them.

She left the bathroom and went back into her bedroom again. Pajamas were her next target. She had a pair of black shorts laying on the end of her bed waiting for her. She stripped out of her jeans and slipped them over her pale legs, a feature every red head has to deal with. Then, she pulled her shirt over her head and got down to a white tank top. Her normal apparel for every night of sleep, even in the winter.

Finally, she crawled back into bed, tossing her soiled pillow to the other side, swapping it out for the clean one she kept on the side of the bed she didn't sleep. The light switch was on the wall across from her and she reached out to turn it off.

She pulled the cover to her shoulders and tried to hold back whatever tears were left in in her eyes. It would be a long night of forcing herself to get some sleep and she couldn't let herself cry throughout most of it.

Her cell phone sat next to the alarm clock and she

grabbed it from the nightstand. As she unlocked the screen, she checked for any missed calls or text messages. Of course, there was nothing, not even a call from her dad. She wanted to call Colton, she needed to hear his voice. She had to force herself from going to the call log on her phone or the message center to send him a text. All she had to do, was keep herself from contacting him or seeing him for a while. She knew it was going to be a full time job in order to do those few simple tasks.

Thirty Two

The next few days were a complete blur. Colton didn't do much of anything, other than go to work, come home, then go to bed only to wake up the next morning and do it all over again. By the time Friday hit, he was more than ready for the weekend off. He wouldn't have to start working a weekend until the play was finished and he would have to clean up after the show. That was still a month away.

He left work and went home to eat dinner with his parents. It was a quiet, awkward meal and his father kept glancing at his watch the whole time. He was on call again and was almost expecting to get one. Denise was busy reading a gossip magazine and didn't bother starting up a conversation. Colton would have loved to hear anything besides the silence.

All week, he found himself bothered by something, a person actually. He expected to hear from her, to get a random text or a phone call or even see her out driving somewhere. Every time he checked his phone, there was nothing from her. He did kind of hint that he wanted her to leave him alone, but he still figured she would try to apologize for what she's done. Actually, he wanted her to do that. A part of him wanted to hear her voice saying she was sorry over and over again. He missed talking to her or meeting up with her to hang out for a little while. It wasn't even strange to him that he really didn't know too much about her. It seemed natural for him to miss a girl like Sidney.

When dinner was over, it was close to seven. Seth wanted to meet at the bar for a few drinks, but Colton refused and reminded him about what happened last weekend. He didn't want to risk getting too drunk and crashing into something on the way home. That's when Seth offered to pick him up and would even pay for the cab ride home if it came down to it. There was no way Colton could say "no" to that offer and, besides, he needed to get out of the house and clear his head with a few drinks.

Seth parked his SUV across the street from the bar and the two of them headed inside. Colton couldn't help but glance at the few cars parked along the street downtown. It was busier than the last Friday he was at the bar. He didn't see the car he was searching for and felt both at ease and upset about it.

They went up to the bar and ordered a couple beers, "Haven't seen you out in a while, Colton. What's the deal?" Seth asked.

Colton shrugged, "Nothing really. Just been busy with work and everything. Trying to find an apartment so I can get out of my parents' basement. I hate knowing that I'm one of the lucky ones who got to move back home."

Seth let out a laugh, "Can't say I'm jealous of you on that one. I would hate to move back home."

"Thanks for forcing me out of my house tonight though. After the week I had, I need to get drunk." Colton stated, taking a big gulp of the beer. "I found out who had been following me home."

"Really? Who?" Seth seemed genuinely interested.

"Sidney. She told me all about it on Monday when I ran into her here. Said she was in love with me or some bullshit." Colton said, sounding tougher than what he felt about the subject.

"Damn. Now, I am jealous of that. I would kill for that girl to fall in love with me and follow me everywhere I went. She is one fine piece of ass." Seth said.

Colton chuckled as he finished his first of many beers of the night. He didn't care how fast he was drinking or how drunk he was getting. He needed to feel some sort of relaxation in order to stop thinking about Sid. She replaced his every thought of Amy and he wasn't sure how he could ever get her out of his mind. Beer would be a good way to help with that for the time being.

"So, is she gonna leave you alone now?" Seth asked. "I mean, did you tell her to?"

Colton nodded, "Kinda. She sort of figured I wouldn't want to see her anymore and I haven't heard from her since. I actually thought I'd see her here tonight."

"She is normally here like every night. Always writing on that laptop of hers." Seth said. "But enough about her. We need to focus on getting plastered or shitfaced or whatever the kids are calling it these days."

"We are still the kids, Seth. We aren't that much older than those young girls standing in the corner." Colton pointed to a corner of the bar.

There were six young women, wearing the shortest shorts or skirts they could have possibly found. Three of them were wearing low cut shirts with their cleavage popping out to everyone. Another one had her hair pulled back in a tight ponytail and wore black framed glasses giving her that sexy, teacher appearance. The moment Seth turned his head to check out the lovely ladies, he was practically drooling over them. He always had a soft spot for a beautiful girl in extremely tight clothes.

"Oh man, look at all the sexy bitches over there. Which one do you want? I'll save her for ya." Seth asked.

Colton shook his head and Sarah set another beer in front of him, "No thanks. Still don't think I'd be very good company with a woman right now. I'll stick with a few more beers, but you go right on ahead."

Seth raised his hands like he was surrendering, "No, this is guys' night. We do things together or we don't do anything at all. If you're not ready for a new girl, neither am I."

Colton snorted as he took a drink, "Ha, I'll believe that when pigs fly."

"Hey now, that's not very nice. True, but not nice." Seth added. "Let's get some shots."

"Totally." Colton said, knowing he would soon regret everything he was about to do

Sarah brought over two rounds of shots for each of them and set them on the bar. Seth opened a tab for both of them, knowing full well he would be too hammered to remember to pay at the end of the night. Then, at the same time, they put the first shot to their lips and let the vodka slide down their throats. Colton immediately went for the second, letting his chest burn as the alcohol poured into his system.

"This is gonna be one hell of an awesome night." Seth exclaimed.

"I hope so, 'cause I really need this." Colton added, then ordered another round.

Thirty Three

The two of them stood by the bar for a few hours. Colton was almost finished with his sixth beer, but has had quite a few shots in order to feel more than just a buzz. Seth kept his eyes glued to the girls in the corner of the room until the one with the glasses walked toward him. She winked at him as she ordered herself another fruity drink and made sure to brush up against him.

The second she walked away, Seth turned to Colton and said, "Sorry, man. The lady beckons."

Colton waved his arm for him to go with the young woman. He finished his beer and turned around toward the bar. He could see himself in the mirror across from him and smiled. His hair was a mess and his grey shirt wasn't exactly the most appealing thing in the world. A good reason why Seth got picked over him. Not that he was willing to go anywhere with a strange woman.

"Sarah!" Colton shouted across the bar for her attention. "Gimme another beer."

She passed him a smile as she approached him, "How many have you had?"

He shrugged, "I don't know, maybe six maybe seven. And a few shots Seth forced me to do."

She shook her head as she took the bottle from his hand, "Sorry, I can't let you drink anymore. It's midnight and you've had enough. Maybe you should worry about finding a ride home or something."

"Awe, your no fun. I'll just wait for Seth to come back and he'll make you get me more drunk." Colton wasn't exactly sure if he said that right, but he knew it made sense in his head.

Sarah giggled in that extra cute way she has done her entire life, "I think Seth isn't going to come back for you. He's too into those girls over there."

She walked away and went to the next patron waiting for a drink. Colton spun around, almost falling to the floor. He caught himself on the stool next to him and let out a quiet laugh. He hasn't gotten that drunk since the day he got his job in New York City. Jake took him out and made sure to get him wasted to celebrate.

He began looking around the slightly spinning bar. The place was packed with a few people he knew and more he didn't. He didn't want to ask any of them for a ride home and he didn't want to call for a cab. Waiting for Seth would be a waste of time. Sarah was always an option, but he didn't feel like bothering her with that problem.

The bell above the bar's entrance jingled and his eyes darted in that direction. Her red hair made him snarl. She happened to catch his eyes and was just about to turn back around to leave, but stayed when Colton almost fell over. He laughed while she walked up to him and helped him stand up straight.

"What the hell are *you* doing here?" he asked, snidely.

"I came for a drink, but I'll leave if you don't want to be in the same room as me." Sid commented.

"Oh no, you can stay. I'm 'bout to go home anyway."

Colton retorted and she could tell how drunk he was by his voice.

He started to stumble away from her, heading for the door to leave. He didn't get too far from the bar before running into someone. Sid quickly stepped over to him and pulled him away from the bigger man who looked like he was going to bust Colton's face open for bumping into him.

"Oh my god, come here." Sid demanded. "If you really want to go home at least let me take you. You can barely walk and I'm sure you'll be less than useless trying to call a cab."

He glared at her and rolled his eyes, but he willingly let her help him to the door and she pulled it open. Once they were outside, he slipped away from her and tripped over his own feet, crashing to the concrete.

"Colton, are you okay?" she knelt down to his side to help him up.

His only response was drunken laughter. She shook her head, put his arm over her shoulders and pulled him from the ground. The warmth of his body was the only thing she was noticing about him. She didn't care that he was absurdly drunk and the smell of alcohol from his clothes was burning her nostrils. All she cared about was how close their bodies were to one another. She wanted to be *that* close to him forever.

Sid carefully walked him to the passenger side of her car and let him lean against it. She dug in her purse for her keys and unlocked the door. When she opened it for him, he began to protest.

"I'm not sure I want to go with you, Sid, you're fuckin' crazy." Colton's words were beginning to slur.

"I know, but I'm the only one sober enough to take you home. Get in the car and put your seatbelt on, please." She insisted.

He rolled his eyes in anger, "Fine. Just remember that my dad knows you're crazy so you'll be the first suspect on his list when I go missing tonight."

Sid let out a sigh as he got in the car. She slammed the door shut and walked around to the other side. She started the engine once she was safely buckled into her seat.

"You're not gonna go missing tonight. I'm taking you straight home, then I'm going to my own house. I shouldn't have come out tonight anyway. You obviously didn't want to see me." Sid replied as she pulled away from the bar.

"Oh, quit whining." Colton said, shifting in the chair a little.

"Hey, you don't have to be rude to me. I'm giving you a ride home. I'm *trying* to do the right thing after I so clearly fucked things up." Sid argued. "Just believe me, after I take you home, you won't have to worry about seeing me anymore. I'll make sure to keep my distance."

She followed the same route Colton took every night after he left the bar. It was something she would never be able to forget, because she followed him enough to get the way memorized. It took a few minutes before she was turning onto his street and could see his house coming into view. She parked the car right outside his house and shut off the engine.

Colton fumbled with the seatbelt, trying to unbuckle it. Sid rolled her eyes then did it for him. Next, she unbuckled herself and got out of the car. She knew there was no way he would be able to walk inside the house by himself. She pulled the passenger door open and held out her hand to help him from the car. Reluctantly, he took it.

"Give me your house keys." Sid ordered as she helped him.

He let out an annoyed sigh as he dug in the pocket of his faded jeans, "So demanding tonight."

She rolled her eyes, secretly enjoying having to take care of him. He stumbled away from the car and slammed the door shut. She quickly caught him before he fell on the ground again. She hated seeing him so drunk and disoriented, yet at the same time, she loved being the one to make sure he got inside safely. It was almost enough to make the last few days of sulking alone in her house worth it.

Colton leaned against her with all of his weight as she helped him to the front door of his house. It was quite difficult having to carry him to the house. He could barely walk straight and it was forcing her to stumble around the yard as well. It took longer than normal to get to the front door and even longer to unlock it. He kept trying to fall into the bushes next to the small stoop, taking Sid with him.

Finally, she pushed the door open and let the fresh scent of lavender fill her nose. She's never been inside Colton's house and spent many hours picturing what the inside of it looked like. She imagined it dressed up with beautiful furniture his mother picked out. Everything was in its place and kept neat and tidy. Except Colton's room, she could never picture that room. It was always something she would have to see for her own two eyes.

"Where's your bedroom?" she asked, quietly so she didn't wake his parents.

"Downstairs." He practically shouted.

"Shhh, I'm positive your parents are sleeping and I really don't think we should wake them up." Sid replied.

Colton smiled as he put a finger over his lips to quiet the place down, "Okay," he whispered, "I'll be quiet." Then let out a slight laugh.

Sid couldn't stop the smile from crossing her lips as Colton showed her the way to his bedroom. He was still hanging over her shoulder, making the trip down the stairs even harder. His bedroom was off to the left when they hit the bottom of the stairs and she walked with him to his bed then he took his arm away from her.

She flipped the dim light on and looked around his room. It was that of a high school student, filled with old posters of bikini wearing babes and a twin sized bed barely big enough for one person. There were books and old photos sitting on the bookshelf and a small TV that seemed ancient in a world of flat screens. She *loved* his room.

"You know Sid," Colton began, speaking loud again, "you are so crazy. I don't get it."

"I know. You don't have to keep telling me this." She stated.

"I don't get why you are so crazy one minute, then a sweetheart the next." A hiccup escaped his throat. "I mean, I *really* like you. You're hot and funny and smart and you love me for no reason. But, you're just so damn crazy. It's like you can't take no for an answer and I kinda like it."

She walked over to him in an ill attempt to make him go to bed, "I can tell you have no idea what you're talking about. You need to get some sleep."

He gently grabbed her wrist and looked into her eyes, "I do know what I'm talking about, Sid."

With his free hand, he brushed a few strands of hair from her face, then carefully pressed his lips onto hers. Sid had no choice other than to kiss back. There was no chance she would force him to back away from her, no matter how much alcohol she could taste in his mouth. This was the man of her dreams and she would kiss him no matter what the consequences were.

While still fused together at the lips, Colton slowly began backing up toward his small bed. He took a few staggering steps, leading Sidney to his destination. She willingly took one step along with him before snapping to her senses. She opened her eyes and slowly pulled herself away from him.

"What's wrong?" he asked, quietly. "I want you to stay with me tonight."

Sid shut her eyes as she shook her head back and forth, "As much as it kills me to say this, I can't. You're really drunk and I can't be that person to take advantage of you. I'm sorry, believe me I am. We shouldn't even be together right now. I need to go."

She returned his house keys and forced herself to walk away from him. Refusing to do the one thing she so desperately craved was one of the hardest things she's had to do. She just couldn't, in the right mind, give in to his drunken gesture and stay the night with him.

She climbed the stairs and went back outside through the

front door, closing it quietly behind her. She ran her fingers through her hair on her way to the car. There was a white mini van parked a few doors down that caught her eye. It wasn't there when she pulled up to the house with Colton, she was sure of that.

The second she walked around to the drivers' side, she froze in her tracks. The side view mirror was completely busted off, sitting in the shards of glass and plastic on the concrete. The window of the drivers' door was completely smashed, leaving pieces of glass all over the street and inside the car. That was just a minor blip on her radar while her eyes were fixated on the words scratched into the paint. A key lined scratch was dug into the length of the car along with the words "He's Mine" written on the drivers' door.

A sly smile crossed her lips as she stared at the words. She had a gut feeling who they were from. There was only one other girl she's come across with that same look of desperation she sometimes found on herself. She whipped her head around and took a long look at the van a few houses down. She could hear it running and thought about approaching it. But she had something better in mind.

"He's yours, huh?" she said to the van. "We'll see about that."

While keeping her eyes on the van, she tousled her hair a bit and began breathing faster. The smile faded from her face and she slowly stepped away from the car. She made sure that whoever was in that van would get a good show out of the clever vandalism they came up with.

She jogged back to the front door of Colton's house and banged on it a few times, hoping Colton would be the only one to hear. After a few seconds, she could hear someone rushing to the door. Luckily, Colton *was* the one who pulled it open.

"You change your mind?" he asked with a smile.

"Someone messed up my car." She said in a panic.

"Wh...what do you mean? What are talking about?" Colton said, clearly trying to sober himself up.

"Come with me. Someone smashed my window and keyed the side of my car." Sid took his hand and dragged him toward her car.

She glanced toward the van, hoping they had a good view of things. She kept her little panicky act going all the way to the other side of her car. Colton stumbled up behind her to examine the damage up close. He was able to get a good look of things with the streetlight shining down upon it. His eyes caught the words scratched into the paint and his heart began beating nervously.

"See what I mean? They really fucked it up." Sid exclaimed.

Colton hung onto her in order to keep his balance, "This isn't one of your sick jokes to get to me, is it Sid?"

She frantically shook her head, "I left you inside like two minutes ago and I *love* this car. Why the hell would I destroy it? I swear to you I did not do this."

"I don't know." Colton couldn't look away from the words written on the side of the car.

He didn't want to believe that someone else was after him. Didn't want to think that Sidney wasn't the only *crazy* person who wanted him all to herself. He looked away from the car and glanced down the street, turning his head to the left and the right. He recognized his neighbors' vehicles and shrugged them off. He saw the white van parked a few doors down and remembered seeing it the other night. It was the only one that struck him as suspicious.

"Umm, grab your purse and stuff. I don't care what you say, you're staying here tonight." Colton sounded a bit demanding.

She nodded, "Okay," silently hoping the driver of the white van heard what he just said.

Thirty Four

Around noon the next day, Colton forced himself awake. His head was pounding as he lay under the covers. He rubbed his temples in an attempt to regain whatever memory he had of the night before.

He recalled Seth dragging him out of the house to go drinking. He knew he drank *way* too much, which he now regretted. He was having trouble putting pieces of the night together. Parts of the night were a blur, until he rolled over and caught a glimpse of red hair lying on his pillow. At that moment a big chunk of the night came crashing back.

Sid came to the bar for a late drink. There was no way she would have known he was there since he rode with Seth. When he got too drunk, she was the one who brought him home safely. He couldn't remember how he got inside the house, but was beginning to see flashes of the words scratched on the side of her car. They flashed through his mind and his heart began to race.

He was hoping it was a dream. He wanted it to be something his mind made up after the past few weeks. Sid following him around town and calling him in the middle of the night was one thing. Having someone vandalize *her* car because they were seen together, that was something completely different. That meant there was someone else watching him. Someone else wanting to have him. He could handle Sid's small amount of crazy. He wasn't sure if he could handle somebody else who *already* appeared worse.

He felt the bed move slightly and his eyes crossed over to her body. She was lying on her stomach with her hands shoved under his pillow. Her shoulders were left uncovered and he could see the spaghetti straps of her tank top along with the star tattoo on her left shoulder. He moved his eyes up to her face and she was staring back at him. Even after a long night's sleep, she still woke up in the morning just as beautiful as when she closed her eyes. He tried to smile, but his mind was too focused on the possibility of another person after him.

"Are you okay over there?" Sid asked, propping herself up on her elbows.

Colton shrugged, "I don't really remember what happened last night."

"Well, if you want, I can tell you." She suggested and he nodded his head. "You were too drunk to get home on your own, so I forced you to let me bring you here. You made me help you inside the house and down here to your room. Then you kissed me and wanted me to stay."

"I kissed you?" he asked, scratching his head.

She nodded, "Yeah and you even tried to get me in bed with you. That's when I tried to leave."

"I am so sorry." He said with sad looking eyes. "What else happened? I remember something about your car."

She nodded, "Yeah, someone messed with it and it freaked you out enough to make me stay here in case something bad were to happen. I'm glad you're such a good guy even after I was such an idiot."

"A *crazy* idiot. You can't forget that." Colton tried to

joke.

Sid rolled her eyes and shook her head. She stared into his eyes for a long moment. As much as she wanted him to be hers, things still felt awkward since he found out about her stalking him. She wanted to be lying in bed next to him every single night. She also knew that her time with him was limited. Any moment and he'd come to his senses and kick her out. It was best if she beat him to the punch.

She sat up on the bed and ran her fingers through her tangled hair, "I think I'm gonna head out. I'll need to get my car to a shop soon and call my dad about it."

Colton watched her toss the blanket aside and reach for her brown, leather boots. He sat up slowly and his headache grew worse and the room spun for a moment. He took a breath as he rubbed his head with his hands.

"You can't go, Sid." Colton stated.

"Why?" she asked.

Colton licked his lips, trying to come up with the best response. She might have been the one whom he thought was crazy for following him, but he liked what he remembered about his night with her. He liked knowing she was there to get him home safely and make sure he didn't die along the way. He even enjoyed knowing that *he* was the one who kissed her.

"We have to tell my dad about your car." He said, thinking of the best possible answer. "He'll need to see what happened so he can file a report."

Sidney passed him a sideways glance and said, "I really don't think that's a good idea."

"Why?"

"Didn't you tell him it was me who's been following you? I'm sure I'm the last person on the planet he wants to see coming out of his son's bedroom." She replied as she stood from the bed.

"I don't care. You might be this crazy girl who got a little too obsessed with me in the beginning, but I don't see that anymore." Colton said, standing up with her.

"What do you see, then?" she asked.

Colton stood up straight and focused his eyes on hers. He didn't see the girl he met at the bar a few weeks ago. He didn't see the charming girl he was happy to call his friend. He didn't even see the person who'd been stalking him for a while.

"I see someone who knows what they want and won't take 'no' for an answer. That's how you managed to go from the nice girl I met, to this stalker chick, and now you're the girl standing in my room after spending the night. You might be a little crazy at times, but I think I might be just as crazy as you are about things."

Sid smiled, "Thank you."

He shrugged, then went to his dresser and changed into a fresh shirt. He doused himself with body spray in an ill-attempt to mask the smell of alcohol. Sid finished making herself presentable as well, pulling her t-shirt over her head then smoothing her hair. Before leaving the bedroom, she grabbed her purse and followed him upstairs. Her heart was pounding harder with each step and she wanted to run through the front door as they passed it. She knew they needed to tell his father what happened with the car. Even though *she* wanted to find the culprit before some cop got involved, she knew telling the sheriff was the right thing to do.

Carl was sitting on the couch putting his black, work shoes on while Denise was dusting a shelf in the corner of the room. Colton cleared his throat, catching their attention and Sidney hid behind him at the top of the stairs. Both of his parents stopped what they were doing and turned their attention to their son. The look on Carl's face changed from calm to angry the second he caught sight of the red head standing with his son. He stood from the couch and stomped across the living room floor.

"What the hell do you think you're doing, boy? Isn't that the girl who's been harassing you?" Carl seethed as he stepped closer to them.

162

Sid held her breath, praying his father wouldn't arrest her. He had no reason not to. She could be considered a stalker and could be charged with harassment. Colton wouldn't take it that far, but she had a gut feeling his father would.

Colton stood in his father's way, "Dad, I know what you think. Believe me I know I shouldn't be around her. But I got really drunk last night and she brought me home."

"And took advantage of you! How could you be so stupid?" Carl shouted.

"It's not like that, dad. I was the one who was trying to take advantage of her. She was trying to leave, but someone messed with her car and I made her stay here. I couldn't be the reason for her getting hurt." Colton retorted.

Carl looked past his son, staring directly in Sidney's nervous eyes, "If this isn't true, you can find yourself in a whole mess of trouble that you'll never be able to get out of."

Sidney kept quiet and simply nodded her head. She knew the kind of trouble she'd get in if she said or did the wrong thing. She's been there before, with her last boyfriend. She wasn't about to ruin things with Colton, especially after things were beginning to look good for the two of them.

"Come outside and we'll show you what I'm talking about." Colton demanded.

Carl moved his eyes between his son and Sidney. He had no reason to believe a single word that came from either of them. He also knew his son was afraid to lie to his face.

"Fine, I'll play along. Show me what you're talking about." Carl finally said.

Colton let Sid walk in front of him. Denise joined them as they walked through the front door and followed Sid to her car parked on the street. The moment she stepped foot outside and saw her car, she knew something wasn't right with it.

"Are you kidding me?!" she exclaimed as she jogged to the car.

One of the headlights was busted out along with the passenger side mirror. Another car length scratch was dug into the black paint on this side as well. "I'll win in the end" was carved into the paint on the door. Those words were the only thing that caught Colton's eye as they approached the vehicle. He knew Sidney couldn't have possibly been behind them. She was in his bedroom the whole night.

Carl walked around the entire vehicle, making a mental note of everything that was done to it. He saw the words scratched on the other side, along with the broken window and mirrors. Sid ran her fingers through her hair, hoping her car insurance would cover the damage. She was going to hate that call, but would hate the call to her father even more.

"This doesn't prove that you're not lying to me." Carl stated, still scoping out the car.

Colton sighed and said, "Dad, I'm not lying to you."

"If you're not, then this girl," he pointed to Sid, "put you right in harm's way. She brought someone else to our doorstep and is threatening you even more. She needs to stay the hell away from you. Whoever this other person is, clearly doesn't want her to be around you."

Colton took a step closer to his father and said, "I understand what you're saying, but..."

"But nothing." Carl snapped, then turned to Sidney, "If I catch you anywhere near my son, I will not hesitate to arrest you. Do you understand that?"

Sid kept her gaze at the man and nodded her head.

"Good. Now, Colton get back in the house and I'll take care of it from here."

Colton shook his head, "No. I am an adult. I can do whatever the hell I want and hang out with whoever I want."

"Excuse me?" Carl stepped toward his son. "You are living in my house and you do what I say. This girl put you in danger. I don't care if it wasn't intentional, she is responsible for every bad thing that happens to you from here on out. So get in the damn house, boy."

Colton stared at his father for a moment. He knew nothing was going to get him to back down. His father always stuck to his guns, especially when family was involved. He glanced behind the man and caught Sidney standing quietly by her car. His father was right about a few things, but not her. She wasn't some person who put his life in danger. She was the reason he was able to get over Amy and want to move on with his life. As strange as it was for him to think it, he might even consider moving on with Sidney.

He sighed and ran his fingers through his hair. His father wasn't going to move out of the way and let him do whatever he wanted. It was best to give up on certain things and do what his father wanted him to do.

Colton nodded and said, "At least let me talk to her for a minute."

Carl rolled his eyes and stepped aside for his son to pass, "One minute, then she leaves."

"Yes sir." He walked passed his father and approached Sidney.

She forced a smile to her lips and said, "I really hope you know how sorry I am for everything. I know I shouldn't have done what I did, I knew it was wrong as I was doing it. I just take things too far and it always ends up hurting the people I care most about. Just ask my last boyfriend."

"I think I can get over it. I didn't get hurt or anything." He replied.

"My car sure did." She took another long glance at her damaged car and grimaced.

"Yeah, maybe you should leave that here. My dad can check it out later and I'll bring it by when he gets everything he needs. You can take mine." Colton says, digging in his pocket for the keys.

"Thanks." Sid took the keys from him. "I guess I'll talk to ya sometime."

He nodded, "Yeah, I'll text you or something."

"I really am sorry, Colton. I never meant anything bad to happen." She said. "I just like you too much, I guess."

He smiled, "I really think I can get over it."

"I hope so." She said, as she walked by him and headed for his car.

Thirty Five

Sidney pulled away from the house, trying not to grind the gears in Colton's car. She was never the best driver when it came to a five speed. Her father tried to teach her. They spent hours going over how and when to change gears. The basics stuck with her. The rest of his instructions flew out the window when she got an automatic.

In the rear view mirror, she could see him standing on the lawn outside his house. His parents were standing by his side, watching as she drove away. She was positive they were making sure she wasn't going to circle around and go back. Colton's father made it pretty clear that he did not want her around his family, *especially* his son. She would have to respect that, for the most part.

She couldn't very well stay away from the man she was in love with for the rest of her life. Colton was finally starting to come around and show her that he might not want to be just friends anymore. He was actually showing her a side of him that cared about her as well. It might not be love right away, but it would build into that. It would take some time and they would need to get rid of his new stalker first.

Sidney didn't know for sure, but she had a gut feeling of who was responsible for destroying her car. It was the only other woman in town who seemed even more obsessed with Colton than she did. She could have told the sheriff before she pulled away. That would have been the logical thing to do. Sidney was more into doing things for herself in order to get to the bottom of it. And, when it came to the love of her life, she wanted to handle it personally.

She wasn't going home right away. Eventually she would have to get to her house. She'd need to shower and get cleaned up. Then call her father and explain how someone damaged her car so he could wire the money to get it fixed. She would leave out the important details, of course. That was a problem she didn't want to deal with and her father would make it a much bigger deal.

She turned the corner at the end of the block and drove toward her destination. She knew exactly where to find the person responsible. One of the reasons she loved living in a small town, people always knew each other's business and it wasn't hard to find out where someone worked.

She pulled into the gas station and found a parking spot up close to the door. A truck was parked at one of the pumps with an older man showing his son how to pump gas. She turned her head the other direction and saw who she was looking for. A smile crossed her face as she shut off the engine, grabbed the keys, and stared into the station for a moment before getting out.

The front of the building was mostly glass windows. The doors were glass and there were two huge window panes on either side of them. The window on the right was the one she kept her eyes on. She could see the cashier perfectly. That short blonde hair and those hideous glasses covering her face. Then there was that annoying smile as she spoke to another employee. It reminded Sid of the night in the bar and how that girl hung all over Colton. But he wasn't her prize to take.

167

He belonged to Sidney.

There were a million things going through Sid's mind that she would love to do to that woman. Like taking her head and smashing it into the counter or ripping every strand of hair from her head and shoving it down her throat. That seemed a little *too* crazy, even for Sid. She was trying to get Colton to fall in love with her, not scare him off by bringing physical pain to another human being. She was more into the emotional torment than anything.

She finally opened the car door and stepped outside. The warm summer air flowed through her hair as she approached the glass door. Her hand gripped the metal handle and pulled it open.

Whatever happy tone was in the gas station suddenly vanished when Sid entered the building. It was like the devil walked into the room and was choosing which soul she wanted to take. Sid had her eyes on the one she wanted as she strolled to the cooler to get herself a drink. The eerie silence followed close behind her.

Sid opened one of the cooler doors and took her time picking out which drink she wanted. There was soda, water, or juice she had to choose from. She didn't go for any of those. Instead, she chose her favorite energy drink and let the door slam shut as she walked away.

The other employee walked away from the counter to go back to whatever menial duty he had to perform. He grabbed the mop from the corner of the room and starting cleaning up the place. Sid kept the devilish smile on her face as she set her drink on the counter and waited to be rung up. She noticed a snide glare coming from the cashier as she took her time scanning the drink.

"Energy drink, huh?" Betsy glanced down at the can. "Did someone have a long, lonely night?"

"Exact opposite actually. Had a great night with an even greater guy. Just need this to wake me up after the long night I spent with him." Sid replied, the sly smile plastered on her face.

Betsy scowled at her as she scanned the bar code, "That'll be four-fifty."

As Sid dug inside her purse for the cash, Betsy glanced through the window next to her and stared at the car parked outside. She would recognize that car anywhere and seeing it in the hands of the red head had anger surging through her. She gritted her teeth and balled her hands into fists.

Sid set the money on the counter, maintaining her smile. There was a long, tense moment between them while Betsy put the money in the cash drawer. One could almost see the anger searing off each of them. There was a battle going on in their eyes, something that would only end when the other was gone for good.

Sid grabbed her drink and Betsy spoke up before she could leave, "You know, I have to ask. What happened to your car?"

There was a playful tone to her voice and the smile faded on Sid's lips, "I'm sure you already know that."

Betsy raised her eyebrows, "I have no idea what happened to that piece of shit. I'm assuming it got what it deserved and maybe now it'll learn to stay away from what doesn't belong to it. This is a game I know it won't win."

"I'm pretty sure I won that game last night when I stayed with Colton and you were sitting outside like the little bitch you are." Sid turned and walked to the door, "Oh and before I go, you are right about one thing."

"And what's that?" Betsy had to ask.

"You *will* win in the end. You'll win the chance to see me walk away with what belongs to me and that is a prize to cherish forever." Sid blew her a kiss, then pushed through the glass door.

Without looking back, Sid went to the car and sat down inside it. She knew the war between her and Betsy was just beginning. It would get worse and part of her was counting on that. There were things in life she was great at doing and getting what she wanted was at the top of that list. She never backed down from a fight and never gave up trying. Taking "no" for an answer was not in her vocabulary. Her father knew that, Colton was beginning to understand that about her, and very soon Betsy would come to learn the same thing.

She backed out of the parking spot and drove away from the gas station. She accomplished what she went there to do. It wasn't much, but she knew she was able to get inside Betsy's head and give her a piece of her mind. Betsy would retaliate, soon most likely, and Sid would be prepared for whatever punch she had to throw. At the moment, she wanted to concentrate on getting even closer to Colton. Last night couldn't have gone any better even if she planned it.

Thirty Six

Colton spent the rest of the afternoon trying to get Sidney's car cleaned up. She left him the keys for the sole purpose of returning it and he felt the need to clean it up. He vacuumed the glass out as best as he could. He even took the door panel off in order to get the glass out of the door so it didn't rattle when it's shut. With a broom, he swept up the shards on the street and tossed them in the garbage can. There wasn't much he could do about the scratches on the doors or the broken mirror and headlight. Sid would have to take the car to a shop in order to get that taken care of.

It took him a lot longer than he wanted to get the car cleaned up. Every time someone drove or walked by the house, he got nervous and hid on the other side of the car hoping whoever it was wouldn't see him. He almost ran inside when the neighbor kids were being picked up by a tan SUV with tinted windows. Then, he laughed at himself for letting a few ten year olds frighten him like that.

He was putting the door panel back on when his father

pulled into the driveway. It was dinner time and he was hoping he would be done by the time his father got home. He stayed in the drivers' seat as he heard the footsteps walking toward him. He didn't want to hear another lecture from his father about how he was making a mistake by helping out the person who drove him crazy for two and a half weeks.

"Been out here all day?" Carl asked, standing by the car door.

Colton nodded, "Can't have all that glass in the street. Someone's bound to get a flat tire that way."

"Good idea." Carl replied.

Colton screwed in the last screw to keep the door panel in place, "Yeah, I'm not *that* reckless, dad."

"Never said you were." Carl replied. "But it is getting late. You can take the car back tomorrow. For tonight, pull it in the driveway close to the house. Hopefully no one's stupid enough to mess with it there."

"Okay." Colton said.

He glanced at his hands. They were scratched and bleeding in a few places from picking up the glass. He couldn't believe he was in that situation. He couldn't believe someone would go *that* far to show how much they wanted him. The thought scared him more than being followed home by Sid every night. Even her late night phone calls were no match for the fear of someone worse out there.

"What are you thinking, boy?" Carl asked.

Colton shook his head, "I don't know what to do. I thought moving back home was a good idea and with all that's happened over the last few weeks, I'm starting to think it wasn't."

"I understand that and you might be right. But this is the choice you made and you have to learn from things like this."

"I know, dad." Colton pulled himself out of the car and brushed past his father. "It's my fault this is happening to me. It's my fault there's some psychopath out there who wants me. You don't need to rub it in my face that I fucked up and now I'm stuck living with the consequences."

He gently shut the car door, hearing a small amount of glass still rattling around in the bottom. He rolled his eyes as he walked around the car and headed for the front door. Carl followed him and grabbed his arm to stop him from getting too far. Colton spun around and faced his father.

"What is your problem today, Colton? I get that you had a bad night last night, but that's not a reason to get pissed off at me." Carl stated.

"Why isn't it? You yelled at me this morning for letting Sid stay here last night. She didn't have much of a choice, dad. You're the one who's always telling me to look after the people I care about just like you look after me and mom." Colton retorted. "That's what I'm doing. I know you think it's wrong and part of me does too, but I care about that girl and I can't be responsible for something bad happening to her."

Carl shook his head, "I know you think you did the right thing by letting her into our home, but she could have hurt you last night. She could have taken advantage of you while you were drunk off your ass. Maybe if you would quit coming home so goddamn wasted all the time, you wouldn't be stuck in the situations you find yourself in."

Colton rolled his eyes, "Nothing happened last night. If anything, I'm the one who tried taking advantage of her and she stopped me before I went too far. She's not this horrible person you think she is."

"I really hope you're right about that."

"I am. I know she did something stupid and she apologized for doing it. I *believe* she's not the person you think she is." Colton turned away from his father and headed inside the house.

Denise had dinner ready, lasagna and garlic bread. She was busy dishing out three plates of the meal for each of them. Colton walked into the kitchen and sat down at the table. As much as he didn't want to, he knew he had to sit at the dinner table and force himself to have an awkward meal with his father. He wouldn't hear the end of it if he picked up his plate and left the room to eat in his bedroom.

Carl entered the kitchen and sat down across from Colton. Denise sat between them and no one said a word throughout the meal. The only sound came from their forks clanging against the glass plate and the small dog begging at their feet for scraps.

It was a long meal and when it was over, Colton practically ran out of the kitchen. He dug in his pocket for the keys to Sid's car and walked outside. The sun was starting to set and the blue sky was slowly turning into a purplish black color. He got inside the car and started the engine. He threw it in reverse and backed up far enough so he could easily pull it into the driveway. He glanced at the house and saw his father standing in the doorway.

"Can't even move the damn car without someone babysitting me." He said quietly while scowling at his father.

He pulled the car close to the garage door, parked it, then shut off the engine. Before getting out, he sent Sidney a quick text telling her he would swap cars out in the morning sometime. Then he pushed the door open and climbed outside.

"At least rain isn't in the forecast." His father stated as he looked toward the sky.

"Yeah, that is a plus. I don't think Sid would like it if I put duct tape and plastic on her car." Colton replied as he walked back to the front door.

Carl put his hand on his son's shoulder and said, "Listen, Colton, I know you're pissed off and scared about whatever happened last night. I'm sorry you have to feel that way. You just have to realize that whatever rules I want you to follow are for your own good. You do understand that, don't you?"

Colton glanced down at his feet and nodded, "I do."

"Good." Carl said. "Let's go back inside. You're mom wants to make brownies for dessert."

"Sounds yummy." Colton added, sarcastically, as the two of them went back inside the house.

Thirty Seven

Colton stayed in the rest of the night and went to bed early. His father woke him up around ten Sunday morning so they could return Sidney's car and bring his back home. Having his father go with him wasn't exactly in his plan. He wanted the chance to talk to Sid about things and hopefully clear some of it up. With his father's presence, he knew none of that would happen.

Carl wouldn't even let him go to the door to exchange keys. He made sure Colton went straight to his car and waited. He could see her from the street when she answered the door. Her hair was a mess and she was still in her pajamas. She must have just woken up, but she still looked amazing. Colton tried passing her a smile when their eyes met, but his father stepped between their gaze and stopped them from seeing each other.

After the awkward drive home, Colton went straight to his room and locked himself inside. He felt like a teenager hiding from his parents after doing something horrible. Like the time he and his friends got caught smoking pot behind the school during lunch. Then there was the time he got drunk at his seventeenth birthday party and his father waited up for him. He felt like a prisoner then and that feeling was slowly making its way back to the surface.

He was actually happy when Monday arrived, a rare occurrence for most people. It meant he was finally able to leave the house and get away from his dad. Unfortunately, there wasn't much work to be done at the theater so he was sent home two hours earlier than normal. He got to his car and climbed inside. As he sat in the chair, he heard a slight crunching sound coming from beneath him. He leaned to the side and felt on the chair, coming up with a folded piece of paper.

Colton held the paper out in front of him and stared at it. His name was written in cursive writing with small red hearts surrounding it. Similar to love notes children would send to each other. Nervously, he unfolded the paper and stared at the note. He didn't recognize the hand writing and was positive it wasn't the work of Sidney. He's seen her writing and it wasn't as neat as what was on the page in his hands.

"Colton,

I can't seem to keep you off my mind. I see you every-where I go. You're in my dreams, my thoughts, my heart. I can't wait until we can be together and run away from this place. I know that's what you want. I see it in your eyes every day. It's the same look I see on my own face, the look of love."

The note wasn't very long, but it was enough to make his heart race. There wasn't a name at the bottom where someone would have signed it. No indicator of who put the note in his car at all. He lowered the paper and frantically looked around outside. The only other car around belonged to the owner of the theater and he was still inside working.

Colton read the note one more time, then started the car

and pulled away from the building. As he drove, he folded the note and shoved it inside the glove box. He wanted to keep it hidden and didn't care to bother his parents with something else that was going wrong in his life. He turned onto the next street and expected to see someone come up behind him. He was lucky enough to make it all the way home without that happening.

His feet carried him from his car to the front door of the house. Behind him, he heard a car coming down the street and, out of sheer instinct, he turned his head to see who it was. Very slowly, a white van drove by the house. He recognized that van as the one parked across the street a few nights ago. He couldn't see the driver, but he could practically feel them staring at him. There wasn't a doubt in his mind that whoever was in that vehicle, was the person who put the note in his car.

He didn't know why so many bad things were happening to him. He didn't do anything to anybody in order to receive that sort of torment. He wasn't sure if his heart and mind could take the racing and fear anymore. First Sidney and now this new person who seemed to be worse. He constantly found himself wondering when the madness would be over.

The front door to the house opened, startling him a bit. He looked away from the street and his eyes met with his mother's. She was on her way out, with her purse in one hand and car keys in the other. Colton quickly walked past her and got inside the house.

"Is everything alright?" she asked, following him into the living room.

He shrugged, "I don't know. Work was kinda boring and I think it's going to be slow all week." He didn't want her to know about the note he received or about the van which just drove by.

"I see. Isn't that play coming up soon though?" Denise asked.

Colton nodded, "A few more weeks of rehearsal, then production two weeks before school starts."

"Then you'll be busy," she said, "I have to go to the store for a few things. Will you be okay here by yourself or do you want to come with me?"

"I'll be fine by myself." he replied.

"Okay, well call me if you need anything." Denise said, then left the house.

He stood in the living room, listening to the sound of her minivan as she pulled out of the driveway. He waited until he saw her drive down the street, then ran to the front door to make sure it was locked. He couldn't admit to his mother how nervous he was about being left home alone and he couldn't bother her by going to the store with her. He would take his chances at home and pray nothing bad would happen.

Thirty Eight

The rest of the week was the exact same as Monday. Every day after work, Colton went to his car to find another love note either in the drivers' seat or shoved under the windshield wipers. The notes weren't very threatening. Whoever was responsible for writing them, just needed to tell him how much they were in love with him. How much they couldn't wait until they could be together forever. Colton noticed that the person thought that day would be coming soon and he had better be ready for it. That was the only thing which seemed threatening at all.

Other than the notes hiding in the glove box, he saw the same white van driving slowly by the house every night. Sometimes they would stop and sit on the street for a few seconds while Colton stared at them from the living room window. His father was never home when that happened and he didn't want to worry his mother about it. She would do something to make Carl leave work early which would mean more prison time for Colton. He was more than fed up with not being able to leave the house. He couldn't take it any-more.

By Saturday, Colton was more than exhausted. He didn't get much sleep during the week nor has he had any contact with the outside world, other than work. When his dad was home, he made sure to listen in on whatever phone conver-sations he had. He had to give his parents just about every detail that went on during the day, only leaving out things that would cause them to worry. He knew telling them about the notes would have been a smart thing to do, but he couldn't take any more of their constant worrying.

He was sitting on the couch, next to his mother. His father chose another western movie to watch for the night. Colton rolled his eyes at the TV and let out an exasperated sigh every few minutes. His phone was sitting on the coffee table and he wanted to grab it. He wanted to call Seth or Jacob to see how they were doing. He even wanted to call Sidney just so he could hear her voice again. She's been on his mind for most of the week and he hated not being able to do anything about it. He's had his limit of watching old movies with his parents.

"You can complain all you want, Colton, I don't care." Carl said, as Colton let out another sigh.

He rolled his eyes as he answered his father, "Glad to know you don't care about torturing your son right now."

"Call it whatever you want, but it's safer to be here with us, than out there where that maniac can find you." Carl replied.

"Why? It's not like they're doing anything besides driving by the house at night. That hardly makes it dangerous for me to leave." Colton admitted without really wanting to.

"You didn't tell me *that* was happening." Carl stood from the couch and walked to the window. "That should have been brought to my attention, Colton."

"Shit." Colton said, under his breath. "I know and I'm sorry for not telling you. I just can't take any more of your damn rules. You won't let me leave, you won't let me call my friends or get on my phone at all. It's like I'm sixteen and grounded all over again."

"Well excuse me for trying to be a good parent by making sure your safe." Carl stated. "I'm sorry it's such an *inconvenience* for you."

Colton let out a sigh, "Whatever, dad."

"You better quit talking to me like that." Carl argued.

Colton rolled his eyes again and leaned forward. He grabbed his cell phone from the table as he stood up. He unlocked the screen and scrolled through the contacts. Being cooped up in the house was driving him crazy and he needed to get out.

"You're not calling that Sidney girl, are you?" Carl asked, following his son through the house.

"It's none of your business who I fucking call. If I want to call her, I can all I want." Colton said.

"Will both of you just calm down!" Denise spoke up from the couch. "I've had enough of this."

Carl ignored her comment as he took a few steps closer to his son, "Do you not understand that you cannot talk to her anymore? For all we know, she's behind this other person who's stalking you."

"You are so wrong it's not even funny. Why would she go through all this trouble when I already know she did it to me once?" Colton said, giving up on his phone and shoving it into his pocket.

He turned away from his father and moved toward the basement stairs. Carl was right behind him and stopped him from going too far.

"You need to listen to me on this, son. That girl is not someone you need to get involved with, emotionally or physically." Carl said.

"Well, what if I want to? What if I can look past the stupid shit she did and want to be with her? You can't stop that from happening." Colton stated. "And I'm not going to sit in this goddamn house another minute. I can't take it anymore!"

He turned around and walked away from his father one more time. He didn't make it very far before Carl grabbed his arm and forced him to turn around. Colton found his heart racing as he stared into his father's angry eyes.

Carl leaned in close so their noses were mere inches apart, "You do not walk away from me like that. I am your father and you will respect me. You have got to get this through your head that I am trying to help you. I am trying to get you to see the mistakes you are making. I'm trying to get you to understand that whatever happened last weekend, was some sort of trigger for something worse to come your way. I can't let you make another mistake by letting that girl into your life only to have someone else come in and ruin everything for you."

Carl let go of his son's arm and took a step back. Colton could feel the pounding in his chest and just wanted to go downstairs to hide in his bedroom like he used to do when he was in high school. Whenever his father got that angry with him, he found it easier to hide than to face him. He was an adult and couldn't act like a teenager anymore. He had to face his father like a man and deal with whatever problems that were coming his way.

"Do you understand what I'm trying to tell you, boy?" Carl asked.

Colton nodded, "I do and I know I made a mistake. I shouldn't have gone out last weekend and I definitely shouldn't have let Sidney bring me home. But knowing the mistake I made doesn't change the way I feel. Neither will you."

"And what do you feel? You can't possibly tell me that you have feelings for this girl who basically stalked you." Carl almost shouted.

"Maybe I do, I don't know. I'm not going to let you force me to stay home and not see her at all. I'm not going to let you control my life like you tried to do when I was a kid. I know someone else is out there following me and probably planning something horrible, but I can't stay in this house all day waiting for it to happen." Colton argued.

"It's only been a week. All I'm trying to do is make sure you're going to be safe. Why don't you get that?" Carl was seething with anger.

"Just let me go. I don't want to be around you anymore."

"Fine. Go hide in your goddamn room like you always do." Carl stormed away from him.

Colton turned the corner and went downstairs, slamming the basement door shut along the way. He started to pace around the room, his mind was racing over what to do next. He didn't want to stay in the house. Not while his father was upstairs trying to control everything. There just weren't too many places he could disappear to.

He heard his father stomping around upstairs and into the kitchen. His voice echoed through the floor and down into Colton's room. His parents were talking, arguing about what happened. Colton couldn't tell if his calm mother was trying to stick up for him and he honestly didn't care. He was tired of doing everything his father demanded of him and he needed a break.

He got out his cell phone and went through the contacts again. There was not a chance in hell that he was going to spend the rest of the night locked away in his room with his father upstairs guarding him like a hawk. He found the person he was looking for and clicked on the name to call. It rang a few times before someone answered.

"Hello?" Seth answered and Colton could hear a few girls talking in the background.

"Hey, what's up?" Colton asked. "Are you home right now?"

"I am home and if you can't hear, I have a few guests over." Seth replied.

"Oh, are they gonna be there long?"

"Well, I'm hoping they are. Why? What do you need?" Seth asked, annoyed.

Colton sighed, "I can't be at my house tonight. I was wondering if I could crash at your place."

There was a slight pause, followed by one of the girls' laughter, "If you want one of these gorgeous young ladies hanging all over you, then come on over. But, I know you've been in this sort of funk since you found out Sid was following you, so this doesn't seem like your thing."

"Yeah, that's the last thing I want right now." Colton said. "Thanks anyway man."

He hung up the phone and shoved it back in his pocket. There weren't too many of his old friends that would be willing to let him stay the night. He wasn't catching up with them like he thought he would. There was, however, one place he could go and he knew his dad would be irate if he found out where that place was.

He strolled across the room and picked up an old backpack that was lying on the floor next to his dresser. He emptied the bag and tossed the contents on the floor. Then, he pulled open a couple dresser drawers and grabbed a pair of jeans and a t-shirt along with everything else he would need for the next day. He shoved his clothes inside the bag, then pulled the phone charger from the outlet by his bed. He flung the bag over his shoulder and headed out of the bedroom.

On the way upstairs, he pulled the keys from his pocket and opened the basement door. He knew his parents would hear him leave. In that house, it was impossible to get out the front door without them hearing. He didn't care anymore.

He shoved the basement door open and reached for the door knob on the front door. He slammed it shut after he walked outside, then quickly walked through the grass to his car. Before he could make it, he heard the front door open behind him. He quickly looked over his shoulder and saw his father coming after him. There was anger written on the man's face and Colton quickened his pace to the drivers' side of the car.

"Get back here, Colton!" his father shouted as he came after him.

Colton quickly climbed inside the car and started the engine. He locked all the doors just as his father reached for the passenger door handle. He could hear his father ordering him to open the door. They were empty threats that he's heard over and over again. They meant nothing and he put the car in reverse and hastily backed out of the driveway. He didn't bother looking back as he put it in first and sped away from the house.

Thirty Nine

Colton parked the car on the street outside of her house. He shut off the engine and opened the door, grabbing his backpack on the way out. His feet carried him up the few stairs to the door and he lifted his hand to the doorbell. He could hear its chime ringing through the house.

He waited a few seconds, hoping she would answer the door. He didn't see her car parked on the street anywhere, but still thought she would be home. He rang the doorbell again, getting a little impatient. The only other option he had was spending the night in his car and there was no chance he would do that.

A few more seconds ticked by and he finally heard someone rushing to answer the door. He heard the lock click, the doorknob twist, then she opened it.

"Colton?" Sid seemed surprised to see him, "What are you doing here?"

He took a deep breath, "I can't be at my house right now. My dad is...he's just too much for me to handle tonight."

Sid nodded as though she understood what he was going through, "So you want to hang out here?"

He nodded, "I don't have anywhere else to go."

"You know we shouldn't be seen together. It's a bad idea." Sid answered. "I think you should go back home, Colton."

He put his hand on the door so she couldn't close it on him, "I'm not going anywhere, Sid. Either you let me come inside or you're forcing me to sleep in my car tonight. You know what could happen then." Colton argued.

Astounded, Sid moved out of the way and let Colton enter her house. She saw the bag on his shoulders and knew it was going to be an overnight thing. She closed the door behind him, locking it as soon as it latched shut. She followed him into the living room and stood at the end of the couch.

She was finally getting what she wanted.

She wanted him to *want* to come to her house, to *want* to be with her. A part of her enjoyed the fact that he didn't want to be anywhere else. He would rather spend the night with her than stay at his house where he would be safe with his parents around. It was what she wanted, but for some reason she felt unsure about everything. If his father came looking for him, which she was positive he would, it would mean trouble for her. The kind of trouble her own father would get involved with and she didn't want to deal with him. But, seeing the man of her dreams walking through her house like he owned the place, made getting in trouble worth it.

She watched as he tossed his backpack on the couch. He was stressed and nervously pacing around the living room. She was partially to blame for his tension and fear at the moment. If she would have left him alone, his life would be fine and he wouldn't have to deal with someone else bothering him. She'd never be able to forgive herself for doing something her mind and heart forced her to do.

"Will you please just talk to me, Sid?" Colton demanded. "Ask me something. I don't care."

"What happened to make you come here?" Sid asked.

He exhaled, then said, "My dad. He doesn't get what I'm going through. He thinks you're the bad guy because you followed me home and you're to blame for this other person."

She took a step closer to him and said, "And what do you think?"

He shrugged, "I don't know. When you told me you were in love with me, that's all I could really think about for a little while. You've kinda been stuck in my head a lot lately and I don't know how to get you out."

"Sorry," she said, looking down at her feet, "I guess my greatest flaw is driving people crazy enough to think about me."

He stared at her for a moment, trying to look past whatever flaw she saw in herself. Her big green eyes stared back at him and he could feel something warming in his heart. The fear of someone else coming after him disappeared for a moment and all he saw was Sidney. She was the only thing he wanted to see and he couldn't understand why. He had plenty of reasons not to be standing in her living room and not want the things going through his mind. He shouldn't want to trust her, yet at the same time, he wanted to.

He moved closer to her, removing some of the gap between them. He could smell the perfume coming from her skin and he thought he couldn't get enough of that scent. He couldn't get enough of being in the same room with her. For some reason, he wanted more.

"Why do I feel this way?" he asked after the long silence.

She shrugged, "I asked myself that question a hundred times after meeting you and never found the answer."

"I shouldn't feel this way. I shouldn't want anything to do with you, but it's really hard not to." He stated.

"I know." She whispered as he got closer.

He lifted his hand and ran his fingers through her soft, red hair. He looked into her eyes as he put his hand on the back of her neck. Her lips were beckoning to him, begging him to caress them with his own. He moved in closer for the kiss. He could feel her breath on his face and the two of them closed their eyes. Before he could seal the gap, a loud vehicle was outside revving up the engine. Colton's heart began to race as he opened his eyes.

The two of them glanced toward the window behind the couch and could see a pair of headlights shining down the street. Sidney moved away from Colton and leaned over the couch. She slid part of the curtains aside to get a better look at who was causing the noise.

"How would they know I came here?" Colton asked as he stared through the window.

Sid stared at the white van as anger filled her heart and soul. She pulled herself away from the couch and stomped through the house to the kitchen. She kept an aluminum base-ball bat next to the backdoor. Something her father wanted her to have in case there was ever a home invasion. She never had a reason to use it until she saw the white van parked outside.

She grabbed the bat, then headed for the front door. She unlocked it and yanked it open. The street lamp was dim, but she could still see the blonde hair of the woman in the drivers' seat. Sid stepped onto the front porch then jumped down the few steps. Her feet carried her along the sidewalk and she clutched her fingers around the bat. She could feel the anger surging through her as she made her way to the van. The driver caught sight of her and the tires spun as they drove away.

"Come to my house again, bitch." Sid said under her breath as she watched the van disappear down the street.

She turned back to the house and walked to the door. She gently closed and locked it before going into the living room. Colton was sitting on the floor, holding his head in his hands. She's never seen a man as upset as he was. He was shaking with the fear that was coursing through him. She set the bat on the floor and strolled over to him. She slid against the wall as she sat down.

"That van drives by my house at night when I get home from work. They left a love note in my car every day. Now they know I'm here with you."

Sid nodded, "They're gone and hopefully they won't come back."

Colton swallowed hard, "What am I going to do? I've never been *this* scared of anything before."

She shrugged, "I wish I knew what to tell you, but I'm normally the one doing the following. I've never been on this side of things."

"Can you promise me something, Sid?" he asked.

She nodded, "Anything."

"Promise me that nothing bad will happen tonight." Colton said as he looked into her eyes.

She licked her lips as she stared back at him. There was no way she would be able to promise him something like that. She couldn't control what happened over night while they slept. But, she knew he wanted to hear her say it.

"I promise and I will do my best to keep it." Sid replied.

"Thank you." Colton said, then leaned his head on her shoulder.

Forty

"I didn't know you wear glasses." Colton stated when Sid came out of the bathroom after changing into her pajamas.

She shrugged, "I only wear them at night, if I remember to take my contacts out."

She was wearing a pair of short, black shorts and a white tank top. Her black slippers looked like a comfortable pair of moccasins. The glasses she was wearing had a plastic purple frame surrounding the small lenses. In Colton's eyes, she looked like a hot nerd who always got what she wanted.

Sid sat on the couch next to him and propped her feet on the coffee table. On TV was an old rerun of some family show. They weren't really watching it. They just needed the noise to keep the quiet out of the house.

"Are you absolutely positive you want to stay here tonight? I have a bad feeling that you are going to be in a hell of a lot of trouble tomorrow." Sid asked.

"I'm not going home. My dad can do whatever he wants, but I would much rather be here with you instead of spending another night stuck in my room. I was seriously about to go *crazy* all week without some kind of contact with the outside world. He wouldn't even let me use my phone for anything other than work or emergencies, like I'm a teenager again." Colton replied.

"Yeah, I get that. My dad was pretty protective of me too. It might have something to do with how I'm not very good when it comes to having a boyfriend. I always take things too seriously and it gets out of control." Sid said.

"Is that what happened with your last boyfriend?" Colton asked.

She shrugged, "Sort of. You already know some of the story, I'm sure."

"Not really." He shook his head.

She took a deep breath. The story with her last boyfriend was never an easy one to tell. So many regretful things were done on her part and no matter how many times she'd call him to apologize, he still wanted nothing to do with her.

"Well," she began, "we dated for a while and I thought for sure he was the one. I was the first one to say 'I love you' and I was the first one to suggest moving in together. Maybe things were going too fast and he wasn't ready for that kind of relationship. But, you know me, I can't handle rejection. When he broke up with me, I kinda went berserk. I followed him everywhere. On his way to work, when he was going to the gym, even when he went to the damn doctor. I made sure I saw him at least once every day. I just couldn't get over him and I guess it made me a little crazy."

"And that's when you moved here?" Colton asked.

She nodded, "That's when my dad found me this house and *made* me move here. I forced myself to move on and I was doing really good. Until I met you. You kind of threw me off track and I just couldn't handle it when you said you just wanted to be friends."

Colton smiled, "I got that when you started following me home every night."

She took a deep breath, exhaling slowly, "I don't know

192

what goes on in my head to make me act that way. Maybe it has something to do with my mom, she was a little crazy too."

Colton kept his eyes on her face. She wasn't looking at him, she was looking past him at the wall. He could see the sincerity on her face. She was more than just a girl who did something crazy at one point in her life. She was something different and he was finally beginning to see that. He wanted to see more of it.

"I don't think you're crazy, Sid." Colton finally said.

"Yeah right." She said, unconvinced.

"I mean it. I don't think you're this crazy person you claim to be. There's obviously someone a little crazier than you out there. Just look at your car for proof." Colton said with a slight smile. "I think you're this person who had something bad happen and it changed the way you look at things. When you lose something you care about, it isn't just a small ordeal that can be fixed easily. You see it as something you'll never get back, that's why you couldn't handle that breakup and probably why you couldn't handle it when all I wanted was friendship. There's more to you than meets the eye, Sid, and I think I'm starting to see that."

She smiled back at him, "Do you even realize how charming you are when you say stuff like that?"

"It just sort of pours out of me. My ex-girlfriend couldn't see it, but I'm glad you can."

Sid kept her eyes on him. She loved the way he was looking back at her with the same sense of sincerity and care she felt for him. It's been what she wanted since that first night in the bar. The love, the caring, the tenderness only he could give her. She knew in her heart that he was the only man for her and she was positive he was beginning to realize that she was the only woman for him. Being with him was what the world wanted, what it needed. There was no other way she could go on with her life unless he was in it.

Colton stared back at her, still trying to comprehend the feelings that were bubbling up inside. Even when he was with

Amy, she never made him feel like the whole world was gone and it was just the two of them. There was something about Sidney that was bringing certain emotions to the surface. He knew it wasn't right to fall for someone who lied to him right away, but to him, it *was* right and everything else seemed wrong. She was definitely doing something to him and he was slowly growing more and more willing to let her.

He swallowed hard, keeping his eyes glued to hers, "Sid."

"Yeah," she whispered.

He smiled, "What the hell did you do to get me to fall for you?"

She shrugged, "I don't know. Do you not want that?"

Before he could answer, a loud banging came from the front door of the house. Instantly, Colton grew nervous, his heart started pounding in his chest. Sidney was instantly annoyed with whoever was knocking on the door. She was so close to finally having what she wanted and her moment was ruined.

She rolled her eyes, let out a sigh, then stood from the couch. Her feet carried her to the front door and she looked through the small window to see who it was. If it had been anyone else, she wouldn't have answered the door. She already had problems with this person and she didn't need things to get worse. She unlocked the door and pulled it open.

"Where is he?" Carl Wischmeier shouted in her face.

She stepped aside, letting Colton's father enter her home. He stomped into the living room and his angry eyes caught his son relaxing on the couch. Sid closed the door gently and went back into the living room.

"Dad, what are you doing here?" Colton quickly got to his feet.

"I've been looking for you all night. You wouldn't answer your damn phone and you weren't down at the bar. Why the hell would you come here after I warned you not to?" Carl argued.

Colton shrugged, "I don't know. She's the only person I

want to be around."

"It's not safe to be around her. You don't know what she could do to you. She followed you for days and called you in the middle of the night just to hear your voice. If she was that desperate to see you, there's nothing stopping her from taking things further." Carl said.

Sid stood behind the sheriff without saying a word. There was nothing she had to say. Everything he was saying was the absolute truth and she couldn't do anything to defend herself.

Colton shook his head, "You're wrong, dad. She's not that person."

"Really?" Carl turned to face Sid. "I got ahold of your father tonight, Sidney, just to get a little bit of a background on you."

"You called my dad?" she asked, shocked.

"It is my job as a sheriff and a father to know who my son wants to be involved with." Carl replied. "Your father told me about your last boyfriend, how you stalked him and when he got a restraining order against you, you *still* went after him. Even before that, you followed every guy you wanted to be with until they couldn't stand it anymore. Your parents knew you needed help, but no therapist in Chicago was willing to work with you because you didn't listen to them. Your dad told me how your mother suggested sending you to a special hospital to take care of the problem. I guess he didn't like that and moved you here instead."

Colton stepped in front of his dad and stared at Sid, "You told me your mom was dead."

Sidney hated thinking of her past. She didn't have an easy life with her parents always down her throat on what she should do with her life and who she should spend her life with. It was enough to drive her a little crazy and she took things too far. Every man she found, automatically became the love of her life. When they wanted someone else, she made it impossible for them to get that. Her mother made things worse by wanting to lock her away like she was a lunatic. When her father moved her a few hours away, she never had anything to do with her mother again.

"Sidney?" Colton said.

She turned to him, "It's all true. I can't handle things the way you or anybody else can. When I don't get my way, I go too far and mess everything up. I lied about my mom because she wanted to ruin my life and send me to a place that would change me. My dad hated the idea and thought it was best to send me somewhere she couldn't find me. Forgive me for wanting to lie about my mom, than admit to how she wanted to send me away."

Colton walked away from her and grabbed his bag from the floor by the couch. He flung it over his shoulder and followed his father. Carl opened the door, but before they went outside, Colton turned around. He saw the tears in her eyes, the sadness written on her face. There was so much sorrow built up inside her and it was seeping out through every pore on her body.

"I'm so sorry." She spoke, but he could barely hear her words through the pain in her voice.

He shrugged his shoulders and shook his head, "I really don't think it matters anymore."

He took one last look at her before his father urged him to go outside. Deep inside, he knew it was better that way. Better that he didn't get too close to the person who lied to him, who followed him around town for her own personal gain. He just wished it was easier to admit to it being better, because he was hating how much his heart was hurting as he walked away from her.

Forty One

Colton stayed a few car lengths behind his father on the drive home. He wasn't in a hurry to get back to the place he still didn't want to be. All he could think about as he stared at her house in the rear view mirror, was how much of an idiot he was to fall for her lies. Sidney toyed with his mind and he was a fool to think she was sincere. He should have known that everything she said to him, everything she did was nothing but a lie. A ruse so she could have him all to herself.

He turned the corner and he could no longer see her house. If his father wouldn't have drove him crazy, his night wouldn't have ended so badly. The lies Sid told him, would still be lies and he would know no better. His thoughts were starting to consume him and he was losing focus on the things around him. His father was getting further and further away and he didn't notice. As much as he didn't want to, the only thing he could think about was Sidney. It was like she was still playing her little games with him. She was still winning, because she was still on his mind.

From the very beginning, when he saw her at the bar, he noticed how beautiful she was. Then the kiss at the mall and how he hated to admit that it wasn't the mistake he wanted it to be. Even when she began following him, seeing her car in his rear view mirror was all he could think about. He didn't know it at the time, but even then she imprinted herself in his brain. He could try a million times over and she would never leave his thoughts.

Colton drove down a few more blocks before realizing he passed the street he needed to turn onto in order to get home. He let out an annoyed groan as he kept going to get to the next street so he could turn around. At the stop sign, he checked both ways before doing a U-turn in the middle of the intersection. The streets were strangely empty and it was only ten at night. There should have been a few other people out roaming around.

He finally got the car turned around and headed in the right direction. Coming toward him in the opposite lane was a vehicle with the headlights turned off. He raised an eyebrow out of confusion then flashed his lights at the other driver. They weren't responding, so he flashed them once more. He knew it was common courtesy to let someone know when their lights were off.

The driver of the other car clearly wasn't paying atten-tion. Colton simply rolled his eyes at his failed attempt of doing the right thing. Just as he was about to pass by the other car, they flipped the headlights on bright, nearly blinding him. He raised his hand to shield the light and squinted his eyes as he tried focusing on the street.

"Goddamn asshole!" Colton shouted at the car, knowing they would never hear him.

He didn't get a good look at the other vehicle and didn't really care who it was. He figured it was a bunch of dumb kids playing a prank on everyone they came across. Then he heard the squeal of their tires and he quickly looked over his shoulder to see what was going on. Whoever was driving the other car, was now coming up on his tail fast. The headlights were starting to shine right in his eyes as they reflected off the mirrors of the car.

Colton stepped on the gas a little, hoping to put some distance between himself and the crazy person behind him. His turn was coming up and he thought he was going to miss it again. He quickly spun the steering wheel, drifting on to the street. The vehicle behind him slowed down in order to make the turn. Then, they quickly caught right back with him.

They stayed on his bumper and he was failing to go fast enough to get away. His heart was pounding and he could feel the sweat trickling down his neck. The car behind him got close enough to the back of his and he felt a tap against the back bumper. That was followed by a bigger tap causing him to jerk forward a little.

"What the fuck is going on?" he shouted.

He tried downshifting to a different gear, one that would let him accelerate much faster. Unfortunately, the gears began to grind and he shifted into the wrong one and slowed down quite a bit. Enough for the vehicle behind him to slam against the back of the car. He heard the crunch of metal and was positive both taillights were busted. That was the least of his worries.

He glanced in the rear view mirror one more time. The headlights were keeping him from seeing the driver, but he was sure it was the owner of the white van he's been seeing. Sidney might have lied to him about most things and did some crazy things before, but he knew she wouldn't go this far. This was the work of someone else entirely.

His house was coming up and all he had to do was pull in the driveway and slam on the horn to get his father's attention. All he needed to do was get away from the car behind him. The other driver had different plans.

Everything happened so fast that Colton wasn't sure if it even happened at all. He felt the last hit between his car and the other. The force was strong enough to take control of his car and he lost his grip on the steering wheel. The Honda started to spin out of control and the world rushed by him in a blur. He slammed his foot on the brake pedal, but the car was already going too fast for it to make a difference. The only thing he could do, was brace himself for the inevitable crash.

The tires squealed as he slid into the opposite lane. He bounced around inside the car, hitting his head on the frame above him as the car went over the curb. The car finally came to an abrupt halt when it hit head on with an oak tree. The force of the stop jerked Colton forward only to be caught by his seatbelt locking up and cutting into his chest and shoulder. The airbags deployed and slammed into his face, knocking the wind completely out of him. The windshield cracked instantly, but didn't shatter in on him.

He was still conscious when the airbag slowly deflated and he tried catching his breath. His ears were ringing and he thought he could hear the tires of the other car squealing as they sped away from the scene. His head was pounding and there was a strange ache in his eyes every time he turned them to look at the damage.

His car was completely totaled. The front end of it was smashed and smoke rose from the engine. He glanced at the house whose yard he ended up in and found himself staring at his own house. At that moment he remembered a saying he's heard his whole life, "the worst accidents always happen closest to home". He never thought something like that would ever happen to him.

He reached down to unbuckle the seatbelt, wincing as a new pain spread into his left hand. With his right hand, he tried gripping the door handle, but couldn't find the strength to open it. He thought for sure something was broken. His whole body was in pain so he couldn't pinpoint which bone it could be.

"Colton?" his father's voice broke through the ringing in his ears, "Please tell me you're okay."

Carl ripped the door open, nearly pulling it from the hinges. He knelt down beside his son and put a hand on his shoulder. Colton slowly turned his head and could see his mother standing nearby, tears in her eyes as she held a phone to her ear. His neck hurt with every slight movement he made and he winced from the pain.

"We gotta get you to the hospital." His dad couldn't have sounded more worried even if he tried.

"Dad?" he whispered.

Carl knelt down beside him and said, "Yeah, son?"

"Someone ran me...off the road." He spoke with pain in his voice.

His father nodded his head, "I know, I saw everything from the front door. I'm going to find out who it was and make them pay for this."

Colton took a deep, pain filled breath, "I'm sorry I didn't listen you."

Carl shook his head, "It's okay. This isn't your fault."

"An ambulance is on the way." His mother said as she rushed to the vehicle.

Colton rested his head on the headrest and closed his eyes. He could hear his dad trying to calm his mother down. He knew his father would find the person who ran him off the road and get to the bottom of everything.

Forty Two

The doctors in the emergency room made Colton stay overnight. They gave him plenty of wonderful medicine to take
the pain away. Something which had him speaking in slurs
and nearly passing out the second his head hit the pillow. He
got lucky and made it out of the accident with no broken
bones like he had thought. His wrist was sprained and his
neck was cut from the seatbelt tightening after he struck the
tree. There was going to be a nasty bruise across his chest
from the belt as well and his neck was going to be sore for a
while. But, he survived and that was the important thing.

His parents stayed with him through the night, not
leaving his side once. Even when he assured them he was fine
and could handle being at the hospital alone, they refused to
leave. Denise fell asleep on the recliner while his father slept
on the uncomfortable couch in the corner of the room. Colton
would never admit to them, but he was actually happy they
stayed with him. He didn't really want to be alone, even in a
hospital full of people.

When morning came, a nurse appeared in the room with a tray of soft oatmeal for his breakfast. His doctor walked in behind her to check on him. He put the cold stethoscope on Colton's chest, listening to his heartbeat. Next, was the blood pressure test, followed by the bright light shining in his eyes.

"Everything looks better than it did last night, Colton. Your heart is beating regularly and your blood pressure is normal. What's your pain level?" the doctor asked as he read over Colton's chart.

He took a deep breath, "Umm, there's some pain in my chest still, not as bad as last night. My neck hurts, but I think it might be from this stupid brace and I have a headache."

The doctor smiled, "I'll have the nurse take the brace off so you can relax and eat your breakfast. I'll give you something for the pain in your chest and that will also help with the headache."

"When can I go home?" Colton asked.

"Soon." The doctor said, then turned to leave.

The nurse stayed behind and set his tray of food on the table next to him. She came over and gently took the brace from around his neck. The stiffness went away, but the pain remained. She helped him lean forward in the bed so he could sit up while he ate.

"Thanks." He said before she left the room.

She passed him a smile then walked away. Denise stood at the side of his bed and brought his tray closer so he could eat. Cinnamon oatmeal was in the bowl before him and he grimaced at the sight of it. Oatmeal was never a favorite of his. It reminded him of baby food mixed with vomit. But, he knew if he wanted to leave, he had to eat what the doctor ordered.

"Don't worry, I'll make you a real meal when we get home." Denise said with a smile.

He took a bite of the mush and forced it down his throat. His father joined them at the side of the bed. He was still pretty worried and upset with the whole ordeal. The wrinkles on his face were deeper when he was stressed about something and it really showed as Colton stared up at him.

"Hon, can you give me a minute with Colton?" Carl asked his wife.

"Yeah, I'm gonna take a trip to the little girls room anyway." Denise answered, then headed for the door.

Colton shoveled more oatmeal into his mouth. His father sat on the edge of the bed, not taking his eyes off his son for even a second. Colton knew something was wrong and he didn't want to hear it.

"You need to tell me what you remember from last night." Carl ordered.

Colton gave him a slight nod, "I was following you and I got distracted thinking about Sid. I missed the turn and got blinded by that idiot who ran me off the road. They turned around and came up behind me and bumped into me a few times before I crashed into the tree. I didn't see what the other car looked like, though."

"I saw it. It was a white van. I was heading inside when I saw you crash into the tree and the van sped away." Carl stated. "I should tell you, after you went to sleep last night, I sent an officer to Sidney's house."

Colton set the spoon in the bowl and said, "Was it her?"

His father shook his head, "No, it wasn't her. She was on the phone with her father for most of the night and she even called him again to clarify. The officer said she was pretty upset and shaken up after he told her the news.

"I see." Colton said, then went back to eating his mushy meal.

That didn't set his mind at ease. He already knew Sidney would never hurt him. She had a strange way of showing how much she cared about him and seeing him in pain wasn't part of that. This was the work of someone worse. Someone who wanted him so badly, they didn't care how they got him.

Two hours crept by before the doctor came back to release him. His father drove the three of them home in his mother's van. Colton was still sore and his neck muscles were cramped up from being in that brace all night. His father drove slowly in order to keep his pain level low.

When they turned onto their street, Colton caught a glimpse of his wrecked car sitting in the yard. Someone pushed it away from the tree, but he would need to get it towed to a junk yard since it probably wasn't worth saving. The hood was wrinkled up toward the cracked windshield and both headlights were busted. The front bumper was barely hanging on and the left side rested on the grass. The back end was dented up as well and he could see the frame was bent in the middle from the harshness of the hit.

There were so many memories he spent with that car. Driving it off the lot, feeling proud of himself for paying for it all on his own. He picked Amy up for their first date in that car and made out with her for the very first time in the front seat. Memories which seemed to be wasted as he stared at the wreck sitting on the lawn.

He heard his father let out an exasperated sigh, "You have got to be kidding me."

He pulled the car in the driveway and Colton saw what he was talking about. Sidney was leaning against her car, parked on the street. He couldn't believe she was there waiting for him after everything she's done to him. If it weren't for all her lies, he wouldn't have been in an accident and stuck in a hospital bed all night.

Carl shut off the engine and quickly got out of the car. Colton moved as fast as his sore muscles would let him and got out as well. His father didn't seem as angry as he should have, but he still stormed across the lawn toward Sidney.

"Dad, wait." Colton shouted, getting his father to stop.

He turned around to face his son who was gradually making his way through the grass. He looked past his father and saw how tense and nervous Sidney appeared. Her hair was a mess and she wasn't dressed to the nine as she always was. Instead, she was wearing a plain blue t-shirt and jeans with tennis shoes.

"Let me handle this, dad." Colton said after taking a breath.

"Are you sure about that?" Carl asked.

"Yeah, you can stay out here if you want, just let me talk to her alone." Colton stated.

Carl nodded and let his son walk by him. He joined his wife at the front door and remained outside to keep an eye on things.

Sidney took a step away from her car and said, "I know I shouldn't be here, but I was up all night worried about you. I just needed to see that you're alright.

"I'm fine or as fine as I could be." Colton replied. "How long have you been here?"

"Not long, I swear." She said. "Listen, I know you never want to see me again and I understand completely. I just have to tell you something before I walk away and never come back."

"Okay, I'm listening." Colton said.

"I'm sorry again, for everything. For following you, for calling you in the middle of the night. I lied to you about some really important things in my life and I shouldn't have. I'm ashamed of my past and I knew you would never love me if you knew everything about me. The relationship I have with my mom and what I did to the last guy I was with, is horrible and I hate thinking about it. But, that was all I lied about. The feelings I have about you, how I'm in love with you, that's the complete and honest truth." Sidney said.

Colton stared at the tears forming in the corner of her eyes. It wasn't another one of her games to get him to feel something for her. He could see the sincerity in her eyes and hear it in her voice. Her honesty wasn't enough to change anything. His mind was already made up and he never wanted to see her again.

"You know, Sid," he began, "I appreciate you making sure that I'm okay and coming here to tell me all that. I can't give you whatever it is that you want from me. I can't keep falling for you only to find out it was just part of your little plan. That's not the kind of relationship I want."

"I understand." She said, then turned to her car. "Before I

go, I just need to know one more thing."

"What?"

"You know it wasn't me last night, right? You know I would never hurt you like that, don't you?" her eyes were pleading for his answer.

He gave a slight nod of his head, "I know."

"Good," she stated, "because I would rather die than let anything like that happen to you."

Colton watched as she got back in the car, then he turned around and headed for the house. His mother opened the front door for him, letting him walk by her. He walked straight into the living room and went to the window. Carl joined him and the two of them watched as Sidney drove away from the house.

Forty Three

Colton called his boss later that day and was fortunate enough to get the next week off. He tried explaining the situation and said he shouldn't need that much time away, but the man insisted and Colton wasn't going to argue. Carl thought it was be best for him to take that time to relax and focus on other things. Things that didn't involve members of the opposite sex. Mainly, his father wanted him to erase a certain person from his mind.

That was proving to be a hard task to complete.

She stayed on his mind for the most part of Sunday night as he lie awake in bed. Every time he closed his eyes, all he could see was her face. Her red hair flowing in the wind and those eyes that beckoned to him. He even tried thinking of Amy, but it didn't help. She was there to stay. He knew it was wrong to have any sort of feelings for Sid, especially after everything she did and all the lies she told. He really wanted to hate her and never think of her again. His mind and heart wouldn't let him win that battle.

When Monday morning came and went, he was still finding it hard to push her from his thoughts. He spent two hours cleaning and straightening his bedroom, which helped a little bit. For a while there, all he could think about was why he had so many relics from his years in high school. He kept most of his notebooks and found a shoebox full of old love notes from former girlfriends. He laughed at many of them, then figured it was time to throw the box away. There was no room for things like that in the new life he was hoping to lead.

Monday was gone and Tuesday came along. He was sore from cleaning his room so soon after his accident and was sitting on the couch, trying to relax. His mother brought him his meals so he didn't have to get up and move around. He noticed that every time he sneezed, there was an all-new pain brought to his neck and holding it back only made it worse.

Denise sat on the couch next to him after bringing their small lunch into the living room. She brought him a grilled cheese sandwich along with a soda. She was enjoying all this extra time with her son. His injuries meant he stayed home with her and she got to take care of him just like she did when he was younger. Colton was secretly enjoying it as well.

"Thanks for making me lunch, mom." He said, then took a bite of his sandwich.

"You're welcome. How are you feeling?" she asked for the third time since he came upstairs.

"I'm good. I think by the end of this week I'll be perfect again." He joked.

She smiled, "I hope so. You know, tomorrow is our wedding anniversary."

"Yeah I know. Is dad taking you anywhere special?"

"Yes, your father made dinner reservations for seven o'clock tomorrow night." She replied. "Do you think you'll be alright by yourself or should we have someone come over and sit with you?"

"I don't need a babysitter, mom. I'm pretty sure I can handle a night alone in the house. I am an adult you know."

Colton replied, sarcastically.

"I know, I'm just thinking about everything that's been going on and I have to make sure you'll be okay." Denise said.

"I'll be fine. I'll keep the doors locked and my phone with me at all times. If anything suspicious happens while you guys are gone, I'll have Seth come over and take care of me." He chuckled at the thought of seeing Seth in hand to hand combat with anyone.

He took another bite of his meal and stared at the TV for a second. There was only one time he's ever seen Seth in a fight. It was the fifth grade and some kids from the next town over were there for a baseball game. They were picking on Seth's little sister and he tried to stick up for her. He got a few swings in, but lost in the end and walked away with a bloody nose and black eye. Ever since, he's avoided physical contact, unless it was with a beautiful woman.

Colton glanced at his mother. There was a look of concern on her face as she tried to eat her lunch. He hated seeing his parents so worried about him. They shouldn't have to be. They should be out enjoying this time of their lives instead of staying at home to make sure nothing bad was happening to his. He was old enough to be taking care of himself and shouldn't have to rely on them anymore.

"Mom, I'll be fine." he said, reassuringly. "You and dad raised me right and I can take care of myself. Whatever anyone throws at me, I know I can handle it because of what you guys taught me."

A smile crossed her lips, "You surprise me sometimes, Colton. I forget you have this side to you."

"We'll just keep it a secret. Dad can't know about it." Another joke.

They finished their lunch and watched a few hours of television together. There was an old western on just like the ones his dad loved to watch. They had a good laugh at the bad puns and the not so great acting. His father came home just in time for dinner and brought a pizza with him.

It was an early night for his parents, but he stayed up a little while longer. He sat in the living room with the TV on and the volume turned down low so they could sleep. The only light came from a dim lamp sitting on the end table next to the wall.

While he sat on the couch, he took his phone from his pocket and scrolled through the apps he had on it. Of the few games he had downloaded, none of them seemed interesting enough to play. He went through the photos he had taken and smiled. Most of them were of New York City. The skyscrapers and landscapes. Everything he missed. There were a few of his car on the day he bought it. He was so proud of himself for owning a car instead of having the endless payments. That car was totaled now, being forced to rot for eternity in a junk yard.

He continued scrolling through the pictures until he came across the ones with Amy. Her smile lit up the screen. He almost missed that smile. It used to make his whole day better. Then she ripped his heart out when she dumped him and made things worse when she said she never really loved him.

As much as it hurt him to do it, he selected every picture he had of Amy, including the ones when they were together, and hit the delete button. He hesitated when the phone asked if he was sure about deleting all twenty-five photos. There were parts of their relationship he didn't want to forget. The times when he was sure they were going to last forever. Those memories weren't enough to keep him from deleting the memories he had on the phone.

"That cleared up a bunch of space." He said to himself.

He wasn't very happy about erasing that part of his life, but it needed to be done in order to move on. He tossed his phone on the couch next to him, then looked at the TV. There was nothing on, besides reruns, so he found himself watching an old cartoon show.

It reminded him of Sidney, those were her favorite shows to watch. He liked that about her, that she was honest with him about a childish part of her life. Not too many people admit to certain things which might be embarrassing. But he loved that she wasn't afraid to admit those things. He also hated that he loved certain things about her.

A car pulled in front of the house and the headlights caught Colton's attention. Lately, every time a car drove by the house slower than normal, his nerves shot through the roof. That same eerie feeling crept up on him as he watched the headlights shine down the street and his heart was beating faster in his chest.

Slowly, he leaned over and flicked the lamp off and the room went dark. The light from the television was enough to guide him to the window. His father kept the white curtains closed so no one could see inside, but he could still see things outside. He gripped both panes of the curtains and peeled them open a crack so he could peek through.

The van was parked on the street in front of his house. He could hear the motor running as he stared at the black windows. They flipped the headlights off and he quickly closed the curtains. The driver most likely saw him, but he still ducked below the window sill. It hurt his back to kneel on the floor like that, but he felt better knowing the driver of the van couldn't see him anymore. If he knew they wouldn't speed away from the house, he would run and wake up his father. He wasn't an idiot and he knew the second his dad got outside, they would be gone. He'd never get to the bottom of who that person was and he'd be stuck living in fear forever.

Forty Four

Colton didn't get much sleep that night. He stayed upstairs and slept on the couch with his mom's dog with him. He couldn't bring himself to go downstairs with that creep just outside his house. All he could think about, was someone breaking in and quietly taking him away. He felt safer on the same floor as his parents with a little dog that would be worthless in a protective situation. His father didn't question why he slept on the couch or why he left the TV on all night. Carl let him go about his day instead of bombarding him with a million questions.

Colton spent the day in the same spot on the couch, staring outside. He took a quick shower, got dressed, then went right back to the couch. He was hoping the white van would show up during the day so he could finally get a good look at it. Any hint of who the driver might be, would be better than him constantly wondering and worrying about it.

His mother cooked him a steak dinner before she headed to the restaurant with his father. She felt the need to cook him a nice meal since they were going to a nice place for dinner. She even brought the plate and silverware to him so he could eat at the coffee table instead of getting up to go to the kitchen. Then she disappeared into her bedroom for a few minutes to get changed for the evening.

His father came into the living room, dressed nicer than normal. He had on a dark blue, buttoned down shirt with a light blue tie. His black slacks matched his shoes and he even combed his hair. After she was ready to go, his mother came out wearing a black dress and a set of pearls around her neck. Her hair was curled perfectly, not a strand out of place, and she had a silver shawl to wrap around her shoulders.

"Well, you two look nice." Colton said as he finished his meal.

"Thanks, sweetie." Denise said, then gave him a kiss on the cheek.

"We'll be home around eleven. The restaurant has a band playing tonight and we're going to stay for the whole show." Carl chimed in. "But, if you need anything, call and we will be home as soon as we can."

"Dad, I'll be fine for a few hours." Colton said, simply.

"I know, but we'll still be here if you need anything. If you feel like someone's right outside the house, you give me a call and I'll be home." Carl said.

"Okay, dad." Colton said as he rolled his eyes. "You two just go out and have good time. It's your anniversary and you deserve a night out."

"Thanks, son." Carl said.

He set his plate on the coffee table next to his phone, then followed his parents to the front door. He let his mother give him a hug before walking through the door. Without waiting to see if they got to the car okay, he shut the door and locked it. He was nervous about being in the house alone. Even with his father asleep, he still felt safer knowing he was there if he needed anything. He just couldn't bring himself to say how nervous he was. That would ruin their night.

He went back into the living room and grabbed his plate

from the coffee table and finished the last few bites of his meal. Then, he took the empty dish to the kitchen sink and headed back for the couch. When he sat down, his mother's dog hopped up next to him and climbed on his lap. At least he wasn't completely alone.

Over the next hour and a half, he watched two shows and part of a movie. The little dog fell asleep on his lap and every so often there would be a quiet snore coming from the little guy. Colton couldn't help but smile whenever the dog snored. He thought it was kind of cute, especially coming from a ball of fluff.

Outside the house, dark clouds were taking over the sky and lightning flashed through the air. No doubt rain was in the forecast. Colton could hear the thunder rumbling in the distance and it added to the nervousness he was already feeling. Having someone constantly following him made this oncoming storm seem much worse. He stare through the front window, watching the lightning brighten up the neighborhood.

The street lamp outside the house went out and the street was painted black. Another clap of thunder and the TV went out because the satellite dish lost signal. The house was completely quiet, even the dog woke up. Colton kept his eyes glued to the window, watching the storm roll in. Something crashed just outside the house and he knew it wasn't thunder. It was some type of glass being shattered. It wasn't a window, the sound from that would have been louder. It sounded like someone was smashing bottles in the driveway. Another clash of glass shattered and the little dog jumped up and began barking. He jumped down onto the floor and Colton stood from the couch.

He took his time going to the window, unsure of what he would see in the driveway. His fingers moved the curtain slightly out of the way and he peered outside. No one was out there. No one was breaking glass in the driveway as he suspected, but he could still hear it and wanted to figure out where the sound was coming from.

215

Colton walked away from the window and headed for the front door. He flipped the front porch light on so he didn't have to go out in the dark. Then he unlocked the door and pulled it open. His mind was screaming at him not to leave the safety of the house. There were bad things outside in the dark, but his feet weren't listening to the message his mind was trying to send.

The warm air filled his lungs as he stepped outside, closing the door behind him so the dog wouldn't get out. The sound of breaking glass got louder as he took a few steps away from the door. It seemed like it was coming from the street, so he headed that way. He looked up to the sky, the dark clouds covered up the moon and the stars. He could smell rain in the air and knew the sky would let loose at any second.

He strolled across the lawn and his eyes darted in every direction hoping to spot one of the neighbors outside. No one was crazy enough to be out during a possible rain storm. The lights were on in the houses around him, but he couldn't see anyone walking around inside or sitting at their sofas. He stepped off the curb and onto the street. The sound of glass ceased and the only thing he could hear was the wind blowing through the trees.

He looked to his right, staring down to the end of the street. No one was there. He turned his head to the left and everything was much darker that way. He squinted his eyes, thinking he saw a light shimmering off something metallic. It was most likely a car parked not far down. He stared at it a second longer, then the light disappeared behind what looked like a figure moving around in the darkness.

"Hello?" he called out nervously. "Who's out there?"

The figure didn't respond, only sending his beating heart into overdrive. He was too afraid to turn and run back to the house. It was like he was frozen at the end of the lot.

The dark figure moved closer and he was beginning to make out features of them. This person was slender and a bit shorter than he was. Colton thought it was a woman by how

216

they were walking. They seemed too feminine to be a man. Their hands were behind their back, as though they were hiding something. The figure got closer and he could see her blonde hair and a fraction of light bouncing off her glasses. He let out his breath, unsure if he should be relieved or afraid.

"Betsy? What are you doing out here?" Colton asked. "You scared the shit out of me."

"I'm sorry, I didn't mean to frighten you." She replied.

"What the hell are you doing here?" he asked.

A smile came across her face as she spoke, "I'm so glad to see you, Colton. My car broke down a few houses from here. Could you come help me?" she seemed much too calm for Colton to feel relaxed about helping her.

"Yeah, let me go inside for my phone. I'll call you a tow truck or something." Colton said, not wanting to go with her. "I'm in no shape to help anyone with stuff like that."

She shook her head, "Just come with me. I'm sure you can fix it."

There was something in her voice that seemed a little off to him. He couldn't pinpoint what it was, but he certainly didn't want anything to do with it.

"I can't," he shook his head, "I have to get back inside."

She let out a loud sigh, "I don't think I can let you do that, Colton. I can't let you get away from me again."

"What are you talking about?" he asked, confused.

Without saying a word, she lifted her hand and Colton caught a glimpse of the small, wooden bat just before she slammed it against the side of his head. He didn't have time to react and fell to the ground, unconscious before he could shout for help.

Forty Five

Carl and Denise cut their night short due to the rain. The sky let loose and huge rain drops fell from the sky. They laughed as they ran from the car to the front door of the house, soaking wet with water dripping from their hair and clothes. Carl stuck his key in the lock on the door and turned it, not checking to see if the door was locked. He pushed the door open and they both walked into the living room.

The lights were still on and the TV set was on standby. Denise made sure to lock the door and quietly followed her husband through the house to their bedroom. It was late and, since Colton wasn't sitting on the couch, she assumed he was in the basement asleep. Neither of them wanted to wake him after the long week he's had. They disappeared into their bedroom and changed out of their wet clothes into something more comfortable before going to bed.

Morning came and rain still fell from the sky. The thunder stopped, but the storm was expected to last another day or two. Carl was never one to trust the weatherman and always went by whatever the sky was telling him. He shared a nice breakfast with Denise after he put on his uniform for work, then walked into the living room.

"I suppose we should wake our son up so he doesn't sleep the day away." Denise said as she followed Carl.

He nodded, "Yeah, I'll head down there before I go."

Something buzzed in the room and both their eyes turned to the coffee table. Colton's phone was vibrating on the glass top and a little green light was flashing in the upper corner of the screen. Carl stepped to the table and grabbed the phone. He made the screen light up and noticed Colton had a few missed calls from his friends over night.

"I guess he forgot his phone up here last night." Denise said, over Carl's shoulder.

He raised a confused eyebrow and said, "I guess he did."

He clutched the phone, then turned away from the coffee table. Colton was having some issues at the moment, but he wouldn't have left his phone upstairs. There was the real possibility of something happening and he would need it to call for help. Carl let his feet carry him to the basement door with his wife following eagerly behind him.

"He's just asleep and his medicine must have made him forget it." Denise said, a slight hint of worry to her reassuring voice. "That's all this is."

Carl nodded, but continued to walk down the stairs, "Colton?" he called into the dark basement.

He flipped the light on, not getting an answer and quickly made his way to his son's bedroom. The door was wide open and the room was being lit only by the light coming from the windows. The bed was neatly made, without a body lying under the sheets. He clutched the phone a little tighter as he stared at his son's empty bedroom.

"Where is he, Carl?" Denise asked, her voice filled with worry. "Where is my son?"

He turned around and placed his hands on her shoulders. He brought his lips to her forehead and pressed them against her smooth skin. When he pulled himself away from her, he

219

saw tears building in her bloodshot eyes.

He took a deep breath, before saying, "I'm going to find him. I'm not coming home until I do."

He gave her Colton's cell phone and quickly walked away from her. His heart was pounding as he climbed the stairs and headed to the front door. He gripped the knob and began to wonder if the door was locked when they got home from the restaurant. He never checked before going inside the house.

The rain splashed on his head and clothes as he ran to his squad car. He climbed into the drivers' seat and slammed the door shut behind him. Once he had the engine going, he backed out of the driveway and sped away from the house.

His mind was racing along with the car he was in. There was nothing that could stop him from being a good parent and finding his son. Whether someone had taken him or he was just out with his friends and had forgotten his phone, Carl was going to find him and bring him home.

It didn't take more than a few minutes before he pulled in front of his destination. Lights were on in the house and he could see her shadow walking by the front window. His son ran away to this house before and he thought for sure Colton would do it again. He left the car running as he got out and ran to the front door and started pounding on it with a closed fist.

"Sidney!" he shouted. "Open the damn door!"

A few seconds went by and the door flew open. A confused Sidney was standing on the other side of it, still dressed in her pajamas. Without saying a word, Carl forced his way into her house and frantically began searching the place.

Sidney shut the door and followed him, "What do you think you're doing?"

From the middle of the kitchen, Carl spun around and glared at her, "Where is he? I know he's here somewhere, now tell me where my son is!"

She shook her head as she stared at him, "Colton isn't

here. I haven't seen or spoken to him since Sunday morning."

He took an angry step toward her and gripped her shoulders, fiercely backing her up against the kitchen wall, "I know you're lying. Tell me where he is!"

Fear was flowing through her mind and body as she spoke, "I swear to you, he's not here. You can tear my house apart and you won't find him. I'm not lying."

"Then you have him hidden somewhere!" he shouted at her.

She jumped a little in his grip, "No. I didn't do anything to him. I promise you, I would never do anything like that."

He shoved her against the wall, then let her go. He stomped through the rest of her house, still searching for his son. Her bedroom was empty along with the spare room and the bathroom. He didn't see any stairs that could take him to a basement and there wasn't a garage.

She wasn't lying.

They were the only people in the house. Disappointment flowed through him as he walked back into the kitchen. Sid was still leaning against the wall where he left her, too afraid for her life to move a muscle.

"You swear to me that you had nothing to do with him not being home?" he ordered, tossing her an angry glare.

She nodded, "I swear."

Carl began pacing through the kitchen. His every step angrier than the last. Sidney watched him, keeping her eyes on his pistol the whole time. She was afraid he would use the weapon on her, but she had a good feeling he wouldn't. He wasn't that kind of person to threaten her with death just to find out that she was telling the truth.

"Is he really missing?" she finally asked.

"I don't know." Carl said, calming down a bit. "He wasn't home, but he left his phone on the coffee table. I thought for sure he would be here, but I'm guessing that other bastard took him."

She kept her eyes on him, watching him walk back and forth across the tiled floor. The tension on his face brought out the veins of his forehead and he looked much older than he really was. Sidney might know the solution to his stress and could end it so easily. All she had to do was tell him about the only person on the planet that was crazy enough to steal Colton away from them.

The sound of his boots clicked away against the floor, sounding almost like a clock. Sid stayed close to the wall, contemplating her next move. She had an idea of where Colton could be. She might even know the name of the woman who was behind his disappearance. It would be easy to open her mouth and tell the sheriff everything she knew. A confession such as that would take the joy of revenge out of the game. That woman stole something from Sidney and she needed to be the one to get it back.

"Before I leave," Carl stopped pacing and looked her way, "is there anything you need to say? Anything at all you think would help me find him?"

Sidney leered into his eyes. They were bloodshot and she could see the tears building in them. It was her last chance to say the name of the person who has been driving the white van. The only suspect that could have done this. Instead, she shook her head from side to side.

"I'm sorry, I don't know anything." She was praying he couldn't see through her lie.

He sighed as he shook his head. He thought Colton would have gone to her house to hide from whomever had been following him. In a way, he was hoping that was where he'd find him. At least he'd have an answer, instead of walking away with nothing.

Forty Six

Colton slowly opened his eyes and was instantly blinded by an overhanging light on the ceiling. He was lying on an air mattress in a small room. Some place he didn't recognize. A musky smell filled the air around him and he squinted his eyes trying to figure out where he was. He sat up and pain filled his head. He let out a slight groan and put his right hand to his head where he'd been hit earlier. He felt the cut on his head and wiped away some of the dried blood in his hair.

"Shit." he whispered, then recalled some of the night.

There was the sound of glass breaking, which caused him to go outside. Then he stood in the street and someone was walking toward him. He saw her face, the smile she wore as she smashed the bat against his head. As much as he tried to, he couldn't believe Betsy would have done something like that to him.

His eyes wandered around the room again. In front of him was another, smaller room off to the right and he could the rim of the toilet seat poking out.. Across from that, was a sink with soap sitting on the edge and a towel hanging from a bar on the wall next to it. He came to the conclusion that he was locked in a bathroom somewhere. It was a depressing bathroom. The ceiling was bare revealing the beams of the floor above him and a few wires going to the lights. The walls were painted an off-white color that had faded over the years. The floor was nothing but smooth, grey concrete, the kind you would find in a basement or garage, and the shower was grimy and filled with mold.

Colton took a deep breath as he carefully stood from the mattress. His head was still pounding and he kept a hand pressed to his wound. There was a mirror on the wall above the sink and he approached it. The cut on his head wasn't as bad as he expected, his hair covered most of it. He grabbed the towel and turned the faucet on to get it wet. Then he began wiping the blood off his face and out of his hair.

As he stared in the mirror, he could see a hallway leading out of the bathroom. He dropped the towel in the sink and turned around. He rushed to the hallway, hoping he would find his way to freedom. All he had to do was get out and pray Betsy wouldn't be there waiting for him.

He didn't get very far. Where a door should be, were tall, steel bars connected together to make a door. It reminded him a jail cell. There were hinges on one side of the door and a pretty big lock on the other, forcing him to stay in the bathroom like he was some kind of animal in a cage. His heart raced as he gripped the bars and tried pushing on them, hoping the door would open. Of course, it didn't move at all.

Outside of his little jail cell, was an even bigger, nearly empty room and he was able to tell he was trapped in a basement. There was a futon against the wall opposite of the bathroom and a mini refrigerator next to it. The futon was made with a few pillows and a big blanket for someone to sleep and also keep an eye on him. A wooden table with two chairs on either side of it, sat next to the wall to his right. The tabletop was rid of anything and there was absolutely no sign of anyone else in the room with him. He couldn't see what was to the side of the bathroom, but could tell it went further into the basement.

He felt around the outside of the bars for the lock. A huge padlock hung from it keeping the door connected to the wall so he couldn't get out. With both of his hands, Colton tried pulling it. When that didn't work, he banged it against the metal bars, sending a loud sound echoing through the room. He ignored the sound and kept trying to find a way out.

Out of nowhere, someone slammed a wooden bat against the cage door, connecting with one of his hands. He let out a cry of pain as he quickly held his injured, left hand with his good one. He stammered away from the door, cursing under his breath.

Betsy stepped in front of the bars and glared at him, "That noise drives me fucking crazy!" she shouted at him.

Colton backed away from the bars, still clutching his hand. He could feel his knuckles swelling up and was positive something was broken. As he looked at Betsy's face, he could see rage building in her eyes and could feel the fear rising through his chest. He's never been afraid of a woman before, especially one who was shorter and skinnier than he was, but Betsy was really dragging the panic out of him.

"I'm glad you're awake, Colton," her entire mood shifted to something filled with desire, "now we can talk about our life together."

"Wh...what do you want with me?" he stammered.

She licked her lips, "I think you know what I want, Colton. I've been dreaming of this moment ever since you got back to town."

He shuddered, then said, "You've been dreaming about kidnapping me and locking me in a goddamn bathroom?"

"I really am sorry about doing that last night. Hitting you like that wasn't how I wanted to do this. You just weren't making this easy for me." She said with a smile. "But now we can finally be together."

"Are you insane? I don't want to be with you. Especially not now." Colton retorted.

"You're just confused, sweetheart. Everything will be okay. You belong to me and I'm not going to let you slip through my fingers again." Her voice was calm.

"You can't keep me locked in here. My dad will be looking for me, the whole fucking town will be out there searching for me. Sooner or later, they'll figure out you're the one who has me." Colton argued. "You just need to let me go and end whatever madness is going through your mind."

"I can't do that." Betsy whined. "I love you too much and I *need* you here with me. If keeping you in that room forever means that I'll get to have you, then that's exactly what I'm going to do. I can't let you go and know I'll never get to see you again. Don't you understand that?"

He nodded his head, "I understand that you are a fucking lunatic."

Betsy gritted her teeth as she let out a loud screech. Her hand gripped the baseball bat and swung it against the metal bars again. Colton jumped back a step until his back bumped the wall behind him. There was nothing he could do to keep her from coming into the room to hurt him. He felt so helpless. With a now injured hand and still sore after his accident, he wouldn't be very useful in a fight, even against her.

Betsy lowered the bat and her face calmed as she spoke, "You don't need to be afraid of me, Colton. Whatever happens after this moment, happens only because I love you. You'll learn to love me, so we can live the rest of our lives together and be happier than ever."

"I think I'd rather die than love you, Betsy." Colton said quietly.

A small chuckle escaped her throat as she reached into her pocket, "You really shouldn't say things like that."

She pulled a key from her pocket and shoved it into the padlock on the door. With one flick of her wrist, the lock came undone and she removed it from the metal latch it was hanging from. She pulled the door open and Colton's nerves shot straight out of his body. There was nothing to stop the tears from forming in the corners of his eyes as Betsy took one step into the room, baseball bat in hand. She pulled the metal door shut behind her and put the key back in her pocket.

She smiled, "I hate it when you lie to me, my love. You need to know how angry it makes and I hate being angry with you." She stepped closer to him, gripping the baseball bat tight in her hands.

His eyes stared at her and he started to plead with her, "Please, Betsy," he backed away, moving further into the bathroom, "I...I take back what I said. I swear."

"I think it's a little late for that." She said as she backed him up against the wall by the sink and raised the baseball bat.

He raised his hands over his head just as she brought the bat down against his shoulder. The pain shot through him and he felt like he was going through the car accident all over again. He dropped to his knees, keeping his hands over his head in order to protect himself. She hit him with the bat three more times, each swing slamming against his back bringing nothing but pain flowing through his entire body.

"Maybe now you'll learn to show me some respect." Betsy said when she was finished.

As he fought the pain in his back, he lowered his arms and looked up at her. She was standing over him like she owned him. There was that look of determination in her eyes, one that seemed much worse than when he saw it in Sidney's. Once again, he felt more helpless than ever. He *felt* like she owned him.

A smile crossed her lips and she spoke, "Why don't we go upstairs. I'm sure you're pretty hungry." Her voice changed into that sweet tone again.

It wasn't much of a suggestion, more like an order. She reached down and grabbed the collar of his shirt and forced him to stand. Then she pulled him with her and walked out of his dungeon.

Forty Seven

"Before I let you eat, I want to show you around *our* house. I think you'll find it quite pleasant." Betsy kept a firm grip on his hand as she led him upstairs.

Colton kept his eyes on the baseball bat in her other hand. He never would have expected her to be a strong, malicious woman. She never acted that way before and always had an innocent demeanor at times. She was doing a bang-up job proving him wrong. The way she handled the baseball bat and how forceful she was being, Betsy *definitely* wasn't the girl he remembered from grade school.

At the top of the stairs, they turned left into the kitchen. Colton got a good look of the place, taking in anything that would be useful to him. The yellow countertops were completely bare and there were no dirty dishes in the sink. Pots and pans hung from a rack above the stove next to the refrigerator. The ceiling and walls were cracked in places and the paint was fading to a dull, grey color with mildew in the corners. They passed by the sink and Colton noticed the window above it had been nailed shut. There was no hope of escaping through that one.

"Come with me," Betsy demanded, "I want to show you our bedroom. At least, it will be our bedroom when you learn to love me."

He swallowed hard and took a deep breath. He couldn't figure out why she was so obsessed with him falling in love with her. He wanted nothing to do with her. She was this crazy woman who kidnapped him in hopes of forcing him to love her. He wanted to be as far away from her as possible. He just needed to find a way to do that.

She held his hand and pulled him through the rest of the kitchen and into the dining room. The table and chairs were spotless and the smell of pine scented cleaner filled the air. There were two places setup right across from each other with plates of eggs and glasses of milk sitting in front of them. Steam rose from the plates and Colton grimaced at what used to be a good meal to him. If he was able to get out of that mess, he wasn't sure if he could look at certain things again without being reminded of Betsy.

They walked through the dining room and into a dreary family room. The couch and chairs were covered in plastic and the television set was ancient. The carpet was a dinghy brown color, stained in a few places with something Colton didn't want to recognize. The windows had been painted black to block any light from shining through. He could see nails sticking out of the wood around the frames. Another shot of escape ruined by Betsy's preparedness for the situation.

They headed down a short hallway. There were three doors that were shut and padlocked. Another door was wide open and Colton could see into the bathroom. The white porcelain surrounding the sink stood out in the darkness. She pulled him along and they walked into the last room in the hallway. The door was wide open and the room was pitch black before she flipped the switch on the wall.

"Isn't it wonderful?" she said with a smile, "I designed it

just for us."

Colton stared at the horrific scene in front of him and shook his head. Photos covered the walls, all of them were of him. Through various years of his life before he moved to New York and even after he came back. Most of them, he had no idea were taken. From high school, with his friends, to the few he took with Betsy when they dated in middle school. He even spotted a few of him at the bar with Seth right by his side.

Above the king-sized bed, were pictures taped to the ceiling to give her something to look at before falling asleep. He recognized one of them. It was taken when he was at the mall with Sidney. He was walking through the hall and could see a bit of red hair in the corner of the photo by his arm. The rest of her was cut out, leaving jagged edges behind.

He moved his eyes up and down the rows of pictures plastered to the walls. Betsy was more obsessed with him than he thought. She'd been following him for years and was much sneakier about it than Sidney ever was. He preferred Sidney compared to what he was seeing in the room.

"Do you love it?" she asked, turning her attention to him.

He stared at her, with his mouth agape and slowly shook his head, "This is sick."

"No, this is beautiful." She replied.

"You and I have a very different definition of that word." Colton stated. "This isn't normal, Betsy. You need help."

She rolled her eyes and said, "That's why you're here. You're the only person who can help me with this. You're the only person I've ever loved and I need you here with me. You can make things better."

He didn't want to make things better for her. He wanted to go home, to be with his family where he knew he was safe. He just *had* to be an idiot and rush outside to see what was going on. The situation would have been different if he stayed in the house and been afraid until his father got home.

She clutched his hand tighter as she stood right in front of him. She licked her lips, then backed him against the wall.

He knew where she wanted things to go and he didn't want to go there. She slowly moved her face closer to his and he felt her breath against his cheek. With his free, injured hand, he grasped her shoulder and gently shoved her away from him. A look of anger crossed her face and the baseball bat fell from her grip. She quickly reached up and wrapped her fingers around his hand and ripped it away.

Pain shot through his fingers, soaring up his arm. Being hit by a baseball bat only moments earlier made things much worse and he could feel the tears forming in his eyes as she squeezed his hand. He hated feeling helpless. He hated being taken advantage of by her as she shoved her lips upon his. Her body pressed against his, wanting to be closer. Colton was pinned against the wall with her surprisingly strong grip holding both of his hands and the only choice he had to make was to kiss her back.

She licked her lips as she pulled herself away from him. A smile formed on her face as she finally let go of his injured hand. He let out a sigh of relief and watched her retrieve the bat from the floor.

"Maybe we'll get to sleep in here together sooner than I thought." She spoke, her words tearing through him like knives.

Betsy flipped the light off in the room, then pulled him through the house once more.

Forty Eight

Colton sat at the table across from her. She was busy shoveling her breakfast into her mouth while he let his get cold on the plate. He had no appetite for anything she had to feed him. He'd rather starve to death if he knew there was no other way of getting out of the house. He was holding out hope for his father to find him, so eating could wait.

"You need to eat." Betsy said after taking a drink of milk. "I'll be at work for most of the day and you won't get anything while I'm gone."

He shrugged, "I don't care."

She rolled her eyes and said, "If you want your time to be more enjoyable, you have to do what I say. I don't think you want me to hurt you."

"If you love me as much as you say you do, why would you want to hurt me?" Colton retorted. "Why would you run me off the road and make me hit that tree? Why would you hit me with a baseball bat and practically break my hand?"

She smiled, "It's because I love you. That's why I do

these things. When I saw you leaving that *whore's* house, I needed to teach you a lesson. You needed to know that you *can't* do that to me. You can only be in love with me. I can't have you out there, falling in love with random girls anymore. I'm the only one for you."

Colton shook his head, "You're insane if you think I'll ever be in love with you. This is just a sick fantasy of yours and one I'll be out of very soon."

She choked back a laugh and her voice changed from sweet, to a little more tense, "And how do you expect *that* to happen?"

"My dad is looking for me and I know it won't take him long to find me. Then you'll be locked away for a very long time." He replied.

She shook her head and said, "You're not a little boy anymore and daddy isn't going to come after you."

Colton shoved her empty threats aside and turned his head away from her. He knew his dad would find him. There was nothing that would get in the way of that.

As he stared at the room around him, he tried searching for something he could use as a weapon. The walls were bare of pictures or hooks. The two windows in the dining room were painted black, just like the ones in the living room. He could see the nails keeping them closed. The only thing on the table, were their plates and silverware, but those were made of paper and plastic. He was completely void of anything he could use to make an attempt at escaping.

He let out an exasperated sigh and his fingers through his hair. He glanced to his injured hand. His knuckles were swollen and cracked, with dried blood on his skin. He was positive Betsy broke something when she swung the bat at him. Even when she struck his back, he could feel the bruises forming already. He rolled his eyes, looking away from his hand. The doorway out of the room was behind Betsy, otherwise he'd be headed back for the basement. He knew the front door to the house was somewhere by the living room, he just needed to find it.

"Will you please eat something?" Betsy demanded, drawing his focus back to her.

Colton looked down at the food on the table. The eggs were going cold, along with the toast she had prepared for him. The cup of milk next to the plate was filled to the rim. He lifted the cup and stared at it for a moment. It was plastic and the milk was cold inside. He held it for a few, long seconds, then came up with a plan.

With the cup in his hand, he took a deep breath, then flung it across the table. The cold liquid struck Betsy's face, blinding her long enough for Colton to get out of the chair and run through the dining room. He moved as fast as he could, listening to her screaming as he went into the living room and turned away from the hallway leading back to the bedrooms. There was another, shorter hall with stairs going up to the second floor of the house. Beyond them, was exactly what he was looking for.

He ran to the door and gripped the handle. He twisted it and pulled, hoping the door would swing open. The knob just kept spinning, but he continued trying to open the door. He slammed his body against the wooden door over and over, praying the latch would give. The door never budged and he took a step back to examine the thing. At the top, were two padlocks, both of them locking him inside the house. He reached for one of them and pulled on it.

"C'mon, open." He pleaded with the lock.

He tugged on both of them as Betsy screamed his name through the house. He ignored her and slammed his body against the door a few more times, ignoring the pain in his back. The old door was stronger than he was and refused to open. He let one of the locks slam against the door, hitting the metal latch it was attached to. At that very instant, a loud blast echoed through the house and he quickly dropped to his knees with his arms covering his head. He could recognize the sound of a gunshot anywhere and the bullet hit the door mere inches from his head.

"What the hell are you doing?" Betsy shouted as she

stormed closer to him. "You think you can get away from me!"

Colton uncovered his head slowly and noticed the black hand-gun in her grasp. Milk dripped down her chin and soaked her tan colored shirt. She looked furious and the mascara running down her cheeks added to her demented appearance. He kept his focus on the gun, instead of her face, and his heart started pounding in his chest.

"I told you that you belong to me now!" she shouted. "You think I'm just going to let you leave?"

She stomped across the floor with the gun aimed right for him. He pressed himself against the door, wishing it would shield him from her anger.

"Please, Betsy," he begged, "I'm sorry. I'll do whatever you want."

"Get up." She ordered.

He nodded and pulled himself to his feet. His legs and hands were shaking as he moved. The gun in her hands was the only thing getting him to obey her words. The fear of what she would do with that weapon, could get him to do just about anything. He might have thought that he'd rather die than stay at the house with her, but the thought of dying scared him more than anything else in the world.

She rushed to him and grabbed his shirt, pinning him against the door. The gun pressed against his stomach as he stared into her eyes.

"Please, I swear," he said quietly, "I'll do whatever you want."

She didn't say a word. She kept a firm grasp on him and pulled him through the house, back into the dining room. He forced himself to keep up and not fight against her as they walked through the kitchen to the basement stairs. She never let go of him and he found it difficult to walk down each step without feeling like he was going to fall. They made it to the bottom of the stairs and she forced him to his prison cell.

She shoved him inside the small bathroom and he stumbled until he caught himself on the wall. He caught his breath, then turned to face her. The gun was still aimed at him, along with the glare on her face.

"How could you do that to me?" she said. "You're supposed to love me, why would you want to run away from me?"

"Why won't you let me go?" he asked, knowing it wasn't the answer she was hoping to hear.

She gritted her teeth as she took the door to his cage and slammed it shut. Colton jumped when the metal clanged together and listened to the sound of the lock. She lowered the gun and stared at him for a second. He watched her face go from anger to calm during that short second.

A smile even crossed her lips as she spoke, "I'll be home in a few hours. We can spend more time together and be happy again."

He closed his eyes and leaned against the wall. Her sporadic behavior was a little too much for him to bear. One minute she was angry and the next she was happy. There were no warning signals for him to notice before she changed attitudes and nothing he could do to stop it. He leaned his head against the wall and listened to her footsteps walking across the basement floor. She climbed the stairs and he heard the familiar clicking sound of the light switch. He opened his eyes and the room around him vanished to darkness.

Forty Nine

Carl spent the morning searching everywhere he thought he'd find his son. He went to every one of his neighbors and asked them the same questions over and over again. Each time, he'd get the same response. No one knew where Colton would have gone and nobody claimed to have seen him leave the house. He was positive he'd find him at Sidney's house. He thought he'd go over there and see him sitting on her couch and the whole ordeal would be over with.

He's never hated himself so much for being wrong.

He was afraid to go home and face his wife without something to give her. She's called him at least twice every hour to see how things were going. He never had a good answer for her and he dreaded the sound of her voice during each phone call. She was crying and had been all day. It would take the sight of her son to get her to stop.

By midafternoon, Carl was drained of everything, as well as his car. He pulled into the gas station a few blocks from his house and filled the tank. There were four other cars in the lot and two people running through the rain to get inside the gas station. As he stood by his car, with the pump in his hand he canvassed the area in search of any sign Colton might have been there. The white sedan at the pump next to him, had two small children in the backseat and no room for his son to hide. He couldn't suspect the young mother of kidnapping his son anyway.

The gas pump clicked itself off when the tank was full and he quickly put the nozzle away and the gas cap back on. He walked through the rain to get to the door and couldn't help but look inside the sports car and the small truck parked outside. They came up empty, as he assumed, and he shook his head. He reached for the handle and pulled the glass door open. Before he went inside, he eyed the last vehicle parked next to the building. It struck him as familiar and he took a moment to gaze at the white minivan. The windows were tinted and there was a scratch on the front bumper. Carl took a mental picture, then went into the gas station.

There was an older gentleman, with grey hair and a bald spot, standing at the counter paying for his beer and cigarettes. He didn't strike Carl as suspicious so he walked to the coolers. The last time he ate was breakfast and he could feel the hunger building. He would be less than useless if he ran into trouble on an empty stomach. He knew he at least needed to eat a snack of some kind. He grabbed an energy drink from the cooler and a snack cake on the rack at the end of the aisle. There was a teenaged girl at the counter paying for her candy bar, when he walked back that way. She was too young to be into a man like Colton and was far from his list of suspects.

The teenager grabbed her chocolate bar and walked out of the gas station to the sports car outside. Carl set his items on the counter and dug in his pocket for his wallet. The blonde woman behind the register forced a smile and he couldn't return the favor.

"How are you today, officer?" she asked, a sweet tone to her voice.

Carl shook his head and said, "I've seen better days."

"That's too bad to hear." She replied.

He finally stared into her eyes, hiding behind plastic-framed glasses and saw determination inside them. A gas station clerk might be a good person to ask about his missing son. He thought, maybe she could have seen something or someone suspicious lately.

"I'm actually looking for someone." Carl said, knowing it never hurt to ask.

"Who's that?" the clerk scanned his drink and snack.

"My son, he's about your age with brown hair and eyes. Maybe a couple inches shorter than I am and slimmer. Seen anybody like that?" he asked.

The clerk ran her fingers through her hair and stared at Carl for a long moment. He couldn't tell if she was thinking about the people she's seen all day or if there was something else on her mind entirely.

Finally, she shook her head and replied, "I'm sorry, I see so many people all day, it's hard to remember faces."

"How about anybody acting suspicious around here? Anyone seem like they're hiding something?"

This time she gave him half a smile, "Again, there are a lot of people that come in here. The few people that act suspicious about *anything*, are the kids who think they're sly trying to steal candy. I'll keep an eye out for you, though."

Carl nodded his head and handed some cash to her when he got his total. He knew it was a long shot, but he had to at least ask. He was already feeling like a failure as a father and a cop. If he couldn't find his son, he couldn't bring himself to go home. The house would feel emptier than when Colton was just in New York. Knowing he was missing, made things much worse.

"What's your name in case I call and check with you again?" Carl asked.

"Betsy McMann." She replied.

"Thank you." Carl took his change and his small dinner, then headed for the door.

"I really hope you find Colton soon, officer. I'll let you

know if I see anything at all." Betsy called as the sheriff walked out of the store.

He strolled through the rain until he got to the squad car. He climbed into the drivers' seat and turned on the engine. He checked all of his mirrors before pulling away. There were a few more places he wanted to scope out before heading home to a depressing evening with his wife and no son.

Fifty

It was late and the sky was dark by the time Carl parked the car outside of the bar downtown. The rain let up slightly, but thunder still roared in the sky. It would be a stormy night trying to fall asleep without knowing where his son was.

He walked into the bar and looked around. He eyed a few men in suits sitting in a booth. Two girls were eating a late dinner and laughing the night away. The bartender was busy drying a beer stein and talking over her shoulder to the man in the kitchen. There was one person sitting at the bar and he was whom Carl was searching for. He knew he wouldn't find Colton there, but his best friend would be the closest thing to finding out where he might be.

He strolled to the bar and sat in a stool beside Seth. He waved the bartender away right as she tried asking if he wanted a drink. He couldn't think straight with beer in his system and he didn't want any of that poison at the moment. Seth spun to face him and passed him a huge grin when their eyes met.

"Officer Wischmeier," Seth exclaimed, "What brings you down here?"

"I'm looking for Colton." Carl said, simply.

The smile faded from Seth's lips and he said, "I haven't seen him since before the accident."

"When was the last time you spoke to him?" Carl asked.

Seth shrugged his shoulders and said, "He texted me last night to see what was going on, but I was too busy to text back. That was around 7:30 I think."

Carl nodded, "You don't know where he would be? He left his phone at home and I can't find him anywhere. He's not with that red head, Sidney, and he's not hiding at any of the old spots I used to find him when you kids were in school. He didn't leave a note and the last time I saw him, was before dinner last night."

Seth stared at the sheriff and could see the pain and worry on the man's face. He's not used to seeing his best friend's father look so upset. That man was supposed to be invincible and withstand anything.

"I wish I could say I knew where he was. I would think he went to Sid's too, but he said they haven't talked in a while. I really don't know where he would be. It's not like him to leave like that and not tell someone." Seth replied.

Carl let out a sigh and said, "I know. I just need to find him before I go home. I can't face my wife like that."

Seth nodded, "Yeah, she was always the most worried mom of the bunch."

He was hoping his little joke would make Carl smile a bit. There was no reaction. Not even a nod or shake of his head.

"Is there anyone else you can think of who Colton might be with? Someone he doesn't talk about?" Carl asked after the moment of silence between them.

Seth took a sip of his beer, then shrugged his shoulders, "No one I can think of. I mean, Sid was the only person he ever spoke about. He was into her, I think, until she went a little crazy. You know, she even snapped at this other chick who was hitting on Colton. She got so jealous seeing some-one else with him and was not going to have it."

Carl lifted his head and asked, "Who's the other girl?"

"Betsy McMann. She went out with Colton for like a month in the sixth grade. I don't know if he ever told you, but she's been *obsessed* with him ever since. Always left love notes in his locker and drove him crazy. He still can't stand her."

Carl recognized the name and sat up straight. She was the one at the gas station who claimed she didn't know anything about Colton. She acted like she hadn't seen anyone with his description or anyone that looked suspicious about anything. He recalled the last thing she said to him right before he walked out of the station. She knew his son's name and that was something he was certain he did not mention.

"Betsy McMann?" Carl asked and Seth nodded his head, "You wouldn't happen to know where she lives, do you?"

Another nod, "Yeah, she lives down on Buffalo Road. There's a big, brick house at the end of the lane that was her grandparents' or something. That's where you'll find her."

Carl got up from the stool and put a hand on Seth's shoulder to thank him, "Thank you, Seth. You have my number in case you see or hear from Colton before I do. Please let me know if you do."

"Yeah, anything to help." Seth stated.

Carl stormed through the bar and pulled the door open. He walked outside, listening to the thunder overhead and eyeing the lightning as he made his way to the car. He nearly ripped the door off its hinges as he opened it and climbed into the drivers' seat. He started the car and backed out of the parking spot. He flipped the flashing lights on and sped down the street, running the few stop signs along the way.

Fifty One

Colton had no idea what time it was. The darkness of the basement made everything much worse and the day seemed a lot longer than it probably was. The quiet was starting to get to him and every tiny noise or creak of the house made him jump. The rain pounding on the small, basement window sounded like a machine gun going off right outside the house. Everything was intensified and nothing he could do would change a thing.

He tried picking the lock on the door with a small piece of wire he found on the floor. He spent, what he assumed was a few hours trying to get the lock to come loose with a frail wire. Of course, the thing never budged and he was just as stuck in the bathroom as he was before. When he gave up on that, he moved back to the air mattress and stayed there, staring into the darkness before him. His knuckles were swollen and his back ached. His mind was still baffled at how a woman like Betsy could do something like that to him. She might have been crazy about him in high school, but that should have faded with time. She shouldn't have turned into this maniacal kidnapper, locking him in a basement until he loved her back.

The rain started up again and Colton ran his fingers through his hair. He rubbed his eyes, wiping the few stray tears from under them. The only thing on his mind, other than escaping, was his family. He wondered when he'd get to see them again. His father was out there looking for him, he knew that for a fact. The moment his parents would see that he wasn't home, they would have gotten frantic and started searching the town. As long as it didn't take too long, he knew he would be alright.

Sidney found a way into his mind as well. Being locked in that room had him wondering what life would actually be like with her. She wasn't as crazy about him as Betsy apparently was, but he knew she wouldn't let any other woman look at him or even talk to him. Sid would hold onto him and never let go. She would give him the love he desired. That's what he truly wanted in a relationship, what he wanted when he was with Amy. There was still too much about Sid that he didn't know.

He looked up to the ceiling when the sound of a door slamming shut broke the silence around him. His heart started pounding as he listened to the footsteps on the creaky floor above. Betsy was home and he could hear her walking through the house, heading for the basement. He could just about pinpoint exactly where she was by where the creaks were coming from. An old house like that, was perfect for eerie noises and things that go bump in the night. She was in the kitchen and he could hear her feet on the tiled floor. She was moving things around, opening cupboard doors or messing with pots and pans. He couldn't tell exactly what she was doing.

He heard the basement door open and a bright light filled the room around him. He quickly closed his eyes and covered his face with his hands. The light was blinding after being stuck in the dark for so long. She was walking down the stairs and he counted the seconds until he heard her standing right outside his bathroom prison.

"Colton." Betsy said in a playful voice. "I've been waiting all day to be here with you."

He slowly uncovered his face and opened his eyes, letting them adjust to the light. The metal lock clanged around until it got loose, then he heard the door open. He clutched the blanket on the air mattress and listened to her walk into the room. He got to his feet as she came around the corner and smiled at him. He quickly backed away from her, cornering himself next to the sink.

She smiled even bigger as she spoke, "I missed you so much today, Colton. You have no idea how badly I wanted to skip work and come home to you."

She inched her way toward him and he shuddered when she touched his arm. She pushed her body against his and licked her lips. He turned his eyes away from her and caught a glimpse of their reflection in the mirror and saw something hiding behind her back. As much as he wanted to push her away and make a run for the exit, the gun tucked into the her jeans was making his decision a tough one.

Betsy put her hand on his cheek and forced him to look at her, "Come on, I know you want this just as much as I do."

She put one hand on the back of his neck and the other was rubbing his stomach under his shirt. She pressed her lips onto his, forcing him to kiss back. He closed his eyes, wanting that moment to be over with. He knew the gun was hiding behind her back and it was enough to get him not to fight with her. Getting hurt over a kiss wasn't exactly what he wanted.

"I've been saving myself for you." She broke the kiss and whispered in his ear. "I wish you would have saved yourself for me too."

Her hands trickled down his body and he could feel her fingers grabbing the belt around his waist. She just about had it undone when the greatest noise on the planet broke her concentration. The knock on the door upstairs was loud and sounded angry. Betsy pulled herself away from him and glared at the ceiling above them.

"You have got to be kidding me." She growled, then walked away from Colton.

On her way out of the room, she slammed the door shut and put the padlock back in place. Her feet stomped up the basement stairs and she shut the light off when she made it to the top. She walked through the kitchen, then the dining room, until she got to the living room. The knocking came again and was much louder than before. She rolled her eyes as she made her way to the front door. She quickly unlocked the two padlocks at the top of the door and pulled it open.

A soaking wet sheriff pushed his way into the house and started searching the place. She closed the door and her heart started pounding nervously in her chest.

"Can I help you, officer?" she asked, following him into the living room.

He whipped his head around and glared at her, "Where's my son?"

Her eyes grew wide as she said, "What are you talking about? I'm the only one here."

He turned away from her and started looking through the house again. She quickly followed him and watched what he was doing. He checked everywhere in the living room, behind the couch and chairs. Then he walked to the hallway and opened the first bedroom door.

"I know he's here. You can't play stupid with me." Carl argued.

"I really don't know what you're talking about, but if you come with me, we can talk about this in the dining room. There's nothing in this part of the house anyway." Betsy said, frantically trying to get him away from her bedroom.

Carl slammed the first door shut, then moved on to the second one. Each room was dark and he even checked the bathroom. Betsy followed close, her hand slowly reaching for the gun behind her back. She gripped the cold metal as the sheriff walked in the final bedroom on the first floor of the house. He flipped the light on and stopped in the doorway, staring at her handiwork. His jaw dropped as he stared at the many pictures of his son hanging on the walls. He took a step into the room and Betsy pulled the gun out and pointed it at the officer.

He turned around and saw the gun in her hand and quickly reached for his own. She raised hers higher and shook her head.

"I wouldn't do that if I were you." She said, simply.

"Where's my son?" Carl asked, trying to stay as calm as he could.

Betsy aimed the gun at his head and said, "Give me your weapon and your handcuffs."

Carl nodded and did as he was told. He was fearful of what would happen to his son if he disobeyed her. It didn't matter if he could overtake this woman, he was too worried about Colton to take any chances.

"Please, just tell me where my son is." He said one more time.

"Why did you come here? You weren't supposed to look here." Betsy seethed.

Carl raised his hands in surrender and spoke, "You said his name before I told you what it was."

She rolled her eyes and said, "Everyone in this town knows who your damn son is! You weren't supposed to come looking for him *here*. He belongs to me and now you do as well."

"What are you talking about?" Carl asked.

She held both guns and ordered, "Move."

Carl nodded, quietly hating himself for having to obey that woman, then walked out of the room. He got in front of her and felt her poke a gun at his back. He could hear his handcuffs dangling as they walked through the house. She forced him back down the short hallway, through the living room and into the dining room then the kitchen.

"The basement stairs, move it." she demanded.

She shoved the gun against his back as he kept moving

through the house. He started down the stairs and she hit the light switch. At the bottom, Betsy looked around the room.

She wasn't prepared for someone to come there. She never expected someone to search her house for Colton. It made everything worse when that someone who showed up just so happened to be her lover's father.

There was a support beam in the corner of the basement, right across from the entrance to the bathroom. She pushed her new prisoner to the post then gave him the handcuffs.

"I think you know what to do." Betsy motioned to the post.

Carl nodded and took the cuffs after she took the key from them. He put his hands around the beam and cuffed them in place.

"Dad?" Colton said and Carl was able to see his son locked behind the barred door across the room.

"Colton, are you alright?" Carl asked in a panic.

His son shrugged and said, "What's going on?"

"I came to get to you." Carl replied.

"Both of you just shut the hell up!" Betsy shouted, jabbing the butt of the gun against Carl's side.

He grunted and Colton yelled for his father. Betsy turned to him and walked to the door. She put one of the guns behind her back, tucking it safely into her jeans. Then she reached into her pocket for the key to the padlock and unlocked the door. Before Colton could try running past her, she grabbed his swollen hand and pressed her gun against his side.

"You're coming with me." She ordered.

"No." Colton argued, trying to get away from her and get to his father.

She squeezed his hand and he grunted from the pain, "You will do as I tell you."

"Dad." Colton called out as Betsy pulled him through the basement.

"Just do what she says." Carl said, watching the woman put a gun to his son's back.

249

Fifty Two

Sidney drove down every street in town searching for Colton.
She peered through every car and every open window she
came across. She spent hours driving through the rain trying
to find him. She even went to the gas station where Betsy
worked and came up empty handed. She knew that woman
had something to do with his disappearance. She just needed
to find her in order to get revenge.

It was around nine when she found herself parking at the
bar downtown. She ran through the rain to get to the door and
pulled it open. There was one person that might be able to
help her out and he was sitting at the bar with a brunette
flirting with him. Sid stormed across the bar and grabbed his
shoulder, spinning him around on the stool, away from the
brunette.

"I need to talk to you." She said.

Seth nodded and said, "Okay, what do you want?"

"Tell me where Betsy lives." Sid demanded.

"I wouldn't go there if I were you. Colton's dad went

there about an hour ago. It would be bad news for you if you showed up too." Seth replied.

"I don't care." Sid retorted, "Just tell me where she lives."

Seth shrugged and rolled his eyes. He went on explaining how to get to Buffalo Road. He told her every turn she needed to make and which house she needed to find at the end of the gravel road. Sid remembered everything and, as soon as he was finished, she ran out of the bar without saying a word.

She ran back to her car, not caring about her hair or her outfit getting soaked in the process. There were more important matters at hand. She quickly slid into the drivers' seat and started the engine. The window was still busted, but she covered it with a piece of plastic. She was still waiting for her father to send money to get the car fixed up. He was trying to teach her a lesson by making her wait.

Sidney sped through town, heading to the highway Seth instructed her to. The streets were quiet, making it easier for her to get to where she needed to be. Everyone else in town was probably getting ready for bed or staying inside, away from the rain. A place she'd rather see Colton than where she was headed.

Her heart was racing with every second that brought her closer to her destination. Some of the rain was splashing through the cracks in the plastic where she didn't do a good job at taping it. Her face and clothes were getting sprinkled with rain, but none of that mattered. Her number one priority, was finding the love of her life and making sure he was okay. If something were to happen to him, she wasn't sure how she would live with herself. She knew everything was her fault. If she hadn't followed him and drove him crazy, Betsy might not have gone ballistic and kidnapped him. He might not have gotten into that accident and he never would've gotten hurt in the first place. She would never be able to forgive herself.

There was a small street sign coming up on the right side of the highway and she slowed down in order to turn onto

Buffalo Road. Seth was right, it was nothing but gravelly mush that splashed every side of her car. She saw the brick house coming into view, the lights were glowing in a few of the windows. She shut the headlights off and pulled into the driveway. It wasn't too far from the gravel road to the house and she couldn't risk being seen driving up to the place.

Sid pulled the car off to the side of the driveway, in the grass a little and hidden behind a few trees. She shut off the engine and stared at the house. It was a two story, massive building that had to be at least a hundred years old. From what she could see, the bricks looked faded and the windows were ancient and covered by something black. Parked in front of the door, was the police car she knew she would find. The lights were off and rain had washed most of the mud from the sides of the car. She could see it dripping down and had a feeling it's been sitting there awhile. She had hoped to not see that car and things would already be over.

She turned away from the house for a brief moment to collect her thoughts and search her car for a weapon. She hated guns and her pocket knife was at her house. It was something she always forget to put in her purse. She did know how to fight after taking a few kickboxing classes. Her father forced her to take them and she knew she could lay a decent punch. A weapon would have added a little more sense of security, but she would have to do without.

After gathering her courage, she pushed the car door open and stepped into the rain. She shut the door quietly, then ran away from the car, making sure to keep low in case someone spotted her. Her feet carried her through the wet grass and to the building. She went to the side of the house and ducked close to the ground making sure to stay below the windows.

Sid stayed close to the building as she moved to one of the basement windows. She got to her knees and peered inside. There was a large room just on the other side of the window with stairs on the opposite wall. A table and two chairs sat in one of the corners, but that's not what caught her eye. There was a cage-like door on the right side of the room. It was wide open and seemed like the room was empty. Her eyes caught movement in the room and she maneuvered herself to get a better look. Handcuffed to a wooden beam, was Colton's father. He leaned against the post, fighting the cuffs on his wrist. She was afraid of seeing him like that. At least he wasn't dead.

She took a deep breath then looked around outside when thunder crashed through the sky. There weren't any signs of other people, so she turned her focus back to the window, looking for a way to open it. There was a latch on the inside made of cheap plastic. She shook the window a bit getting the latch to move and, to her surprise, the thing broke loose. A piece of the latch fell from the window and she braced herself for the inevitable sound from it hitting the ground. She held her breath, but never heard a thing.

The window let out a quiet squeal as she pushed it open. Carl heard the sound and turned his head toward her. She ignored him and propped the window open with a small stick she found on the inside ledge. Then she slid inside, feet first, until she landed on something soft. When she was through the window, she noticed she was standing on a futon covered with pillows and blankets. Rain water dripped from her hair and clothes onto the mattress.

"Sidney?" Carl whispered and she quickly turned to him. "What the hell are you doing here?"

She wiped some of the rain water off her face and said quietly, "The same thing you are. Where's Colton?"

Carl nodded to the stairs, "She took him up there right after I got here."

"Where's the keys to your cuffs?" Sid asked.

"In her pocket." He replied, simply.

It was warm and musty in the basement as Sid carefully closed the window. As quietly as she could, she stepped off the futon and started looking around the basement. She and Carl were the only two down there. She didn't see anything she could use as a weapon and didn't bother searching any harder than she had to. She took a step toward the stairs, then instantly froze in her tracks.

Creaky footsteps walked across the floor above them. They grew louder and her eyes darted to the stairs. The door at the top opened lighting up the stairwell. A slight panic went through her as she frantically searched the room for a place to hide. The futon was too low to the floor for her to fit underneath. There weren't any closets or dark corners anywhere. She turned to Carl and shrugged her shoulders.

"Hide in there." His voice was barely a whisper as he motioned to the room with the bars for a door.

The footsteps were on the stairs and she could see two sets of feet descending into the basement. She took a deep breath, then silently ran into the small room. It was a little bigger than she anticipated. Around the corner, she came across a mattress lying on the floor which she assumed was there for Colton. To her right, was a smaller room with a toilet and enough of a wall to keep her out of sight. She darted behind that wall and kept quiet.

"I wish you would have ate something, Colton, it would make you feel so much better." Betsy's voice pierced the silence of the basement like a knife.

Sid heard a sniffle come from Colton as he spoke, "I'm sorry. I guess being kidnapped by a crazy bitch took my appetite away. Maybe if you'd let my dad and I go, I might be in a better mood."

That must not have sat right with Betsy because the next thing Sidney heard, was the sound of something hitting Colton and he fell to the floor. She heard Carl shouting for his son, followed by Betsy yelling at him to be quiet. It took all of Sid's strength not to rush out of her hiding spot and destroy that woman. She gritted her teeth and dug her fingernails into the palm of her hands as she listened.

"You'll learn to respect me soon enough, my love," came Betsy's voice again, much calmer than before.

The room was silent for another moment, then Sid heard the very familiar sound of a kiss. It was a short, simple kiss.

One which was probably forced upon Colton. It was followed by the sound of the metal door latching shut and the lock being put in its place. Sid heard the key turn on a padlock, then Betsy's footsteps as she walked away from the room.

Sidney took a deep breath as she slowly poked her head around the corner. She could barely see Colton on his hands and knees, crawling his way to the air mattress. His hand was held against his stomach and a pained look crossed his face. She knelt down a little then came out of her hiding place.

"Colton." She whispered.

Startled, he lifted his head and spotted her staring at him, "Sidney? What are you doing here?"

She moved toward him, helping him get to the mattress, "I broke in to find you."

He sat up and stared into her eyes, "How did you know I was here?"

"That's not important right now. We just need to focus on getting out of here." Sid replied.

Her eyes happened to catch the dried blood in his hair. A small scratch could be seen through the brown strands. She saw how he held his swollen left hand, cradling it against his chest.

"She hurt you." Sid said quietly, trying to hide the anger in her voice.

"She got me with a fucking baseball bat right outside my house. She got my head, then my hand, next my back, and now my stomach. I'm getting my ass kicked by a damn girl and I don't know how much more I can take. I thought every-thing was okay when my dad showed up, but you can see how *that* turned out."

Sidney looked at his left hand. It was swollen and bloody from being hit. An anger built up inside of her, something she's never felt before. She was used to getting jealous and taking it to a level she shouldn't, but she wasn't used to seeing the man she loved being treated so badly. Seeing him hurt was enough to make her want to kill Betsy for being the cause of his pain.

"Sidney." Colton said, softly.

"Yeah?" she stared into his sad eyes.

"I'm really glad you found me." He said.

"You are?" she asked.

He nodded his head, "Yeah."

"You know this is my fault, right? You're here because of me, because of what I did to you." She stated.

He shook his head, "Then I guess you'll have to make it up to me by getting us the hell out of here."

She took a deep breath, "I'll do my best."

Fifty Three

"How are we going to get out of here, Sid?" Colton asked. "I thought I was saved when I saw my dad down here. Now he's cuffed to that post and we're locked in here. At least she doesn't know you're here."

Sidney ran her fingers through her tangled hair and said, "I'm sorry, I'm not the best at making plans that involve escaping from someone's basement."

Colton nodded, "Yeah, me neither."

Sid stared at him as he solemnly sat on the air mattress. She was still kneeling on the cold floor in front of him, her damp clothes clinging to her cold skin. There was nothing good about the situation. If she would have found a hiding spot outside the bathroom, things would have been different. She'd have been able to come up with a better plan to get out of the mess they were in. The only chance they had at leaving the house at all, was having Betsy open the door for them.

"I hate to say this, but we need to get her back down here. She's the only one with the key for the lock *and* your dad's cuffs. If we have any chance at getting out, that's it." Sidney stated.

Colton let out a sigh and said, "I really don't want to deal with her again. She's pretty strong for a little chick."

"Well, you won't have to deal with her."

He raised his head and stared at her, "What are you talking about?"

Sidney shrugged, "You already said it. She doesn't know I'm down here, so she won't expect to see me. I'll get her to unlock the door and come after me. When you have a clear shot, you run like hell and get outside. Your dad's car is parked right by the front door."

"She keeps it locked."

"Then break a window." Sid suggested. "Look, it's not the best plan in the world, but I would rather do this than have you stuck down here another minute. Whether you are with me or not, this is probably the only shot we've got."

Sidney didn't wait for him to answer as she got to her feet and headed for the door. She could see him rising to his feet as well, but he never stopped her. Her heart was pounding harder with every step she took. It was by far the most extreme thing she has ever done for a man, attempting to save his life while risking her own. With every fiber of her being, she knew it was worth it. She reached her hand through the bars and grabbed the padlock and began clanging it against the bars. It was the only thing she could think of that would get Betsy's attention without having Colton call out for her.

It didn't take long for the angry footsteps to come walking toward the basement stairs. The door at the top burst open and the enemy came stomping down into the basement. A small part of Sidney was really looking forward to what was going to come next, despite how nervous she was about everything.

"Colton, I warned you about making that goddamn noise!" Betsy hollered as she made her way toward the bathroom.

Sidney stopped banging the metal together, brought her

hand back inside the room, then leaned against the wall with a smug look on her face. Betsy came into view and her eyes met with Sid's. She opened her mouth to speak, but no words would form. She raised the baseball bat, let out a shrill scream, the slammed the bat against the bars.

"I can tell you weren't expecting to see me here." Sidney stated, trying to stay calm.

"How the *hell* did you get in here?" Betsy screamed.

Sid shrugged, "I guess I'm just better at getting what I want than you expected."

"Where is he?" Betsy shouted.

"Oh don't worry, he's safe in here with me. In fact, I think it's much better this way."

Betsy lowered the bat and dug into her pocket for the key to the lock, "You're going to regret this. I'm gonna *make* you regret it."

"First you have to open the door." Sid said with a smile.

Betsy gritted her teeth while her hand hovered by the lock with the key. Her eyes were trying to burn a hole in Sidney's head so she could see what she was thinking. There was something to her voice giving Betsy a slight suspicion that something would happen the second the door was open. She had to keep the situation under control. She couldn't let anyone steal the power away from her.

She lowered the key and said, "That's what you want, isn't it? You want me to unlock this door so you can take Colton away from me. Too bad for you, I'm not that stupid."

Sidney raised an eyebrow and asked, "Are you sure about that?"

She pulled herself away from the wall and walked backwards a few steps. Colton was still hiding by the mattress when she reached out and grabbed his shirt, pulling him toward her. She turned him around, gently shoved him against the wall, and pressed her lips to his. Her eyes closed tight as she wrapped her arms around him, adding more spice to the moment. With Betsy's extreme jealousy, she should be bursting into the room any second and all hell would break loose.

Sid felt Colton's hand on her back, running it up and down her spine. The sound of the metal lock came from behind them, but neither of them bothered to care. They were both lost in the moment of whatever sensation was driving them to keep their lips locked together. The whole world disappeared during their kiss and the danger they were in seemed to stop.

Colton kept his arms around her, feeling like he never wanted the short moment to end. He knew it was wrong to keep falling for her, but there was something telling him they were meant to be together. Whatever crazy things she has done since they met, she did it for him. In a strange way, he loved knowing that she was willing to do anything for him.

The wonderful moment didn't last and Betsy pulled the door open and stomped into the room. Sidney felt her grab a handful of her hair and yank her away from Colton. She was dragged away from him and thrown onto the floor in the basement. She rolled a couple times, stopping right next to Carl. She lie on her stomach, fighting back the pain she felt in her arms and legs. She heard the footsteps approaching and saw the feet standing right in front of her.

"You really shouldn't have done that." Betsy seethed as she raised the baseball bat above her head, standing directly over Sidney.

Sid braced herself for whatever blow that was about to come her way. She even watched as Betsy started to lower the bat, quickly. She brought her arms up and covered her head and face. Colton ran up behind Betsy and stopped her before the bat would have struck Sid's arms. He wrapped his arms around Betsy and pulled her away from Sid. He tried taking the bat from her, but her grasp was stronger than he expected and she held onto it like her life depended on it.

Betsy let him hold onto her and went willingly as they backed away from Sid. She didn't try to fight him to get out of his grip. Instead, she kept walking with him, moving faster with every step. The wall was only a few more steps and she could use it to get him to let go of her. With all of her might, she pushed him against the wall, hearing him let out a grunt when his bruised back hit against it. He immediately let go of her and she moved away from him. She spun around on her heels and glared at him, readying the bat for another swing.

"How could you do this to me?" she shouted. "How could you let that whore in here and ruin everything? We have something special, something great, and you're ruining everything!"

Betsy raised the bat above her head once more and Colton waited for it to slam down on top of him. He pressed himself against the wall behind him and waited.

"You're blaming the wrong person, bitch."

Betsy turned around just in time to see one of her folding chairs from the corner of the room, being swung through the air. Sidney slammed the chair hard against Betsy's side and watched as her enemy crashed to the ground. The bat fell from her fingers and slid across the floor, rolling underneath the futon. Sid dropped the chair and knelt down next to Betsy, who was trying desperately to catch her breath. She remembered Carl saying how the key to his cuffs was in one of her pockets. Sid climbed on top of Betsy, pinning her to the floor and stuck her hand into her jeans' pocket until she found the key.

"No." Betsy gasped for air.

Sidney ignored her and tossed the key to Colton and he quickly ran to his father. Betsy let out a harsh growl and grabbed one of Sid's hands, digging her fingernails into her skin. Sid turned her attention back to the girl on the floor. Rage was building inside her as she stared at the woman who was responsible for Colton being in danger. The woman who kidnapped the man of her dreams and locked him away from the world in a dinghy basement. She's never hated anyone more than the woman on the floor.

Betsy reached up and grabbed hold of Sid's hair, pulling down on it hard. She forced Sidney to the floor and rolled on top of her. She released the red hair from her grip and wrapped her hands around Sid's throat, squeezing her fingers as tight as she could. Sid was still able to breathe, it was labored, but she was getting air. She lifted her hand and grabbed the glasses from Betsy's face and slammed them against her cheek, cutting it instantly. Blood dripped from the cut as Betsy let go of her.

"You bitch!" Betsy shouted, rubbing her cheek.

Sid dropped the broken glasses and threw herself at her opponent. They toppled over one another, rolling across the basement floor, until Sid wound up pinning Betsy to the cold concrete once again. She balled up a fist and slammed her hand against Betsy's face. She stared down at the woman who tried stealing everything away from her. There was blood on her face and teeth. Her eyes were red with anger and tears. Sid hated the life she was seeing before her. Everything about that woman was horrible and wrong. She didn't deserve to live anymore.

Betsy attempted to reach for Sid's hair once more, but got her hand smacked away. Sid brought both of her hands to Betsy's throat and squeezed her hands tight. She could feel the nails digging into her skin as Betsy tried clawing at her arms. Even as the blood slowly dripped down her arm from being cut, she never released her grip. Sidney was too hell bent on getting the revenge she deserved. The pain in her arms, fueled the fire burning in her heart and she squeezed her fingers even tighter.

Colton freed his father from the cuffs, then turned around. He saw Sidney strangling his kidnapper on the floor with so much anger in her eyes. He had to stop it before it got past the point of no return. He moved as quickly as his pain filled body would allow and approached the two girls. He put his arms around Sidney, one over her arms so she would let go of Betsy's neck.

"I can't let you kill her." Colton said, holding Sidney's arms down. "I can't let you live with that."

He pulled her across the room, listening to her seething with anger. She glared at Betsy lying on the floor, trying to collect herself. That woman didn't deserve to live and Sidney wanted to be the one who saw to that. She wanted to end everything before it got out of hand. But, she didn't fight against his grip. She knew if she killed Betsy, she would never get to see Colton again and *her* life would be over as well.

Carl held the handcuffs in his hand as he approached the two of them, "You guys alright?"

Colton nodded his head and said, "I am."

Sidney kept her eyes glued to Betsy. She watched her roll onto her side, trying to catch her breath and get to her feet. At least she'll be happy knowing her enemy will rot in a cell for the rest of her life.

Sid took a deep, calming breath and nodded her head, "I'm fine."

Colton released his grip on her and let her stand by his side as his father made his way to Betsy. It was his turn to do his job and put that girl in cuffs and haul her downtown. Sidney turned to Colton and looked into his eyes. By the calm demeanor of things, he knew everything was over and things could get back to normal.

"Thank you for saving me and my dad." He said, listening to his father's footsteps.

Sid forced a smile, "I'd do it again."

"It's bad that I know you would." He said as he held her hand.

Betsy rubbed the pain from her neck and caught the sight in front of her. She was losing everything. Colton was staring into the eyes of the red head that she hated more than anything else in the world. He was going to live happily ever after while she was forced to spend *years* behind bars. That's not how she wanted things to turn out. He was supposed to be with her. To fall in love with *her*.

She saw the sheriff approaching with the handcuffs dangling in his grip. Soon, she knew those metal things would be wrapped around her wrists and she would be tossed in the back of a cop car, never to see Colton again. She would never get to touch him or be with him and she wasn't going to stand for that.

The cop was standing right over her, reaching down for her wrist. She quickly sat up and pushed him away, slapping the handcuffs out of his grip. The metal clanked to the floor and she quickly reached behind her back for something she forgot about. She held the gun in her hand and took aim.

"If I can't have him, no one can." Betsy pulled the trigger the second before Carl could react.

The blast echoed through the basement and Carl lunged on top of her, yanking the gun from her grip, but the damage had already been done.

Fifty Four

The next few hours couldn't have gone slower. The ride in the ambulance only made things worse. There was so much blood and the paramedics worked frantically to take care of what they could on the way to the hospital. Carl had one of the other officers take Betsy down to the station and into a holding cell. His next job, was being at the hospital for his son.

The sheriff stood in the exam room as his wife sat on a chair while their son got checked out. Colton's knuckles on his left hand were badly bruised. He'd have to wear a brace for a while to keep the swelling under control. The bruises on his back were looked after and the doctors took an x-ray to make sure there was no internal damage. He would be sore and on pain medications for a few days, but he would live.

After they were finished in the exam room, Colton was told he had to spend the rest of the night at the hospital. They ordered him to get some sleep, but couldn't force his eyes to close even if he wanted to. He sat on the edge of the bed with his legs dangling over the side of the mattress. His father was in the hallway, waiting for one of the doctors to bring him the news about Sidney. Colton's heart was pounding as he waited and his mind kept replaying the night over and over.

The blast sounded like a cannon in the basement and he remembered seeing his father ripping the gun from Betsy's hands. He looked down at his own body, checking to make sure the bullet hadn't hit him anywhere. Then, he felt a tug on his arm and heard her fall to the floor. There was blood soaking the bottom portion of her shirt and he tried to help by pressing his hand against her stomach. The rest of the world blurred by him as other cops showed up with an ambulance and he rode to the hospital with her.

He glanced across the room at the clock hanging on the wall. It was two in the morning. He was getting anxious as the seconds ticked by. They got to the hospital just past eleven and she's been in surgery ever since. His mother stood at the end of the bed, trying to give him reassurance that everything would be okay.

He kept thinking there was a complication. Maybe they couldn't stop the bleeding, she lost a lot on the way. Maybe they couldn't find the bullet or maybe it hit something important. There were so many horrible things going through his mind that he couldn't stop thinking about losing her. As much as he knew he should hate her, he found it exceedingly hard not to. With all of her flaws and the crazy things she did since they met, he knew he could look past all of it as long as she was there for him.

He let out a sigh as he ran his nervous fingers through his hair. He could hear footsteps in the hall outside the room. Every few seconds, he found himself staring at the door, begging it to open with his mind. As long as he heard good news before laying down, he'd be able to sleep.

"It'll be alright, sweetie." His mother said, rubbing his back.

He shook his head, "I hope so, but I can't stop thinking about her. What if she doesn't make it? What if we didn't get to the hospital in time? I can't live with that thought on my mind, mom."

"You got here in plenty of time, the doctor told you that. They are just taking their time to make sure everything is perfect so she'll heal correctly." Denise said as she sat on the bed beside him.

He took a deep breath, trying not to let his bad thoughts overwhelm him. The last thing he needed was a panic attack in the middle of the hospital. He didn't want to cause a scene when Sid needed all of the attention from the staff she could get.

His heart just about leapt from his chest when the door finally opened. He stood from the bed, feeling his mother's touch on his shoulder. He couldn't go too far with an IV attached to his elbow, but he stood by the bed as his father approached him.

"Is she okay?" Colton asked, hardly able to contain himself.

Carl nodded, "She's fine. They said the bullet passed straight through her stomach and missed the major arteries and organs. She's going to be here for a few days, but she'll be alright."

Colton let out a sigh of relief and said, "Thank god."

"Since you refuse to go to sleep, there's someone here who wants to talk to you." Carl said.

Colton nodded and saw the other man walking into the room, stepping beside his father. This man had reddish-grey hair with a thin beard on his chin. His eyes were green, much like Sidney's, and he had the same look of determination on his face.

Colton took a breath, then said, "You're Sid's father?"

"Yes, I'm Charlie Jenison." He replied.

"As soon as we called him with the news, he hopped on a helicopter to get here." Carl added to clarify how Sid's father was able to get there so quickly.

Mr. Jenison took a step closer to Colton and said, "Sidney's told me a lot about you. I know she has issues and

267

a big problem handling rejection. I'm sorry you had to go through this because of my daughter. I'm glad to see everyone's alright, but I'm here to let you know, you won't have to worry about Sid bothering you anymore. When she wakes up and is ready to travel, I'm taking her back home with me and you'll never have to see her again."

Colton shook his head, quickly, "No, you can't do that. I want to see her again. She saved my life and I need to be there for her when she wakes up."

Mr. Jenison let out a sigh, "Why?"

"Because she needs to know that I care about her. That I might actually want to be with her no matter how crazy she appears to be. I get that she has problems and I get that I shouldn't want what I'm feeling, but you can't tell me not to feel this way about her. Believe me, my dad has tried to tell me how wrong this is, but I don't care." Colton replied.

Carl smiled, "It's true. He's a stubborn boy, but when he's passionate about someone, I know he's sincere."

Mr. Jenison glanced back and forth between them. Sidney was so much like her father, Colton was beginning to notice. They both dressed their best, even when times didn't call for it. Charlie was wearing a black suit covered with an overcoat. The briefcase at his side, was leather and in perfect condition. Everything about him screamed perfection which was exactly what Sidney did every day.

"I see that you care about her." Charlie said. "I respect that. I just hope you know that it would be better for you if you didn't get involved with her."

Colton nodded and said bluntly, "I know, but I don't really care."

Charlie smiled, then turned for the door, "I get why she likes you."

Colton sat back on the bed as Sid's father left the room. He wasn't sure if he got through to the man and if he'd be able to see her when she wakes up. All he could do was hope.

Fifty Five

Sidney opened her eyes and found herself lying in a strange room on an uncomfortable mattress. There was a soft beeping sound coming from a machine next to the bed. An IV with clear fluid was sticking out of her arm. Her eyes felt heavy as she looked around the room, getting a grasp on where she was. The last thing she remembered, was being carried out of Betsy's house into the rain. After that, things went black.

The light from the window across the room was almost blinding. She had to squint her eyes in order to see anything. On the wall in front of her was a sink and a few cupboards. Above that, was a flat screen TV hanging from the ceiling. There was a small, leather couch in the corner by the window and a rocking chair next to it. She recognized the man sitting in the chair, staring up at the TV. It's been a while since she's seen him and was relieved he came for her.

"Dad." Her throat was so dry her voice was barely more than a whisper.

He was still able to hear her and quickly stood from the

chair and went to her bedside, "I'm so glad you're awake, sweetheart. I've never been more worried about you in my life. You're mom's worried as well, but she chose to stay home and let me handle this. It's better this way."

"What happened, dad?" she asked, still a whisper.

He set his hand on top of hers and said, "Well, after you got shot and the cops showed up, an ambulance brought you here. They said you passed out on the way. I got a call around 11:30 and hopped in the chopper and got here as fast as I could."

"Thank you for doing that." She said. "Can I sit up?"

He pressed the call button above her bed, then said, "I'll get the nurse in here so she can help you with that."

Not a moment went by and a nurse walked into the room. She was wearing pink scrubs with flowers all over them and she approached the bed with a smile.

"Well, good morning. Maybe I should say afternoon. It is one o'clock by the way." The nurse tried for a joke.

Charlie smiled, "She wants to sit up a bit. Can you help with that? I don't want to mess anything up."

"It might cause her pain if she sits up too much, but I'll get a couple more pillows to put under her back to make her comfortable. Let me just check her vitals and make sure everything's good."

"Thank you." Sidney said, softly.

The nurse went about her job and made sure Sidney was still okay and her heart was beating normally. Then she left the room to go after a few pillows.

Charlie pulled up the rocking chair closer to the bed and sat down next to her. As much as she was glad to see him at the hospital with her, she was hoping Colton would be there as well. She wanted to see his face and make sure he wasn't as hurt as she thought he was.

"Dad?" she asked.

"Yeah, Sid."

"Where's Colton?"

The nurse came back in with the pillows, "Alright, let's

get you comfy." She set the pillows on Sid's legs then said, "I'm gonna have to lift you up a bit then we'll have your dad slide the pillows under your back, okay."

Sidney nodded then took the nurses hand. She couldn't put any tension on her stomach without a searing pain shooting through her body. It didn't last long and her father put a pillow under her back and one at her head. Then, she lay back down and the nurse left the room. Finally, she was slightly comfortable.

"Is that better?" Charlie asked.

She nodded, "You need to tell me where Colton is."

Her father let out an exhausted sigh, "He's alright."

"Can I see him?" she asked.

"You don't need to see him anymore. I warned you about getting hung up on another boy you don't need to be with. You take things too far, Sid, and this little incident from last night, took it over the top. You could have died because of what you did to him." Charlie said.

Sid stared at her father's face, listening to the same speech he has told her a million times. Each time he grew more and more tired of telling her to stay away from men she knew she couldn't have. Colton was different. He was kind and charming and she couldn't let him go so easily like her father expected her to do.

"I'm in love with him, dad." Sid finally said quietly.

Charlie chuckled, then said, "I've heard that before."

Sidney shook her head, "It's different this time, I can feel it. He's not like any other guy I've dated. He knows who I am *and* the things I would do for him. Somehow he's managed to look past it all and I know he wants to be with me too. If you just tell me where he is I can prove it."

Annoyed, Charlie stood up and walked to the door. Sidney heard the latch, then he disappeared out of the room. She couldn't tell what he was doing or see who he was talking to. He kept his voice low, making it impossible for her to hear what he was saying. When he walked back into the room, there was someone following him and her eyes lit up the second she saw his face.

Colton rushed past her father, nearly running to the bed. His eyes were red and a tear drifted onto his cheek as he passed her a smile. He sat on the edge of the bed, without shaking it or making her uncomfortable.

"I am so glad to see you." He said, softly.

"Me too," she whispered, "Did you stay all night?"

He nodded, "Yeah, I was down the hall a few rooms."

"I'm glad you're alright, Colton." She said.

"All thanks to you." He replied. "I hate to say this, but I'm kinda glad you risked your life for me. It sucks that you had to get shot in the process, though."

She gave him a small smile, "I don't care about me. I only care that you're okay."

Colton nodded, then brushed the few strands of hair from her face. He leaned forward and planted a soft kiss on her forehead, which she gracefully accepted.

"I wish I could stay with you all day, but my dad wants me to head home with them so you can rest." Colton said.

"Yeah, it's okay." She replied. "I'll text you later or something."

"Good. I'll be waiting."

He stood up and walked backwards out of the room. Their eyes were on each other until she could no longer see him and the door was closed.

Fifty Six

Colton was given the next couple weeks off from work. He was a little worried if he would even have the job anymore after getting into a car accident, then getting kidnapped and missing so much already. His boss, Greg, assured him that his job would still be there waiting for him. Everyone was just happy to know he was okay and still himself after everything he went through.

He had a doctor's appointment the following Tuesday, almost a week after being locked in Betsy's basement. His doctor needed to make sure he was healing properly and not in any more pain. He was finally able to stop wrapping his left hand in bandages every day and the bruises were almost completely gone. While sitting in the exam room, his doctor made the comment on how Sidney was sent home that morning. They kept her a little while longer, since the bullet was so close to hitting an artery, they needed to be sure she was going to be alright on her own. Colton practically ran out of the hospital after he heard the news.

He longed to see her smiling face, her red hair, and those cute freckles on her nose and cheeks. He wanted to hear her voice again and be in the same room as her. She was all he could think about since he left her at the hospital and he hated every second he couldn't see her. As he maneuvered his mother's van through town, his heart beat nervously in his chest as he thought of what he wanted to say to her. Things that couldn't be said over the phone without having the effect he needed them to have.

He turned onto her street and slowed down to park in front of her house. The front door was wide open, letting the fresh summer air into the house. He shut off the engine and got out of the van, strolling to the door. The sound of the television came through the screen door and he could hear the cartoons talking as he got closer. He smiled, picturing her watching the children's show as he walked up the couple steps to the door.

He didn't bother knocking or ringing the doorbell. There was no need to make Sid get up to open the door when he knew she would let him come in. He pulled the screen door open and stepped foot inside the house. He turned into the living room and smiled when he saw her sitting on the couch in black, yoga pants and a white tank top. He could see the bandages through her shirt from where she was shot.

"You were supposed to text me when you got home." He said, walking over to the couch.

She smiled and said, "Sorry. My dad brought me home and I fell asleep for like an hour."

"It's okay." He said. "I want to talk to you about something."

"Yeah, what's that?"

He sat on the couch next to her. She adjusted herself enough so she could see him a little better. There was a pillow behind her back and her feet were propped up on the table. A throw blanket was draped over the back of the couch and he couldn't help but notice how comfortable she looked. He smiled as he thought of what he wanted to say.

He took a deep breath, "First, I want to tell you again that I'm really glad you're okay. I don't think you could possibly understand just how *crazy* I was going sitting in that hospital room trying to be patient until my dad came in and said you were okay. All I could think about, was what I would do if you didn't wake up."

"But I did wake up. It'll be a few weeks, but I'll be back to my normal, *crazy* self." She stated.

"Good." Colton said. "In case you were wondering, my dad said they are going to get Betsy with kidnapping and attempted murder charges. With any luck, she'll be in prison for a long time."

"That's good, but I know you didn't come here to talk about that stuff."

"You're right, I came here to talk about something else. I wanted to tell you at the hospital, but I didn't have the right words." He replied. "You know, something has been driving me crazy for the last few days. I have just been dying to know how you knew where to find me. I wanted to know how you knew I'd be at Betsy's. But the more I thought about it, the more I don't really want to know the answer. I guess I started not to care about *how* you knew and focused on the fact that you *did* know and you went there just for me. Maybe one of these days I'll ask you for an answer, but not today."

"What do you want to talk about today?" she asked.

He took a deep breath and let it out through his nose, "I can't hate you for what you did to me. As much as I probably should, I can't. Even after finding out how you lied to me and told me things just to get me to feel something for you, I can't bring myself to want to hate you for it. I know you're sorry and I forgave you the second I saw you in that basement to save me.

"You risked your life for me and I love that about you. I love that you can't take no for an answer and that you would do anything to get what you want. I don't want you to stop being crazy and I damn sure don't want you to ever stop following me and calling me in the middle of the night just to hear my voice. That is probably one of the best things about you. That you *want* to be in love with only me and to hell with what other people think of that. I want you to promise me that you will never stop doing that and I'll promise to never stop falling for you."

Sidney stared at him, with tears of happiness in her eyes. It felt like she's been waiting forever to hear him say those words. That's all she's ever wanted from him, to know that he wanted to be with her just as much as she wanted him.

She wiped away an escaped tear and smiled, "I think I can manage that."

"Good," Colton said.

He scooted closer to her on the couch and brushed a few strands of her red hair out of her face. Carefully, he leaned in for the kiss, making sure he didn't make her uncomfortable or accidently hurt her. He put his hand on the back of her neck as she caressed his cheek. With that kiss, the first one of their life together, Colton knew that *was* exactly how he always wanted to feel. Knowing that the person who was kissing him back was in love with him more than he could possibly know was the greatest feeling in the world. He couldn't wait to spend the rest of his life with that feeling.

About the Author

Tahnee Fritz lives in southern Iowa with her husband and husky. She has been writing poetry and short stories since she was in grade school. Her first, published novel, *The Human Race*, was released in late 2013.

trfritz88.wordpress.com

www.ingramcontent.com/pod-product-compliance
Lightning Source LLC
Chambersburg PA
CBHW071121170626
46809CB00002B/450